Scary Kisses

Scary Kisses

edited by
Liz Grzyb

TICONDEROGA
PUBLICATIONS

*To Kate and Kate, who share my appreciation
for romances of the darker persuasion*

Scary Kisses edited by Liz Grzyb

Published by Ticonderoga Publications

Cover design by Amanda Rainey
Designed by Russell B. Farr
Typeset in Sabon and Feel Script

A Cataloging-in-Publications record is available from the National Library of Australia

ISBN   978-0-9806288-4-5 (trade paperback)

Ticonderoga Publications
PO Box 29 Greenwood
Western Australia 6924

www.ticonderogapublications.com

10 9 8 7 6 5 4 3 2 1

Acknowledgements

The editor would like to thank Russell, Shane and Angela, Amanda, Alisa, Kate and Andrew, Debbie, Jacinta, Kate, Terri, Ruza, Lina, Lynne, and all of the wonderful Scary Kisses *authors: Nicole, Ian, Felicity, Shona, Angela, Lisa, Matt, Astrid, David, Martin, Kyla, Donna, Bruce, Annette and DC.*

Contents

Scary Kisses

THE ANSTRUTHER WOMAN

NICOLE R. MURPHY

ALLY smelt the fear as soon as she walked into the old wooden hall. The town was starting to panic.

She stopped just inside the door. When she'd taken over Auntie Maeve's role as the local wise woman, Ally had hoped she would have time to adjust. However, she'd walked into a maelstrom of horror. Small animals—calves, chickens, family pets—were being ripped apart under the cover of night.

Over the past couple of days, concern and anger was escalating into horror and the need for retaliation as more stories came in.

She started to wander through the fifty or so people in the hall. Despite having not lived in Barrengarry for several years, she knew most of them—they were the old families, people who were descended from the pioneers that forged their way over the escarpment from the coast in the early 1800s. Dairy farmers, mostly, although some had diversified into things such as wine making and more exotic animals.

"It was awful," Ally heard Mrs O'Driscoll say as she went past. "We got home from a night up in the Highlands and found it. The poor little lambkin was still alive, its chest heaving, but the dog had taken a huge chunk out of its rear. There was no way to save it."

"It got into my henhouse, I don't know how," Mr Lam was telling his neighbour. "No holes in the wire, no damage."

"You didn't leave the door open, did you?" Mr Harper said and Mr Lam's eyes began to shine with suppressed tears.

"In the rush to get to the big smoke I must have, God help me."

There were a few new faces, and Ally started to make her way around near them. Aunt Maeve had always said that it was important for a wise woman to get to know newcomers as soon as possible, but it was one of the tasks she had let lapse in her old age.

One man in particular intrigued Ally. He was average height, average weight, average colouring. However, he stood with his feet splayed, hands on hips, his chin held high. It was as if he considered himself the best man there, and was waiting for an opportunity to prove it. Nothing about him said anything about wealth, and he certainly wasn't famous. She wondered why he had such an apparent air of superiority.

Ally was skirting a large group when somewhere near the door, someone yelled out, "Tynan Rutherford. About time you showed yourself."

Ally, along with everyone else in the hall, swung to the door. She sucked in her breath at the sight of the man standing there— tall, confident, powerfully built. If it weren't for the black hair and amber eyes, she wouldn't have recognised him.

When last she'd spent time with Tynan Rutherford during a trip home from boarding school, ten years ago, he'd been a gangly teenager, at odds with his body.

He'd certainly grown up well.

He smiled, clapped someone on the shoulder to speak to them. Ally looked around, noting all the eyes trained on Tynan. The Rutherfords were the closest thing Barrengarry had to royalty— their family had been the first to settle in the valley, and at times it was the wealth of their property that had kept the town afloat.

Ally turned back to continue her journey toward the mystery man, and told herself she wasn't irritated that Tynan hadn't yet come to visit her, despite the old connections between the Rutherford men and the women of Anstruther Farm.

"Time to begin, folks," the local councillor, Andrew Dickinson, called out. Ally frowned, disappointed she couldn't get closer to the man and see what she could work out about him. She found herself a seat near the back of the crowd. A shiver went up her spine moments before a deep voice whispered in her ear.

"I'm sorry I haven't been over to see you yet."

Ally looked over her shoulder and had to fight against the pull of Tynan's gaze. "Hadn't you? I didn't notice." She turned back to face the front, warmed by his chuckles.

"I'm taking bets," he said, and despite his ordinary words, his voice shimmered over her senses. "Ten minutes before the call to arms."

She smiled, glad their teenage camaraderie appeared to have survived the years. She turned her head to whisper back to him, "Council won't allow it."

"Think that will stop anyone?"

He had a point. Ally turned back around to pay attention.

"We're all here because we're concerned about these attacks, and want a cohesive plan on how to deal with it." As he spoke, Andrew pulled on his collar. He'd come to this public meeting in full suit and tie, which Ally thought very correct of him. Unfortunately, it was less than suitable for an un-air-conditioned hall in the middle of an unseasonably hot spring. Sweat was already starting to drip down the sides of his round face.

"Amber Kehoe from National Parks is here to take us through what's been reported, and what their advice is. Amber."

The woman who stood was heavy-set, middle-aged and weather-burned.

"Thank you, Councillor Dickinson. There have now been four attacks reported, all on small animals, and it seems clear they are the work of a dog pack."

Ally felt a wave of anxiety and apprehension wash over her. She focussed her energy and located the source—the man she'd noted earlier. Interesting.

"It's unclear at the moment whether they are feral, or whether some household pets from the valley here have joined up at night. Certainly, we need to ascertain where they are from. If they are domestic animals, then the acts fall under the purview of council, but if they are feral, then we at National Parks need to be involved."

"So how do we find out?" someone called out.

"We need to get the message out to everyone in the valley to lock up their dogs at night. If the attacks stop, then we know we're looking for domestic animals."

"And in the meantime? What about our stock?"

Ranger Kehoe ignored the shout. "If it is wild dogs, then we'll look at starting a baiting program."

"If we see the dogs, we can shoot them, right?"

"Damn, I was two minutes off," Tynan murmured.

"This is ridiculous." Ally looked over and Mr Superiority had stood up. "You're all ignoring the real culprit in this. It isn't dogs. It's the panther."

Ally was surprised by Tynan's growl. She glanced over her shoulder, and he quirked an eyebrow at her. She turned back to the front, fascinated that her mystery man had brought up the panther story.

Up and down the east coast of Australia, people have claimed time and again to see big cats in the bush—cats held responsible for stock losses and encouraging fear. Barrengarry's panther had long been considered a fact by the folks in the valley.

"Mr Caan, I'm not ignoring anything," Ranger Kehoe said. "You told me your theory, and I told you there's nothing to back it up."

"I saw it," Caan hissed. "I saw it attack my sheep. I told you that."

"His was the first," Tynan told Ally.

"I know what you think you saw, Mr Caan, but I'm telling you there is no scientific evidence of these being the killings of panther."

"There's never been evidence, but everyone knows it's true." Caan swung around and appealed to the crowd. "You know it's true. You know there's a panther here in the valley."

"That cat's dead, son," one of the farmers said. "Hasn't been seen for a couple of years. Gone up into the bush and died."

"The method of killing is wrong," the ranger said. "Cats kill cleanly, with little injury to the animal, and it's dead before they start eating. These carcasses were badly mauled, and in one case the animal was left alive. There were also signs of different sized jaws being used, a clear indication of a pack. Cats generally don't hunt in packs."

"Household cats can," someone said.

"I'm telling you, I saw a panther." Caan's face was red, his fists clenched.

Ally tipped her head to one side and studied the man, noting the physical signs of his growing frustration. She was certain that Mr Caan believed he'd seen a panther. However, that didn't prove it was a cat responsible for the killings.

"You haven't said if we can shoot the dogs if we see them?" The conversation was brought back to the matter at hand.

The ranger looked at Andrew Dickinson. It was clear neither of them wanted to say yes.

"Landowners are legally required to deal with wild dogs," was the ranger's eventual reply.

"If you shoot someone's legally owned animal, you can be prosecuted," Andrew said.

"I'll be damned if I'm not going to protect my herd," the man shouted. The ranger shrugged. To Ally, the message was clear—if you actually came across the dogs attacking your animals and shot them, you'd get away with it.

The meeting wrapped up quickly after that. Ally had a vision of dozens of guns trained into the darkness that night, ready for a glimpse of a dog, and shuddered. She hoped people would keep their pets in.

As she walked out the door, Tynan appeared by her side. "I've been thinking," he said in the deep voice that resonated with something deep within her, "that since we're neighbours, and old friends, we should get to know each other better." As he spoke, he put his hand on her back and guided her towards her car.

She gave herself a moment to enjoy the shiver of excitement that ran up her spine at his touch. "That's a bit old-fashioned of you, isn't it?"

"I prefer to think of it as opportunistic." As they reached her car, he stopped and turned to her. The setting sun cast a red glow around his black hair and his amber eyes were shining. "I'm very much regretting that I haven't come back to the valley before now."

Ally had experienced attraction before, but nothing with this instant intensity. "You could have looked me up in the city, us being old friends and all."

"I'm regretting not doing that too."

"So, how do you suggest we start this—getting to know one another better?"

"I've got lots of ideas, but I'm thinking the one you'd accept is that we have dinner together. Tomorrow night. I'll be round about seven."

They were standing so close that Ally thought she could just raise herself on her toes and press her lips to his. It was an enticing thought.

"You're assuming I've not got anything planned," she whispered.

"I'm assuming you'll break any plans to spend some time with me."

Wowza, Ally thought as he turned and strode away. She'd hate his arrogant certitude that she'd acquiesce, if he wasn't right. It seemed life in the valley was going to be even more fun than she'd anticipated.

*B*ACK at the farm, she went to check on the animals. Singing Boy, Aunt Maeve's prize alpaca sire, was waiting for her at the fence. He leant his head towards her, begging for a pat.

With a smile, Ally sank her hands into the fur of his neck, enjoying the springy and silky sensation. She'd been delighted when Maeve had decided to move from sheep breeding to alpacas—the wool was so much nicer, not being coated with lanoline like a sheep's was. Alpacas might look strange to eyes used to rams and ewes, with their long necks and legs, but they were interesting and at times affectionate animals and she looked forward to learning to farm them.

She looked over Singing Boy's back to the next paddock, where his latest progeny was following its mother around. The cria was only a couple of days old, and had already lost the clumsiness of a newborn, scampering around its mother's feet and testing its strength. There was no doubt it would be a tempting morsel for whatever was out there, and she hoped that something would come soon.

Alpacas were notoriously vigilant in protecting their herd, and a new mother even more so. Anything that tried to get to the baby would be kicked to smithereens within moments. That would put an end to the attacks.

She shook her head at the violent images that were rising in her mind. They were not the appropriate thoughts for a wise woman. Giving Singing Boy one last pat, she went inside to get dinner ready.

A GUTTURAL, animal screech pulled Ally straight from sleep into the world of the wake. She sat up, focussed and realised the sound had come from outside. One thought slammed into her consciousness—the alpacas.

She jumped out of bed, pulling tracksuit pants and a t-shirt over her underwear. At the back door, she stopped to pull on her trainers. Then she was outside and running towards the barn.

On the far side were the pens where she'd put the mothers and crias—three of each. The rest of the twenty-strong alpaca herd was in the field next to the pens as yet another line of defence.

As she ran around the side of the barn, she saw that she'd been wise to organise the alpacas like that—the herd were in the midst of a brutal fight with four dogs.

Ally stopped and stared. There was something wrong about those dogs—they seemed bigger than they should, and much more determined. Despite the fact each one of them was bloody and torn by the alpaca attack, they were still trying to fight their way through to the babies.

She watched one dog back away, and then try to skirt around the edges of the melee. As it faced her, it stopped and stared at her and she could have sworn a shocked expression crossed its brown eyes. Then it bared its teeth, snarled and lunged at her.

At this point, Ally realised she'd been stupid—very stupid. She'd run out of the house, barely dressed, not at all armed and now an enraged dog was lunging at her. She screamed and turned to run.

She felt something big move past her, behind her, and then heard the unmistakable sound of a dog squealing in pain. She spun back around, and collapsed against the wall of the barn in shock.

There, holding the dog by the neck and growling, was a panther. There was no other word to describe it. It was big—its head was waist-height and it was much longer than her alpacas—and black, with bright yellow eyes.

So, the mythical Barrengarry panther had returned.

The panther dropped the dog, which slinked away whimpering. The cat turned its head, looked over its shoulder and growled. To Ally, the message was clear—get inside, you stupid woman.

Ally turned and ran back to the house. She slammed the screen door closed and locked it. Then she stood and listened.

The panther screamed—an eerie sound to hear in the Australian countryside at night. She strained, and thought she heard the dogs scamper away, barking and howling.

She listened to the alarm call of the alpacas descend into a constant hum, and knew that while they were still stressed, they now felt safe. Then a movement in the shadows. The panther walked into the light cast on the ground by her open door. It stopped and looked at her and she wondered what it would do if she went out there and said thank you. The animal bowed its head, then turned and ran away, disappearing into the inky black of night.

She leant against the door, her heart thudding. So, it seemed that Caan had been right—the panther was back. There was also a pack of dogs and if she wasn't much mistaken, the panther had just protected her flock from the dogs. And saved her life.

She headed over to the fridge for a glass of wine, knowing she wasn't going to get much sleep that night.

IN the morning, she went out to inspect the damage. A couple of the alpacas had bites on their legs, but none of them had been killed. She looked around the yard, and noted that while the paw-prints of the dogs were clear, those of the panther were gone.

Interesting.

On one of the fences, she found a tuft of fur that she thought might belong to the dog that had lunged at her. That dog had seemed darker than the others, dark like this fur. Of course, it could be the panther's.

Ally called the vet out to inspect the animals. Kylie Simpson had been the doctor of choice for valley farmers for a couple of decades now. She patched up the alpacas' wounds, and only got spat on once for her trouble.

"They're getting better behaved," she said as she packed her bag.

"It's definitely dogs, isn't it?"

Kylie looked up with a grin. "You aren't buying the panther story, are you?"

"Around this valley, you can't assume anything."

"True." Kylie stood and then stretched, arching her back. "Did I tell you my very first job here was an alleged attack of the panther?"

"No."

"Although when I say job, what I mean is old Doctor Farrer sent me out there to clean up what was left. It was my test—would I faint at the sight of blood and bones, or would I be fine. Took the sheep carcass back, studied it—a clean kill, mouth over throat and choked it to death before eating about half of it. Quite extraordinary, actually. I back what the ranger said—cats don't kill messy. Dog packs, however, that's a different story. Disgusting, actually." Then she nodded down at the ground. "At least you have the previously missing dog prints. Couldn't quite figure out why there wasn't any at the other attacks. Now, it's dead certain its dogs. The panther is safe from the hunt."

"They were weird looking dogs." Ally shook her head. "No recognisable variety and they seemed bigger than they should be, if that makes sense."

Kylie frowned. "Mutts don't tend to be big, although it does happen."

"Well, these were big. Shepherd sized—no, bigger."

"And not a breed you recognised?"

Ally shook her head. "Like I said, weird. And they just kept going, when they should have given up."

"Sounds like there's a fighting breed in the mix. Whatever, I've never seen a dog that matches that description around the valley, so we can probably assume they're feral. The farmers will be happy—no ramifications if they do shoot one."

"Just what we need," Tynan said as he walked around the corner of the barn. "Trigger-happy farmers." He stopped and looked down at Ally. His eyes scanned her face, his concern apparent. "I heard the news, came to see if you were all right."

"Fine. Me and the herd, still alive and kicking."

"Glad to hear it." He reached over the fence to rub Singing Boy's neck. The alpaca gurgled his appreciation. "Neither of you are any good to us dead. Just make sure you don't take any silly risks."

Ally wondered how much he knew about what had happened here last night. "I only take safe risks."

"That's an oxymoron, isn't it? No such thing as a safe risk."

"I think there might be." She smiled, and her heart thudded when he smiled back.

*H*ER childhood best friend Donna came over in the afternoon to check that things were okay.

"I can't believe it," she said as she flopped down onto the straw chair. "The Anstruther Farm luck has held. How on earth did those dogs not take down one of your animals like they have everywhere else?"

Ally decided that mentioning both her midnight excursion and the panther would bring on too much heat. "Like you said, must be the Anstruther Farm luck."

"Well, I hope you're taking over Maeve's business, 'cause I think I'll bring my charm to get a boost."

"Shhhh." Ally looked around, even though no one could get close enough to the verandah to hear them without being seen. "Same rules apply, D. I choose who I work with, and if you let people know I'll drop you like a hot potato."

"Cross my heart, hope to die." Donna performed the actions.

"So, are we going to have another town meeting, now that we know it's dogs?"

"No, the phone lines are doing a good enough job of that."

"Good. At least that'll save us from the rantings of Mr Caan." Ally shook her head. "How long has he been in the valley?"

"About a year. Kept to himself, seemed a quiet sort of chap until last night. But even if we did have a meeting, we wouldn't be hearing from Mr Caan. All that screeching's gone and given him a throat infection, and he can't speak." Donna grinned. "Jack says he's hurt himself too—saw him hobbling around his verandah this morning. Serves him right for trying to bring the panther back from the dead."

Thoughts started to percolate. "Is he by himself?"

"Has been, although he's got some mates staying with him at the moment. Helen down at the bottle-o isn't too impressed—reckons they're a bit full of themselves."

Ally tapped her fingers on the arm of her chair while she allowed ideas to settle into a pattern that seemed incredibly unlikely, yet made a strange sort of sense. "I think Mr Caan could do with a bit of Anstruther Farm help."

"What? Why? He's not from the valley."

Ally looked at her friend. "No, he's not, and that's why I want to check him out."

"Well, I'm not letting you go there alone." Donna surged to her feet. "I'll drive."

Ally smiled as she went inside and gathered her things. Even when they'd been kids together, Donna had been the font of all gossip.

Caan's property was at the southern end of the valley, and you had to start driving up the mountain in order to reach it. The small farmhouse was built high on a hill and had an incredible view down the length of the valley. As she got out of the car, Ally thought that with the right equipment, this would be a great spot from which to spy on everyone, and note the movements of their animals.

As they started towards the house, Caan appeared. He stopped at the top of the stairs and glared down at them. As Ally looked into his brown eyes, something within her screamed.

"Mr Caan, we haven't met. I'm Ally Bandroy, from Anstruther Farm."

He bowed his head to acknowledge her words, but didn't speak. Ally noted the scarf wrapped around his neck. An unseasonable outfit, she thought as she felt the sun beat down on her head.

"I don't know if you've heard, but my alpacas were attacked last night." She watched him closely and thought she saw his nostrils flare. His eyes remained calm. "I saw dogs, so everyone's decided that's that. But I'm intrigued by what you said last night at the meeting about the panther. My aunt collected stories about the Barrengarry panther, and I'd love to be able to tell her some more. Would you mind if I sat with you for a while?"

Caan lifted his hand to his throat and shook his head. "Ah, yes, I'd heard you have a sore throat. I brought some of my aunt's home-made lozenges. People here in the valley swear by them. There's always a big run after the footy finals." Ally patted her handbag. "I'm sure after one of these, your voice will be much better and we can talk."

Caan shook his head more vigorously.

"Well, that's a shame. Maybe when you feel better." Ally looked over her shoulder and sighed. "It's so lovely up here. You can see the entire valley. I bet you can even see who's at home at night." She looked back over her shoulder. Still no response.

"Well, I guess we'll be going then, leaving you to rest. By the way, where are your dogs?"

This time, his eyes widened and his body flinched. "What dogs?" he hissed.

"Your dogs. I'd heard that you have four of them. I'm surprised I can't hear them. I guess they're out in the bush somewhere. If I were you, I'd get them locked in the house quick smart. The farmers will be toey now, and they're probably going to shoot any dog they don't know." Ally bobbed her head, turned and walked back to the car.

"What were you talking about?" Donna said as she started the car and drove away. "What dogs? There haven't been any dogs sighted at Caan's place."

"Really?" Ally murmured. She leant back in the car seat with a smile. "My mistake." She turned her head to look at the passing bush, and something caught her eye. "Stop."

"What?"

"Donna, stop the bloody car."

Donna slammed on the brakes and the car screeched to a halt. Ally jumped out and ran back down the driveway. Sure enough, caught there in the bush was what appeared to be a big hank of animal hair.

She pulled it off and held up to the light. Was it the same as the hair she'd found on her fence? Regardless, it gave her an idea—a way to confirm her suspicions, and to solve the problem. She pocketed the scrap and then went back to the car, hoping she was right.

WHEN Tynan strode out of the dark to join her for dinner, Ally was standing on her verandah, drink in hand.

"Milk?" she said as he reached the bottom of the steps, holding the glass out.

He hesitated, then looked up at her and grinned. "No thanks. Beer would be good, though. Been a busy day."

"Was a busy night too." She turned and walked inside, heading to the fridge to get them both a cold beer. When she went back outside, Tynan was leaning against the verandah railing, staring out into the inky blackness.

Ally held out the beer, and smiled at the sensation of his skin against hers as he took it.

"I had a very interesting day," she said as she walked past him and leant against one of the posts. "I went to see our friend Mr Caan."

There was a soft growl in Tynan's throat. "You shouldn't have done that. He's not to be trusted."

Ally smiled. "Have you forgotten who I am?" He looked at her, a light frown narrowing his eyes. "I'm a woman of Anstruther Farm."

His eyes travelled over her, and then his lips twisted. "I wasn't sure."

"It breeds true. Just as I think it does in your family." Ally took a sip of beer. "Correct me if I'm wrong, but until recently there hadn't been a panther sighting for a couple of years. How long ago did your father pass away?"

The twist of the lips grew into a smile. "A couple of years."

"And then two weeks ago, the sightings began again, albeit with Mr Caan. How long have you been back in the valley?"

He bowed his head. "As you well know, two weeks."

"And am I right in guessing that your aversion to Mr Caan isn't just man to man, but feline to canine?"

Tynan shook his head, his admiration apparent. "I can't believe I ever underestimated an Anstruther woman."

"Something I'm sure you'll never do again. I think you hurt him last night. He's been telling people he's got a throat infection, but I bet under the scarf he was wearing his neck is black and blue."

"He's lucky I didn't kill him."

"Cats only kill to eat."

"Men kill to protect."

Ally sipped her beer. "How aware of being a man are you as a cat?"

"It's hard, but I can think as both."

"But generally you're just cat."

"Yes."

"I'd like to spend some time with the cat." Ally took another sip of beer.

"Not until the man is satisfied."

The heat in Tynan's eyes sent a shiver down Ally's spine. "I'm sure he will be. But first..." She turned, put the beer down on the table and picked up the envelope that lay there. "Can you tell me what this is?" She held it out.

She liked that Tynan made sure their hands touched as he took the envelope. He opened it and looked inside with a frown. Then he leant down, took a big sniff and reared back.

"Where did you get this?"

"Some from his driveway, some from one of the fenceposts here. It is his, isn't it?" Tynan nodded, and Ally smiled. "Brilliant. I think I can safely say that the animals of Barrengarry will be safe from dog attacks in the very near future."

Tynan frowned. "You can do that?"

Ally reached forward and snatched the envelope out of his hand. "I certainly can. So you'd best keep me happy, my feline friend."

Tynan stepped closer and Ally felt his heat infuse her. "More than happy to do that, witch."

As their lips met, Ally was smiling.

ONE of the disadvantages of the escarpment was how weather seemed to be trapped in the valley, Ally thought as she leant against a verandah post and stared out at the low cloud that covered everything.

Luckily, its ability to trap things was something the Anstruther women had learnt to use to their advantage. One spell could cover the valley, and keep everyone safe.

The phone rang; Ally answered and held the mobile to her ear.

"News," Donna said. "Caan's selling his place. Apparently he's decided Barrengarry isn't the place for him."

Ally made a mental note to send information about Mr Caan out to other wise women. He'd undoubtedly try to find somewhere else to unleash the wild side of himself and his mates.

"Well, it's not for everyone," Ally said.

"So, have you got news for me?" Ally heard the hopeful tone in Donna's voice and almost laughed. She hadn't doubted for a moment that the valley would soon notice the amount of time she and Tynan were spending together.

"Should I?"

"Fine, be like that."

Ally hung up the phone with a smile, then turned and went into the house. It was her turn to cook tonight, and she needed some practice in order to grill a steak to perfection.

The sorrows of falling in love with a carnivore.

FADE AWAY

IAN NICHOLS

Whispers.

She turned and rolled in her bed. She felt her arms, pinched her wrists. Not frail enough yet. Too thick, too earthly, too heavy. The sheets were sticky with her sweat and she lay back, wished that the flesh, the bone would melt away.

Soon.

"But not soon enough." To the air, to the invisible.

Soon.

"Now. Oh, I want you now. Touch me."

With love.

Her back arched and she inhaled sharply through her clenched teeth. She tugged at her nightgown, impatient with the restriction of even that filmy cloth. As it rose over her head and her arms stretched up to be rid of it, a shiver passed down her body. She gasped, touched here, there, as if she traced the path of invisible kisses, every place on her skin, the lightest of kisses, kisses of night and air. The kisses went on and on, insubstantial as the moonlight through her window, molten, flowing into her and burning her until the heat consumed her utterly.

Oh.

Oh.

Only a token of what will be.

"My love, my love, my love."

Yes. I am your love, and you are mine. Eternally.

"Eternally."

HEAT ticked on the roof. Emily picked at the fruit on the plate before her. A cool breeze swept the verandah, shuffled leaves out in the yard. Sere, light as air. That's what she wanted. To be light as air, to go into the breeze and fly around the earth, a gentle breath, as gentle as Derek's touch, his kiss. She pushed the plate away.

"Emily, you have to eat." Her sister walked around the table and put the plate back in front of her. "You're so thin. Too thin. Eat something, for me. I'll worry if you don't."

Emily smiled. "Cassie , you worry about everything. I'm fine."

"You're not." She sat back down. "You look like a skeleton."

"I'm healthy. Since I came here I've lost weight, that's all. Hard work and a healthy diet."

There was truth in that, Cassie thought. There was a glow that shone out from Emily, like a lamp beneath the skin. But it was taut skin, almost stretched. Too lambent, as if it would soon vanish altogether and just the light would be left.

Cassie sat back down and poured herself another cup of tea.

"How has it been out here, apart from the hard work and healthy diet?"

Emily smiled. "It's the best thing I've ever done. A sea change. I'm forgetting the city, the life there, the pace. I love this house, I love this island, I love what I've found here."

"How far's the mainland? It took me two hours on the ferry."

"About twenty kilometres that way." She pointed in a north-easterly direction. "It's not much, an old town with a pub, a church and a few shops. Not many people live in there, but there are a few on the properties around about."

"It's pretty here," Cassie admitted. She looked around at the stone walls of the house. "This place looks about a hundred years old, nice and solid."

"It's convict work. They built like that. This was a meant to be a quarantine station, and then it became a lighthouse, and this was the keeper's cottage. You can see the ruins of the old tower and the beacon down on the point. They shut it down during World War Two, and it collapsed sometime in the late fifties. There's some wild weather here, blowing in off the Southern Ocean. Fishermen used to use it sometimes, but it was bought by some corporate executive and done up as a weekend getaway. He died and his son put it on the market. Now it's the lonely retreat of an aging spinster."

Cassie had heard that word from Emily before. It was usually uttered with a hint of tired bitterness. This time it was light, gently merry, as if she made fun of herself, a private joke.

"Em, what's going on? Have you found a man?" She didn't add "at last". "Is there some secret yachtsman who moors his boat off your jetty? "

Emily looked up at her in surprise, hazel eyes wide. "God, no!" She laughed. "Who'd have me? Fifty years old, skinny and frumpy, that's me. I moved out here to get away from people, not to find a man."

Cassie looked hard at her. Even though she denied it, there was something different about her, some lilt in her voice, some hidden joy that differed from the way she had been.

"Skinny, yes, but not frumpy. You've never been frumpy," Cassie said. And it was true. Cassie had been the plump and jolly one, popular with everyone. Em had been the stand-offish one, tall and elegant, her silky blonde hair always brushed to a glow, her full lips always held in a slight frown. Truth to tell, she'd frightened off the boys at school and at uni. There were one or two men she'd had brief affairs with after she graduated, but nothing ever lasted more than a couple of months. She seemed to have given up trying after that, and devoted herself to being the best lawyer in town. Then the sea change, to this little place a long way from anything. Away from it all. Cassie sighed. "Well, it must be the sea air."

"Maybe it is." She smiled. "I feel this is the right place for me, the place I've wanted to be all my life."

"You've always been a bit of a romantic, Em. But," Cassie said as she looked out to the garden and trees and the ocean beyond, "this is a nice place to be romantic."

"Yes, it is." Em's smile grew a little wistful and she looked down at her lean hands on the white tablecloth. "It's funny that I had to come out here, away from people, to find romance."

"Well, that's what a change is all about, isn't it? Finding something that you didn't have before."

"And, do you know, Cass, I didn't even know what was missing?"

"Peace and quiet?"

"That's part of it." And she said no more.

THEY passed the rest of the afternoon in platitudes and reminiscences, and Cassie left on the ferry around five. "I have to get back to pack," she said.

"It was lovely you could get out to see me before your trip."

"It's a bit far to drive from the city, but since I'm flying out tomorrow, I took a break from organising things for a visit with my big sister. I won't be back for a while, after all. I'll get back late tonight, finish the packing and try to get some sleep. This time tomorrow I'll be on the plane to England."

Romance, Emily thought as she waved goodbye to her sister. *People don't understand what it is. I had to come here to find it.*

But it was only at night, and Emily craved the darkness.

THEY used to call that Poor Derek's Place," the skipper of the ferry called out to her as the boat thumped through the waves.

"What?" Cassie called back. She was the only passenger at the moment. They'd dropped off a few locals at the last island, and they'd probably pick up more at the other islands on the way back to the mainland.

"Poor Derek's Place." The skipper turned around to her. He was a nuggety little man with a scruffy white beard. He had on faded jeans and a thick navy blue jumper that had seen better days. A cap with "Alvin Rods" written on it was pushed to the back of his head, revealing the white hair that circled his scalp like a tonsure. "They called it that after a bloke that died there, back just after the house was built."

"Died?"

"Yeah. Convict, he was. Got left behind on the island, some drunk guard chained him up in the building, and he just got left behind when they were all taken back to the mainland. They'd been building the cottage, y'see, and those guards got pissed on rum. They got in the boat to go back, and just forgot this Derek bloke. The doctor found him when he went to the cottage, a few months later, after the winter storms."

"That's horrible."

"Too right. Too bloody right."

NIGHT. Pastel images cast by moonlight, the sea phosphorescent as it cracked on the rocks, hissed back into the dark. By the jetty it softened, rimmed by the white fire of savage light beyond the breakwater. Emily sat on the sand above it.

Her mind had not left her, but the path of reason had changed. It seemed natural, normal, reasonable for her to walk naked in the night, to sit on the beach, to close her eyes and listen to the orchestra of the waves and wind. To rise, and to writhe in dance, to prance and spin, to let her body demand the motion on motion, finally to curvette at the littoral, tease the ripples and then arch into the chill water, for it to tease at her as she had teased it. To feel the runnels of current trace her flesh, the delicate metaphors of those beyond, in the ocean, that could mould continents.

She ran back.

Well?

"Should I tell you?"

Yes.

"It was as if I was born."

A baptism.

"It was... exciting."

Show me.

"What... ?"

Show me how you danced.

She did. She mimicked the dance on the sand, how she had flirted with the small waves, surrendered to the wind. It warmed her and left her breathless. She collapsed onto the bed.

I loved to dance, until they put me in chains.

She felt his caress, his touch. Stronger. Closer.

I can feel the dance on you. Your breath, your sweat, the beat of your heart.

She reached to touch him, but there was nothing. Not yet. So close.

Soon.

SHE was beyond hunger. Stick-spare, light. No thirst. It was now.

There was chain in the shed. Old, rusty chain. She washed it and oiled it, prepared it as if for a sacrament, as if it was her garb for a wedding. There were padlocks on the shed door and the tool box, another big one on the gate.

The bedroom window had bars set into its stone wall. The chains rattled against them as she looped them around and drew them through. The big padlock secured them. She stripped the bed, put the bedclothes outside. She had made a shift of coarse linen, and she wore this. She put one chain around her waist, tight, locked it. The other went around her neck.

She sat on the bed and closed her eyes. The breeze through the window was laden with scents. The sea, the flowers, bushes and trees. She breathed deeply.

Is it now?

She looked at her hand, where the keys to the padlocks lay. They had a dull gleam, as if it were they that were ghostly, lost in time.

She closed her hand and hurled them away, through the window to lie lost in the yard.

"Yes, now," she said.

Now.

She could feel him, feel him now, touch him as he touched her, but not yet see him. She lay back, holding him to her, closed her eyes and waited for her vision to clear.

WHISPERS.
Derek?
Stillness.
Derek?
Laughter, soft, fading away. Sensation. Loss. Nothing to hold. Nothing.
Softer still. Free. Free from this place.
What?
Softest. Goodbye.
Then nothing at all.

Derek?
DEREK?

Silence.

BREAD AND CIRCUSES

FELICITY DOWKER

*"Already long ago, from when we sold our vote to no man,
the People have abdicated our duties; for the People who
once upon a time handed out military command, high
civil office, legions—everything, now restrains itself and
anxiously hopes for just two things: bread and circuses."*
—Satire X, Decimus Junius Juvenalis

WE live in the graveyard. It's the only place they won't go.
It's not religious. There are no gods left to frighten evil
away. It's not even physical. We've dragged a few of them in to see
what would happen. Nothing much did. They just get pissed. They
get so worked up that they can't function, not even in their usual
shambolic, brainless fashion. And they cry pink-tinged, meaty
tears. We think they have cellular memory of being truly dead and
buried underground, and they don't like it—can't *bear* it.

They would rather stand gazing in and starving. Better that
than to enter the place where the dead used to be imprisoned. So
they lurch outside the cemetery, and we cower within.

My bed is a tomb that was once occupied by SLOAN, MARJORIE,
MAY SHE REST IN PEACE. I guarantee that wherever she is now,

SLOAN, MARJORIE doesn't rest in peace. Nor do I. My lullabies are shuffling thick feet, wet smacking lips, wretched groans oozing from putrescent throats.

It's poetic, I suppose. The outcome of the final revolution. We were the ruling party for so long: living, roaming the world in arrogant freedom. They were the oppressed: dead, planted in dark earth for an eternity of decay and neglect. Perhaps it was always a matter of time until they rose up and fought for our place at the top of things. Maybe their vacant, endless striving for our downfall is fair punishment for our presumption.

It doesn't matter anyway.

I don't hate them. They're too empty to feel anything about, other than fear, revulsion, and crawling fascination.

I hate the graveyard. I hate the Game.

THE Game started a year ago, when we realised we graveyard citizens would survive. That left us with one question: now what? We were alive, there was food for us to stay that way. The countless casualties left behind a lot of non-perishable foodstuffs, and the wilderness brimmed with wild animals for us to hunt. The zombies didn't come inside our graveyard

(prison)

sanctuary. We would endure.

But what was the *point*?

There were suicides. People strolled out of the graveyard and offered themselves to the zombies. Our leaders—men and women for whom managing our village was enough reason for living—saw their

(minions)

community slipping from their grasp. Morale wasn't low, it was subterranean.

The zombies began the destruction of the human race, but we were willing to finish the job ourselves rather than face empty futures.

No religion survived in the age of the walking dead. A few random crazies clung to their philosophical opiate, but most of us understood that eternity and divinity were cancelled when the first reanimated corpse erupted from its grave. Which left... nothing. Just years of well-fed graveyard life, with zombies at the gates.

The lack of joy was killing us more efficiently than any gnashing teeth and tearing fingers could. Our leaders were desperate. In a last-ditch effort to fill our agonising hollowness, they gave bloody birth to the Game, and my fellow cemetery-dwellers were satisfied. That disgusts me more than anything else: they all love the Game. Even though they understand that one unfortunate day, they may be the participants, they're willing to risk it for the rush they get from watching. The proletariat still have to work it for the pleasure of the powerful people, even in the cemeteries of the new world—and *they agree to do it*. I want to scream. I want to die. But I don't want to give them the gift of watching me.

I'm alone since they sacrificed Noelle, and I'm an easy target. The only reason they haven't played me in the Game is because it's more amusing to let me live. Every grinding day I spend here is a joke. They're taking bets on when I'll crack and give myself to the zombies. Or, better yet, when I'll try to attack our little community, take revenge for them killing Noelle. They love a good death-battle. It doesn't matter whose blood is shed. Human, zombie, it's all the same.

A full belly and entertainment. That's all the savage human virus has ever been about, but we've hidden it beneath intricate webs of civilisation until now. In a world ruled by the dead, what need is there to conceal our base selves?

I'm as primitive as the rest of them. The same adrenaline spurts in my bloodstream like liquid fire with each new Game, and I despise myself for it. But I feel something they don't seem to.

Love.

I love Noelle. I miss her.

I don't think they remember love. In that regard, they're already zombies themselves. Every last stinking one of them.

SHE was my girlfriend of five years, and I still thought she was Goddess incarnate. She was tall, dark-skinned, and tough. Without her, I never would have survived the zombies and made it to a cemetery community. I don't know now if that's a good or bad thing. All I know is that Noelle was my angel, my protector, my inspiration. There was beauty in our species while I could stare into her black eyes and kiss her soft pillow lips.

She called me Curly Sue. It wasn't original. It was trite and common. But it was all mine, and sounded so sweet tumbling from her tongue. Nobody calls me anything much now. I'm not sure they know my name anymore. Sometimes I forget it myself. I'm empty and alone. Who cares what my name is?

Noelle did. She cared that my name was Susan, enough to twist it into something that was her own, and make *me* her own.

So I try to remember that I'm Susan. Curly Sue. Not for me—for Noelle.

THERE was no Monday, Tuesday, Wednesday, whatever. Just random time, a series of sun-ups and sun-downs set to the music of milling zombies. Nobody had anywhere to be, so time became redundant. We were cut loose, set adrift in space.

It was horrific.

She kept me tethered to Earth. We lay in the pit we'd dug with our bare hands, five feet into the soft soil in a tree-lined corner of the graveyard. It was warm in there, wrapped around each other. We rose only to eat and defecate. Noelle had been out of the graveyard on food detail. They sent her because she was so strong, she had a good chance of returning. She went without protest. She thought it fair to do her bit. I lay trembling in the pit every time she left, convinced that she wouldn't return. She always did, and I buried my face in her thick dark hair, sobbing tears of relief.

"Relax, Curly Sue," she'd say, stroking my back like the mother-sister-lover-friend she was. "I'm a big girl. I'll always come back to you, little girl. It's fate, and love, and the way things are. Understand?"

I believed, but I worried, too. I knew she was amazing, and amazing things were given only to be taken away.

So they took her, and I can't tell you what day it was, because I don't know. I can't pinpoint the moment it happened, because every moment is the same. That's the most profane thing about it—someone like Noelle deserved to have her death noted in the turning cogs of time.

We were making love. Her long brown legs were coiled around my white ones, intertwined like writhing snakes. She gave off baking heat when we coupled. I basked in it. She was slippery with sweat. I gloried in sliding my fingers around the slick skin of her back. Her tongue danced around my lips, teasing me, and the hard blasts of breath from her nose were a delicious assault on my face.

I ground myself against her, thrusting up, our bodies consumed by a hunger that rivalled the zombies who listened to our carnal sounds. Death and sex, the timeless marriage.

"Two lesbos getting it on in a graveyard while the world goes to shit. Don't that speak volumes," a voice drawled. I looked up over Noelle's shoulder. She grabbed my chin, steering me back towards her, lips roaming my face.

"Ignore them," she breathed in my ear, a wisp of temptation.

But I wasn't that strong. Besides, they'd never intruded on us like this. Something felt wrong.

"Go away," I said, glaring up at the figure above us.

Tom Sheehan. He usually restrained his boorishness to leering at us from the shadows. He was a coward and a bigot. Most of the survivors were. It took a special sort of selfish desperation to evade zombies. Unless, like me, you had a Goddess to deliver you.

"That's not nice," Tom said. Several figures appeared around the rim of our pit. They reached in and laid their hands on Noelle.

"Leave her alone!" I screamed, digging my fingers into the flesh of her back, trying to hold on. She was oily with our lovemaking, and I couldn't keep her safe from them. She thrashed, muscles bulging and the white of her furious eyes vivid.

She didn't speak. She just fought.

It took ten of them to haul her out of the pit. She was big, strong, and enraged. They were all men, the tallest and broadest. They'd known she'd resist. She was powerful. They knew their best chance was to sneak in a mob.

Gutless bastards.

Tom still crouched next to the pit, staring at me. I struggled to my feet, covering my naked breasts and pubic mound with my hands. I felt his piggy gaze skittering across my flesh like loathsome flabby bugs. I forced myself to meet his eyes, and he grinned. I could see saliva glistening on his lips.

"Your hellcat gal pal is for the Game," he said, winking. "She's gonna put on a helluva show. Don't worry, I'll keep you warm at night, after. I've always been a charitable guy."

I grabbed the edge of the pit, ready to pull myself out and go to Noelle's aid. Tom stood and brought his steel-capped boot down on my fingers. The pain was brilliant and nauseating. I heard a crackling sound as the delicate bones in my hands snapped.

I wasn't strong like Noelle. I screamed.

"Stay in there," he said, drawing his boot back and aiming at my face. I cradled my broken hands in front of my heaving belly and tried in vain to see Noelle above ground. All I could see was a mass of jerking backs as the men closed in around her. She still wasn't making a sound.

"Please?"

Tom laughed.

I tried to scrabble out of the pit without using my screaming hands. I must have looked pitiful—naked, crying, climbing using my elbows and feet. Noelle wouldn't have been so pathetic if our roles had been reversed.

"I said, *stay*," Tom said, and kicked me in the head.

Instant blackness.

I WOKE up folded in a corner of the pit. A sharp scent stung my nostrils, and after a moment, I realised what it was. Ammonia. My hair and face felt wet, and I shivered in the cold air. The sun was high, but spared no warmth.

He'd pissed on me. They took Noelle, broke my hands, knocked me out... and pissed on me. This was humanity?

I inspected my hands. They were swollen lumps, skin stretched taut and shiny and already a vibrant shade of purple. As if on cue, my head began to throb and complain. My right eye viewed the world through a thin curtain of crimson where the blood from my head trickled down.

I stood up. They had Noelle. I couldn't do much about it, but I couldn't stay in the pit and let it go unchecked, either.

I used my hands to climb out. I bit my tongue to swallow the pain, gagging on the pulsing blood that flowed down my throat. Everything was red agony, but they had Noelle, and that eclipsed it all.

"Right on time," Tom called as I staggered across the graveyard. He leant on a tree, smiling and beckoning to me like an old friend. Behind him was our entire village, clustered in a thrumming mass near the gates. As I neared them, Tom grasped my elbow. They parted for us, staring with exhilarated eyes. I was crying again. The salt of my tears stung my ravaged face. Tom's hand was a claw, digging cruelly into the tender flesh of my arm.

I didn't think about the zombies stumbling nearby. They were a daydream in contrast to the grotesquery of my fellow humans.

Noelle stood in front of the open gates, groaning zombies pawing the air less than a metre from her. She was still naked, her dark skin mottled with blood and bruises. I saw the imprint of a boot

(I'll kill you Tom, I swear, somehow I will)

in the small of her back and thought I might die from my grief and fury. A ragged sob choked out of my throat, and Noelle turned around, looking at me. One of her beautiful eyes was swollen shut, her bottom lip torn. They'd beaten her. The Game worked better if the participant was bloody and fighting their injuries. Besides, they liked beating on people.

She raised one long arm and pointed at me, resting her other hand over her heart.

"I'll always come back to you, Curly Sue," she said. Her voice was calm and clear. "I love you. Remember."

"Aw, it's so fucking sweet I could cry," Tom said, but he was weak against the force between Noelle and I. I felt it, sparking, connecting us. I pointing at her with one ruined hand, and placed the other on the hollow space that was my heart. They let us stand like that for a moment. Then the machine gunners stepped forward.

Their job was to mow a path through the zombies, to create a space for the Gamer to run through. Noelle stood motionless, watching while they fulfilled their role with aplomb. The undead fell in jittering mounds as the bullets tore into their heads and reversed their reanimation once and for all. The gunners whooped and hollered, sweating, excited, and giddy with the thrill of the easy kill. I covered my ears against the *rat-a-tat-a-tat* of the guns. The result was a bizarre silent movie of exploding zombie heads and falling undead bodies.

The zombies were horrible dead things that should be underground instead of staggering around trying to kill everyone... but they were people, once. They were abhorrent, but mostly they were people who were different to us, and we were mowing them down. They were without intellect, driven by irresistible hunger. We were intelligent, supposedly. We used our advantage to kill easy targets. We were evil.

Although maybe the zombies weren't entirely unintelligent, because after a few minutes of watching their comrades slaughtered by the gunners, they hung back. The path cleared by the bullets stayed open.

It was time.

They gave her a hunting knife and machine gun. I saw her arms shaking under the weight of the gun, and knew how badly they had hurt her. But she walked forward, not looking back, not even at me.

If she'd refused to play, they would have gunned her down where she stood and thrown her corpse out for the zombies to devour. She had a gun, but they had several. The Game was not voluntary. Once chosen, you left the cemetery and greeted the zombies—one way or another.

She left with her battered head held high.

Hidden in the woods outside the graveyard was a metal ball— the Prize. Noelle had to find the Prize and bring it back to win the Game. If she did, she'd never have to play again. She'd never have to go on food detail, muck out a lavatory hole, or venture out for ammunition and blankets and the other primitive and technological miscellanea our village coveted. She'd live in the graveyard with her community taking care of her, revelling in her heroism.

It sounded like a good deal, but nobody had ever won a Game. Nobody except the zombies, the undefeated champions. As I stood watching my love march out the gates and into the sea of churning undead, I dared to hope.

Noelle bolted for the trees. The zombies were cautious,

(unintelligent my arse!)

making occasional grabs with foetid hands, but not rushing forward. She slashed at their seeking fingers as she sprinted past. She looked fearsome, a gore-clad Fury with flying hair, sinuous muscles, and wild eyes. I should have walked away then, sunk into our pit and remembered her in her prime. But I couldn't.

They lunged as she neared the edge of the woods. A pack of twenty surged forward and tackled her to the ground. I saw a child zombie lift Noelle's flailing foot to its mouth and bite off her toes. A dozen sprays of blood arced into the air around the snarling, biting, tearing zombies.

"I thought she'd get further," Tom said. The crowd was

disappointed. I thought I would explode from the hate bubbling and festering inside my veins.

She was dying for their amusement. How could they be so cruel? I loved her, and she was dying, and they didn't care!

But incredibly, my warrior queen was rising to her mutilated feet. In a volley of gunfire and a flash of knife play, she emerged from the clump of undead. They fell like marionettes whose strings had been cut. I saw the child-zombie's blonde head burst open in a cascade of white and red pulp as Noelle took aim and fired. I screeched, a primal cry of bloodlust and triumph.

"Run! Get in the trees and run until you find the Prize and get back here!" I shrieked to Noelle through the bars of the cemetery fence. A man-zombie swiped at my face on the other side, and I laughed at him. I felt spittle trickling from my lips, and knew I was crazy.

For she was lost, whether she made it back or not. They had bitten her, torn at her, infected her. She wouldn't be Noelle for much longer. It was over.

But the Game wasn't over, and she was still my beloved. So I watched, cried, yelled, and screamed. Through it all, she never made a sound, never looked back. She was something else, some other species elevated above humans and zombies. She was perfect.

And still she ran.

She was enveloped by the trees, and as if heeding some psychic call, every zombie turned and followed. They clambered, straining forward, crushing their kin in their rush to chase Noelle. Their groans were jagged and urgent. They had been hungry for a long time, and they, too, loved the Game, for it meant food and purpose for a brief while. They were past their momentary fear of destruction, and their focus was fixed on Noelle.

There was a loud beeping sound, and the crowd gasped.

"I'll be damned. The bitch-giant has done it. Too bad for her that it doesn't matter now." Tom spoke in my ear. I didn't care. I was euphoric, delirious.

It was the Prize monitor going off. She'd picked it up and flicked the sensor switch. She'd got it. Nobody had ever done that before. She was special. She was coming back, and everything would be alright.

Noelle...

I STOOD at the fence for a day and night. Everyone gave up and wandered back to their idle business after a few hours, but I refused to accept it. She had the Prize. She'd won the Game.

She'd said she'd always come back. She made a promise, and she was a Goddess. Somehow it would be ok.

A few women with something vaguely resembling decency left in their shrivelled hearts picked me up and carried me to my

(our)

pit. I think they wanted me out of sight. It was offensive to see me keeping a pathetic vigil at the fence. They didn't want the reminder of their guilt.

The zombies didn't emerge from the woods for several days. Noelle must have been a delight of epic proportions for them. They were even more slow-moving and vacant-eyed than usual after their orgy of ghoulishness. Peeping over the edge of my pit, I could see her blood smeared on them. One held a severed hand, dark-skinned and long-fingered, nibbling on the weeping wrist stump like a juicy canapé.

I couldn't stay in the pit. She should have been there with me, it was our place. Instead, she was splattered across the replete undead. Nothing was right out there, and nothing was right in here. I climbed out and found the most exposed, uncomfortable tomb to lie in (thank you, SLOAN, MARJORIE). It was penance, the least I deserved for doing nothing while they took Noelle. There was nothing I *could* have done, but *she* would have fought for *me*.

I was barren, null and void. Another zombie had been made, without so much as a bite.

I DON'T know how long it's been. I tried keeping track, but the days and nights are greasy things that slip through my clutching mind, and I find myself lost in them. Maybe it's been a year.

When I woke up curled in the foetal position in my dead-bed, I knew today was Game day, and they were going to play me at last. I'd dreamt it, and in the new dead world, dreams didn't lie.

Tom sat on the edge of SLOAN, MARJORIE's slab, staring at me. Was it pain I saw in his moist eyes? He was disgusting, but perhaps even he felt emotion in this weird place. He'd made several advances since Noelle had gone. I'd rejected them. Now they'd sent him to collect me, and he was less than ecstatic about it.

I hated him all the same. If I'd thought I stood a chance of success, I would have tried to pluck the eyes from his murdering skull with my deformed hands that had never healed right. Hands that *he* had ruined.

"Wake up, sleepyhead," he said, voice hard. His eyes continued to give him away. "Today's a special day."

"Is it?" I knuckled the crust of sleep from my eyes. "Am I meant to be shocked? Scared? Sad? Sorry, I'm just bored. You have that effect on me."

His mouth twisted, and one of his hands jerked as if he'd like to slap me.

"You're a stupid bitch. You know that? I could have looked after you. They would have left you alone if you were with me. I tried, but you won't be saved. Will you? Still hung up on that Amazon woman of yours. Well, fine. Take what's coming to you, then. Get up."

"Oh, they'd leave me alone if I was with *you*?" My laughter was a bitter bark in the chill morning air. "*You're* safe from the Games? I think you'll find out one day just what utter bullshit that is, Tom. We're all meat for the beast. Nobody here cares about anyone. Nobody is safe. Nobody is *special*. Nothing matters, not even you—*especially* not you."

He did slap me then, a solid blow that sent my head reeling and thickened my brain. It hurt, but I laughed again. I knew that would bother him.

"Come die then. We'll send you to join your bitch girlfriend. Isn't that what you want, *Curly Sue*?"

He knew how to stop my laughter.

He reached to pull me up, but I waved his hands away. I was determined to go with pride and strength, like Noelle had. I was so terrified that I thought I might lose control of my bladder, but I wouldn't let *them* see. I wouldn't do anything to intensify their enjoyment.

They stood at the gates, waiting. I was clothed, and Noelle had been naked, but I still couldn't muster the quiet dignity she'd emanated. My lower lip was trembling, and my breath was shallow and rapid. I could feel sweat rolling in beads down my brow, despite the morning cold. The gunners stood tensed and ready. Nobody moved toward me. Nobody beat me. It wasn't necessary. I'd been bleeding and broken ever since Noelle died.

I felt hard metal in my hand, and realised Tom was pressing a knife into it. I took it, and he placed a machine gun in my other. It was ridiculous. I had no idea how a gun worked, and couldn't operate it whilst wielding a knife with my other hand—not with my mangled paws. I was no warrior, not like Noelle. The weapons felt heavy and cumbersome, and as useful as if I had been brandishing a frozen fish and a banana. But all that mattered was that I didn't break. No tears. No pleading.

"You're all going to die," I said. They stared back at me, saucer eyes in moon faces.

"We know," a little boy said. I looked at him, and he met my gaze. His face was blank. He couldn't have been more than six years old.

"If I can, I'll come back and kill you all," I said, knowing it was ludicrous.

"Maybe we could give her a break." Tom's voice was behind me, always behind me. They looked at him, pleased. *Here* was some palpable pain. *Here* was the entertainment I was withholding. "She... her girlfriend died this way. Maybe she should be exempt."

Marion, our leader, stepped forward. She was smiling. She looked like a kind old woman, with plump arms you could step into. She had thought up the Game, and she selected who played. She was Grandmother Death.

"Are you volunteering to take her place, Tom? Is that what you're saying?"

There was a pause, stretching out into eternity while I stood holding my useless weapons. Tom coughed. The little boy who had spoken giggled.

Then: "No. I was only saying... I'm sorry. Go ahead. I didn't mean to interfere."

"No, I didn't think you did," Marion said, still smiling.

"Cowards," I hissed through chattering teeth. "You're all cowards."

"Show us bravery, then, Susan," Marion said. She waved one of her small hands at the gates and the zombies loitering beyond.

"Serve your community. Show us heroism, and exhilaration. Entertain us. Feed them. There are no better causes. There is nothing else."

I spat at her, and one of the gunners raised his weapon above his head for a blow. Marion stopped him with a look, and he fell back, glowering. She wiped my spittle from her chest and fixed her pale blue eyes on me.

I looked away first. What good was a battle of wills with this death-queen now?

Marion nodded at the gunners, and they set about their noisy, bloody work. Standing here, so close to them, the sound was deafening. I could hear the cries of the undead with unbearable clarity from my vantage point near the gates. I'd never noticed how animalistic they sounded when wounded. Their cacophony was violent and terrible. I forced myself not to block my ears. This was *my* death, too, and I wanted to be present for it. Every gun blast, every *thock* as bullets tore into zombie flesh, every scream and whimper from the dying undead—I took it in and made it my own.

The legion of walking corpses outside the cemetery fell back. A clear path opened amongst them, snaking towards the woods. The grass was green and fragrant out there, and I remembered that the *world* wasn't dead, only the part of it that was human. Everything else was fecund and free. I had no more time to reflect, because I was nudged forward.

I dropped my gun. It was no good to me, and would weigh me down. The knife I kept, though I had little chance of using it productively.

"What the fuck are you doing?" Tom's voice was a buzzing insect in my ear. "You don't stand a chance without the gun! Are you crazy?"

I ignored him. He was as dead as I was.

I crouched, allowing energy to coil in my haunches... build... climax... and *release* as I sprang into a full-blown sprint. I was out of the graveyard for the first time in years. My feelings were not fear, but giddiness. I'd escaped! Here was *life*!

Then I felt the first cold, moist hand pawing at my torso, and my skin leapt in disgust. I waved the knife wildly around me as I ran, feeling it connect more than a few times, shuddering at the wetness that soon coated my slashing hand. I kept my eyes fixed on the narrowing strip of grass in front of me, and the woods beyond. I didn't want to see the zombies. Confronting them so closely would bring an abrupt end to my running. My legs would seize with horror. So long as I refused to acknowledge their proximity with my eyes, I could keep going.

I heard the villagers cheering me on. They sounded crazed, overjoyed, stunned.

I didn't run for them. I was looking for my Prize, and it was in the woods.

I was small and fast, even after years pent up in the graveyard. I could see trees that marked the edge of the woods metres away. I stretched out my hand, straining for them.

A zombie's hand clamped on my wrist like a stone manacle, and I was wrenched by the force of the grab and my forward momentum. I slammed into the creature, my face smacking into its own. I gasped a lungful of air, felt bile rise in my throat as the thing's dead-stench flooded into me. Its mouth snapped at mine, trying to take in flesh. One of its eyes dangled on the stem, bouncing and brushing my skin as the other stared in frenzied malice. It had no nose, just a ragged flap of skin where it had been. Worms writhed in its patchy black hair, and lice burrowed in its ears. Its flesh was green-grey and damp, coated with mould.

I didn't know if it was male or female. It was just a zombie.

"Rargh," it moaned, a flaccid sound flopping from its rotten throat. "Urgh!"

"Get your hands off me," I said, bringing the knife up with my free hand and pressing it against the thing's soft neck. "I'm sorry, but I have to get in the woods. Let me go."

It mewled, still trying to bite my face, the hand that wasn't gripping my wrist gouging at my chest hard enough to lift the skin in bloody, burning furrows. I could sense its comrades closing in. I had seconds before they were on top of me.

"I'm sorry," I said again, plunging the knife into its throat. The flesh collapsed like moist soufflé. In two stabs, the head dangled by a thin string of mildewed skin. One more rip, and the head toppled off. The zombie's hand came undone around my wrist, and its body slumped to the ground.

A score of hands caressed me, trying to grab, tear, devour. I shrugged them off and threw myself forwards, into the cool darkness of the woods.

My legs spasmed and gave way, and I tumbled to my knees, falling into the aromatic grass and dead leaf mulch on the forest floor. My head spun and my body trembled. I couldn't think straight. I retched until a flood of hot filth poured out of my mouth and painted the undergrowth around me.

My traumatised body had betrayed me. I couldn't even crawl. I flopped onto my back and stared up at the leafy canopy above me, whimpering. I waited to feel the first defiling hands on my body, sobbed as I anticipated the first snaggle of teeth penetrating my skin. My knife lay next to me, useless, accusatory.

I waited a long time, and eventually realised the zombies hadn't followed me.

But *something* was coming for me, shuffling across the ground in lopsided steps. It approached behind my head. I rolled my eyes back as far as they would go, ignoring the watery sting, but saw only a blur.

"Come get me, then," I croaked, throat tight and dry. "I'm an easy meal. Dinner's served."

"Curgh-ee Shoooooooo," the thing crooned, and something in the deepest parts of my brain exploded.

(my Prize)

My visitor reached my side, edged forward, stood over me. I could see it

(her!)

in glorious perspective, a living dead Goddess, looming above me in terrible beauty.

"Noelle?" The word left my mouth before my brain registered it. I couldn't breathe, couldn't think. I was pure emotion, trapped in my fleshy shell.

She was still divine. Her dark eyes were intact, boggling at me from the mess that was her face. Half the skin on her head had torn, and dangled in a large sheet from her chin. But it was *her* skin, that glossy mahogany casing that enclosed everything that was Noelle. It was mottled, and savaged, and paler, but still hers. Her large teeth grinned at me like rickety fence palings. One of her voluminous lips dangled with the skin beneath her chin. Her matted hair was flecked with gore. One of her arms was gone from the elbow down, leaving a stringy stump of gristle and bone. All her toes and parts of her feet were gone. The downy pad between her legs was a mish-mash of blood and maggots. All over her I saw teeth marks, gaping wounds, dangling flesh. A loop of sausage-like intestines protruded from her open belly, wound around her waist like a belt.

She was carnage, pestilence, and decay. But she was still *something else*, something above humans, zombies, and the whole damn mess. She was dead, she was hungry, and she was different, but she was Noelle. My love for her was alive.

No matter what.

Her throat bulged, and she hacked a few times, like a macabre cat trying to dislodge a fur ball.

"It's ok," I said, reaching up to her with shaking hands. "Don't hurt yourself. You don't need to—"

"Uhm bach fuh yooooooo... " she clawed at her neck, frowning. Frustrated. "Ah-wash uhm bach fuh yoo. Curgh-ee Shoo."

A thought occurred to me, and it gave me the strength to sit up.

"Noelle, are you scared of the graveyard?"

She stared at me with lurid eyes. The skin dangling from her face swayed like a grisly beard as she shook her head.

"I didn't think you would be. You're different, aren't you? Different to us all. That's why you can talk to me. That's why you remembered me. You've kept a lot of *you* in there. And maybe, with you by my side, I could do the same."

I saw that her hands were trembling, and every now and then, they would twitch toward me. She kept grabbing at herself— stopping.

"You're hungry, aren't you?"

The enormous flap of skin jiggled again as she nodded, eyes sorrowful.

"No... .urt Curgh-ee Shoo..."

"It's ok, my darling. I *want* you to. It will only hurt for a while, and then I'll be with you forever. And we'll have food and vengeance. We'll go to the graveyard. We'll sneak up on them. We'll give them the best damn Game they've ever had. And for you and me... the food, the Game, and the love will last for eternity. Remember? It's fate, and love, and the way things are."

She had fallen to her knees, and her fingers were fumbling at the blood on my hands and arms. She brought her hand to her mouth and sucked, eyes rolling in her head. I knew she couldn't control herself much longer.

"You're the first Noelle," I said as she bent her face down to mine. "You're the start of something new. I'm lucky enough to come along with you for the ride, but it's always been you that counted. And you're better than all of them. No matter what happens, you're better. *We'll* be better."

We kissed, my lips sliding deep inside the gaping, corrosive wound that was her mouth. Her tongue was furry and soft, and her breath was cold. I felt her hand at my neck, tentative at first, then squeezing, gouging. Her fingers burrowed, laying my throat open under their insistence. She was moaning and panting, like so many times before at the height of passion.

It was going to hurt a lot, but I thought she'd make it quick.

"Uh luch oo," she gurgled against my cheek as her teeth met my skin for the first time. The pain was sharp and brilliant, searing my senses. My face was raw and my nerve endings were aflame. It was so much worse than I had expected, and it was only a little bite. Just the beginning.

"I... love you, too," I gasped, digging my nails into my palms, fighting my urge to scream, to run, to fall apart. Noelle was chewing on a piece of my face, making small sounds of ecstasy in the back of her dead throat.

Her hand around my neck was tight. I couldn't breathe. I couldn't think. The world was receding to bright pinpricks of light in dancing blackness, and in the centre of it was Noelle.

I still had love, and hate, and I took them both down into oblivion.

Remember the graveyard, I screamed inside my fading brain, desperate to cling to purpose. *Remember Noelle, and be with her.*

And kill them all. Humans. Zombies. Just kill them.

I found meaning, purpose and vitality at last as Noelle tore my chest open and grappled with my ribcage to get to my heart— which was always hers.

Now comes the joy, at last. And food, always food. Steaming, dripping, throbbing flesh and red-hot blood. I want it already. I want to see them run, toy with them, hear them beg.

Bread and circuses. Even unto infinity, it's all there is. Even for me. Even for you.

It hurts, and it's horrible, and it's beautiful... and we might as well enjoy it.

BLACK WIDOW

SHONA HUSK

THE new body twitched as Angel's essence took over the warm, empty shell. She poured energy into healing the stab wounds that had caused the woman's death. When the blood stopped flowing she paused, and hoped she hadn't made a mistake in choosing this body. She sucked in a trial breath, the lungs shuddered, but remembered their function. Good, the body would survive. She took a few stumbling steps, her hand skimming the contours of the bricks for support. This body moved differently, but each body she used did. All flesh felt different, like new jeans that needed breaking in. She just needed a minute to get the feel, to get the right fit.

This body was young and flexible, not like the old one, corrupted by age and wear. Her lips moved in a smile that felt alien; she'd ground her previous body down over three decades. Somewhere above her, in a hotel room, it lay crumbled to dust. No life without a soul.

She tipped her head and glanced up at the sky. The neon lights above Las Vegas burned away the dark, a false dawn wrapped over the city. She only had a few hours. She'd wasted too long prolonging the life of the business tycoon whose soul she was tied to, not because he deserved it, selfish prat only interested in money, but because there were no fresh bodies nearby for her to occupy.

Well, none she'd fancied. What fun could she have as a middle-aged man? Female bodies were better built and men were easier to manipulate in them.

Until she secured a soul the new body she'd taken would grow in beauty, a trick to lure in her prey. But without a soul this body would die, again, and she would die permanently. After five thousand years of existence she wasn't ready to leave. Living was too much fun, and humans were too willing to trade their most precious possession for a chance at their dream.

Unsteadily she walked out of the alley. The heels strained her ankles. Passersby took one glance and looked away.

Why?

This body was young and beautiful. The addiction hadn't yet scarred the delicate features of the face. Angel glanced down at the blood staining the clothes and wrinkled her nose. They were terrible; she looked like a whore. Still, it wasn't the first time she'd benefited from a dead hooker. They tended to have a high mortality rate. If she was going to attract the right type of man, she needed new clothes.

No handbag hung from her arm, she had no pockets. Damn, no money. She let the body sag against the wall as she understood the reason for the woman's death. She'd been mugged. No one had come to her aid then, and no one was going to help her now, their eyes cast aside so they could pretend they never saw her blood coated form standing in the alley.

She closed her eyes. She needed money, clothes and a man, in that order. Beneath her feet the Earth turned too fast. She was running out of time and energy. The body trembled around her, the flesh unwilling to die again. It wanted to be used. Angel watched the people pass by. Plenty of men, plenty of money and she was in the perfect body to attract them. Plan made, she retreated into the shadow of the alley and stripped off the top so she wore only a tiny skirt and bra. Then she leaned against the wall and waited, her breath slow as she conserved energy. Pheromones seeped from her pores, modulated for the quick fix she needed. It didn't take long for someone to be drawn in by the promise of sex.

He clutched his groin, a leer on his face. "How much?"

She ran her eye over him. Not her type. She wouldn't share his soul unless she was desperate, and she wasn't there yet. But he could still be useful.

"What do you want?" She played the part he expected.

"Standard." He moved closer and fished around in his wallet fat with green. He'd won too much at the casinos.

"Twenty."

He shoved the paper note at her and unzipped. Her arm moved faster than he could see. The backhand cracked his cheekbone. He dropped to the ground, inglorious and unconscious.

This time when she walked out of the alley she had on a nice white shirt, and a wallet full of cash. He would wake up eventually, maybe next time he would think twice. The traffic stopped and she crossed the street to find a boutique. Usually she would take her time, fuss with the right look to attract the right type of man. Tonight she didn't have that luxury. Black, slinky and simple would have to do. She touched up the makeup on the face she would grow to like. Wide lips, dark eyes. The bleached hair she would fix, but not tonight. She tried on a few smiles, a simper and an eyelash flutter. Her eyes flashed yellow under the fluorescent light, a glimmer of her true self visible for an instant.

No one would think this body had been dying in an alley a mere hour ago, they would be too busy watching her sashay through the crowd, every man wondering if she were available while silently cursing the lucky bastard who would take her hand. She licked her lips and began to cruise the casino floor.

The hunt was on.

Somewhere here, amongst the drunks and gamblers, would be her target. She could smell him, the scent of ambition and desperation was a heady mix, one she couldn't resist. Unlike others of her kind she was picky; she had standards, she wouldn't share just any soul. They had to be special. They had to need her. Although if the sun rose before she had a soul to share she'd make an exception to survive and live another day.

Angel bought a drink and drifted between rows and rows of beeping, flashing machines. The lights reflected in the glazed eyes of the players. She turned away: their souls were already promised. Casinos weren't her usual hunting ground, but she'd never cut a change so close either. She spied the tables, and nodded to herself. That was where men with mettle took their chances. They were eager for their luck to change, and willing to take the offered hand without asking the cost. She cast her gaze over blackjack and poker tables, but found nothing that pleased her eye or the yawning need burning in her belly, warning of the coming day.

She ignored the lingering stares that followed her and walked the floor, guided by the instinct that had kept her alive through thousands of years and countless bodies. Then she glimpsed him, at the bottom of a whiskey, playing roulette. A little scruffy, a little drunk and with too few chips to be anything other than bitter. The aura of wasted drive and unrecognised talent surrounded him, calling out to her, warming her as only the soul of the desperate did. He would do anything to succeed.

Like a moth to a light she flitted to his side. The seat next to him vacated as if by magic and she slid onto it, a smile on her lips. She held her target's blue-eyed gaze for the important moment too long. He had to believe she wanted him, and there was no time for subtleties. He raised a brow and tossed a chip onto red for the next spin. He drained his glass while he waited. His eyes flicked from the wheel to her, his interest growing with each stolen look.

To make this happen she would have to forget about careful and go for broke. The way to this man's heart was through winning. The roulette wheel spun, a haze of red and black and red. Her lips curved as she worked her magic, and dug into her reserves. The man took his extra chips and gave her an appreciative glance. This time she placed her own chip on black. He went red. He won. She pouted and pretended to leave

"Stay. You're my lucky angel tonight." His voice was deep and melodic, even when slurred by drink. His fingers caught her wrist.

Her new heart leaped in excitement sending tingles through her blood. She'd been called many things over the centuries, but that was her favourite. She offered her hand. "Angelique."

He took it, his grip firm. "Zac."

"A pleasure to meet you, Zac. But I can't believe a man like you would ever be down on luck." Maybe she was laying it on too thick but time was pressing its hands on her throat, the sky was warming, if she didn't move fast her existence was over.

He pushed a pile of chips onto red, confident she was his lucky star. She could be, for a price.

"Music is a fickle business." His leg jumped as he watched the ball bounce around the wheel.

Ah, an artist. Her favourite. So much sweeter than stockbrokers and businessmen. The lust for wealth could never reach the highs of an artist seeking success. Such unrestrained need, such untamed desire, this man's soul definitely burned bright enough for two. She ran her hand down his arm. The ball landed. Red. His swelling pile of chips towered between them. She moved closer, close enough to feel the throb of his soul, close enough to burn her tongue with the taste of his ambition.

Zac pushed the chips in front of her. "Pick a number. If you win, you can have what ever you want."

"Then we'll both win," her fingers traced his jaw. "Because I want you." Her voice was more breathy than she'd planned, this body excited by the chance to live. He caught her hand, pressed his lips to her skin.

She moved the chips. Black thirteen. A cliché for some, lucky for others. Always lucky for her.

Hands twisted together, they watched. The wheel slowed, each bounce one step closer. Her muscles trembled like a fledgling fallen into snow, the ache crept into her skull. The ball slowed, one more bounce. Angel gave a final push.

"Black thirteen." The croupier called.

Zac whooped and gathered her into his arms. His mouth closed over hers. Sour with whisky, harsh with need, hungry for success. A spark of his life wound through her. It filled the void and strengthened her connection to the flesh. Power pulsed within her.

As men went, Zac was perfect. Handsome enough for her attraction to be natural, young enough to survive for decades before his soul went cold, sucked dry from sustaining two lives. If he had talent, she wouldn't have to do much to fund his dreams of chart topping success. The less she drew on him, the longer he would live and the longer she would have in this body. As bodies went, this one was nice, shapely. She would try to make it last.

Zac glanced down at her, his blue eyes dazed by the separation of his soul as it split between them. She cupped his face, not wanting to lose contact with him. He lowered his lips to hers, stealing a kiss. The deal was done. She had no need to kiss him again, but she wanted to. She was his lucky Angel.

The February Dragon

Angela Slatter and L.L. Hannett

PRILING did not die immediately.

Her husband's boasting had led to the challenge, to her standing in the arena, almost to term, unable to wear armour because of the great swell of her belly. Priling had been one of the finest dragon-catchers—and killers—in Sepphoris, but that was before this child made her heavy.

The thing she faced was a melding of scale and flame, black and orange, red and gold, with violent flares of blue; the colours flickered like a conflagration. It towered over Priling, spewing forth a hunting cry that excited spectators even as it hurt their ears. She did not flinch.

The crowd roared as the dragon leapt, its attack fierce. The sword Priling plunged into its maw melted in a rush of fire. As if by magic, she avoided the worst of the flames, but the dragon wrenched her arm off with its powerful jaws, teeth easily sawing through her soft flesh. The dragon's blood entered its slayer's wound in the seconds before fire cauterised the spurting arteries. With the dagger in her remaining hand, Priling tore a long hole in the beast's throat, severing its jugular. Black ichor gushed into the sands of the arena. Wranglers were summoned to restrain the dying beast, and afford the Physicks time enough to drag the semi-conscious woman to safety. The audience voiced their displeasure at the abbreviated main event; Priling's husband, face ashen and voice unsteady, did his best to assuage them with promises of better shows tomorrow. He hadn't bargained on giving refunds this day.

It was Priling's nature to fight, and fight she did. Over four days her body gradually turned black and grew hard scales; her hands sprouted claws as the dragon's blood wormed its way through her. It was a poison to the dragon-catcher, but to the child within it was an alchemist's dream. Mother and child teetered on the brink of humanity in the hours before dawn on the final day. Priling fought the venom that could not fully transform her, unable to either remain woman or become dragon. She stayed alive long enough to give birth to a daughter.

And so Casco was born, her father's shame and her mother's final triumph.

"WHERE is she?" Pater Claudio yelled. The old man was so angry that his mane of white hair trembled as if shifted by a sly breeze.

Mirko shrugged. He'd lost sight of his charge ten minutes ago—she'd given him the slip on their way to Verre's House. It wasn't the first time she'd eluded him and it wouldn't be the last. Both he and Pater Claudio knew where she went on these brief sojourns. Mirko was her bodyguard, yes, but if Casco did not want company there wasn't a power known to man or dragon that could make her obey. "She'll be fine."

Pater Claudio's face went an astonishing shade of red. "She's got no cause to go there, Mirko. Slinking around that family, thinking nobody notices her. She's too old to be so foolish. Casco is to be escorted at all times—you know that."

Mirko had never seen such colour in a human countenance; he wondered if his patron's head might pop. "Never fear, Pater. She's bright and sharp—no longer a little girl. And those nails of hers would do for anyone who looked at her the wrong way."

"Those nails," said the older man through gritted teeth, "are precisely what we need to protect, imbecile. The sooner I get her—"

There was a familiar sound at the threshold of the vestibule: the *clack* of bone on stone. A single sharp spur grew from the back of each of Casco's heels. Her boots were custom made to accommodate the protuberance—a hooded gap in the soft leather allowed the spur to remain unencumbered, though not entirely out of sight. Her sharp diamond toenails were easier to conceal. Pater Claudio and Mirko sighed with relief.

Casco both rewarded and disturbed the eye. Her skin was as white as forge-fired glass, so that she seemed to glow in the vestibule's dim light; her eyes were such a deep black they appeared to have no pupils. Her hair, darker still than her eyes, was a series of soft interlocking scales that ran in long waves to her waist, rather like the frills on the necks of the great extinct lizards on display in the House of Natural History. She was beautiful and strange, wonderful and awful; anyone seeing her for the first time felt themselves to be somehow *less* in her presence. Subsequent viewings did not necessarily diminish this sensation.

"Pater," she said. "My apologies. I stopped by the fountain room and forgot to tell Mirko." She lied so smoothly that both men neglected to call her on the untruth.

"See that it doesn't happen again, Casco. You are too important to this House."

"You mean my nails are, Pater," she said archly.

He squirmed on the skewer of her words. "When did your tongue become so venomous, child? Verre's House has cared for you all your life. We rescued you from the Dying Place, my poor dead wife carried you with her own hands, and we've never treated you as anything less than precious."

Casco nodded, a little contrite; but she had heard the story so many times she really wanted to avoid a repetition. Knowing she had been an unwanted baby did not make her feel precious; it made her feel hollow, like nothing more than Claudio's discovery, his commodity.

"And Verre's House will keep you safe from dragons, wolves, witch-lords and time itself," said Mirko, his head low to hide a smile that would belie his sincere tone.

"Valiant gestures indeed, Mirko. And I am ever grateful," Casco intoned.

Claudio looked closely at her, searching for a hint of mockery, then decided it was not worth his while to fight with her. Soon enough he would be in a position to better deal with her little rebellions. He nodded curtly. "Now then, go to your work-cell,

Casco. The buyers will be here at the end of the month to bid for the Empire bottle. It must be finished."

She smiled and the sharp tips of her incisors showed briefly. "The Incantor has finished the spell for the final engraving. I have it here."

She held up a thick creamy piece of parchment covered in precise script interwoven with symbols and sigils, the true meaning of which was known only to the men and women of the Incantors Guild. Casco had made Verre's House famous (and rich) with her unique ability to bind incantation to glass. This latest venture would be Verre's most ambitious; other Houses watched with envy and greed, willing them to fail.

"When did you become so reckless, girl? You blithely wave around our secrets?" Casco's fingernails sheared five tiny furrows into the parchment's top edge when Claudio snatched it from her grasp. Shaking his head furiously, he carefully scrolled the spell, spun Casco around and slid the paper tube into the leather *porte-parchemin* she wore slung across her back. He clipped the case shut, then let his hands slip down her spine, lingering at her waist, the soft curve of her hips, before he caught himself and stepped back. Claudio cleared his throat. "Mirko, ensure that she goes straight to her work-cell. I must have a few words with the Incantors."

Pater Claudio strode out of the vestibule, muttering about young girls and unreliable employees.

Mirko put one large hand around Casco's upper arm. He pinched hard at the soft skin but she gave no sign that he had hurt her. "I won't even bother asking where you were—as if I didn't know. Spying on Daddy-dearest?"

Casco narrowed her eyes. Some days Mirko thought he saw fire there. "You are *not* my keeper, no matter what he says," she hissed. Yes, definitely sparks in the depths, wheeling and forming, flashing and moving, then gone as she controlled her temper.

He sighed and loosened his hold. "There's nothing either of us can do about that, girlie. I *am* charged with keeping you in my sights, whether you like it or not." Smoothing the fabric of her shirt as if trying to erase all evidence of his gruffness, Mirko muttered, "Mark my words, when he gets a ring on your finger he won't be so kindly about your little jaunts."

"Pater has not asked me to marry him."

"Nor will he—he assumes it will happen. Haven't you noticed since his wife died how much he watches you? Did so before too, I swear, but he's less circumspect about it now. So he waits, until the time is right, when it will be *respectable* for him to take his young ward to wife. It will be so tidy: Sepphoris' greatest Engraver married into its greatest House, and Pater Claudio with his bed warmed once more. You'll be a lovely February bride, sweetness. Keep those nails of yours sharp and those britches laced up tight, mark my words."

Casco *had* noticed. The official period of mourning for a wife was one year. She had a month's grace left.

Mirko patted her shoulder. "Just stop hanging around your father's house, Casco. There's nothing for you there and it only enrages Claudio."

"Let me worry about that."

CASCO opened the book. Its covers had been crafted by ancient hands: smooth, polished copper encased the most secret, most puissant spells ever made for Verre's House in its four hundred year history. Not *all* of the spells, for no book could hold so many; the lesser ones lived on in smaller volumes in the Library's folio collection. These ones though—the ones with the power to entrap empires, to ensnare virgin brides in glass coffins, to create dresses of blown glass that felt and fell as soft as silk, to make crystal children so realistic they might even fool doting parents for a time—were collected and wielded by the engravers of Verre's House.

She took the inscribed parchment and smoothed it flat on the table's burnished wooden worktop. Using the diamond tips of her fingernails, she punctured a series of minute holes into the page's edge then inserted it in the very back of the book. Taking up a fine needle and a strand of flexible steel thread, Casco stitched it securely in place. She then propped the book up in the wrought-iron holder next to the table, open at the spell, and placed page-clips at the corners to make sure the leaves did not close. At last prepared, she turned her attention to the House's next great work.

Running a third of the length of the workbench and held firmly in the grip of a giant vice, lay the Empire bottle. The glass was thick and had a slightly green tint to it. Without inscription, the metre long by half metre wide bottle was proof of the Glassblowers' skill, but was otherwise forgettable. However, when Casco engraved the spell upon its body, the bottle would become a weapon: buyers from both sides of the current war would arrive to bid on it.

Casco flexed her hands, cracked her knuckles, circled her wrists like birds tied to a single point in the ground. She took a deep breath. This was the first Empire bottle Verre's House had been charged to build in fifty years; it was the first one Casco would engrave that wouldn't immediately be destroyed as a practice piece. When her task was complete, Casco's beautiful weapon would be capable of sucking an entire civilisation inside it: the ultimate victory for the side that could afford such a thing. She took a final look at the page, her memory catching the design and imprinting it on her mind. This would fund the House for a century, if carefully husbanded. She exhaled slowly, gave her hands a final shake and began.

Her nerves soon settled. Unlike other engravers, who relied on forged implements and unwieldy blades, Casco and her tools were one and the same. Her diamond nails scored even the finest glass without shattering it; her dragon's blood seamlessly guided the Incantors' spells from her mind through her hands and into the glass. *Verba volant, scripta manent*, Pater Claudio always said, and he was right. Spoken words fly away, written words remain. Enchantments hummed through her body like a song while she worked and that song was permanently embedded in the glass beneath her fingertips.

Hours passed, the day shifted from sunshine to the silk-grey of afternoon. Outside her window Proclaimers climbed minarets, calling those who would come to evening prayer. A servant brought her supper tray, then cleared it away again, untouched. Lamplighters came in around five and the torches flared, creating a kind of artificial daylight so she could continue her work. In between reading chapters of a well-loved book, Mirko paced between the room's gaping fireplace and the tessellated fresco on the far wall, which depicted a scene from the Fall of the Dragons. Underscoring all of this activity was a disturbance that gradually, persistently, drew Casco's attention.

"Can you hear that?" she asked Mirko as she straightened up, her back aching. He shook his head.

She frowned, mimicked his gesture. A third of the bottle had been adorned, but it could not be activated until she had covered it, completing the spell. Casco ran a finger across the ridges and valleys of the glass's newly uneven surface while she listened. She became aware, slowly, that she had been hearing the sound for some time—one day, or two? A week? She couldn't be sure; it had dug itself so deeply into her unconscious that she couldn't remember when it hadn't been there.

It was a long rhythmic hum, constant as a piece of machinery, low as a lullaby. Casco's heart raced, and her stomach pulsed with nerves and excitement. The room seemed to dissolve around her as the sound grew in intensity; the workbench, the bottle, Mirko, the nightingale's trill outside—everything faded to black and white as the rumbling bass conjured visions of bright scales rippling, stretched over taut muscles; of flames describing her figure, bare and shimmering with sweat; of someone large, musky, *strong* taking her in his firm grip; of talons encircling her slender waist, the sensation of sharp tips cutting into her torso a mixture of pleasure and pain. All this and more, suggested by the resonant, wordless song. Now she could feel it as a flush in her cheeks, a warmth in her chest that eased the ache perpetually residing there. Its reverberations moved lower until she caught her breath, blushed, embarrassed and swiftly wet. A sigh escaped her parted lips. *Is this how Pater Claudio feels?* she wondered, then shuddered to think of his unwanted, palsied caresses. The world rushed back in a flood of colour, but it paled in comparison to the vivid images the song had fixed in her mind.

"I'll be back in a moment, Mirko." She took a deep breath to steady her voice, to calm herself before she continued. "I need to... clear my head. Don't worry, I'll not leave the House." Her steps were quick and light with only the slightest *clack* as her heel-talon met the cool stone beneath. Mirko grunted his assent, and bent to retrieve the *Book of Oztin* from where he'd tucked it under his seat; Casco knew that before she had reached the door he would be absorbed in the tale of his favourite glass-girl heroine.

She stepped out into the corridor. After the brightness of her cell it took a moment for her dragonish membranes to adapt. They widened to absorb the dim orange light emanating from fire gutters running along the tops of the walls.

Casco felt herself pulled along by the thread of sound. Its cadences threatened to overwhelm her again; she walked as though in a dream, her gaze turned inward and outward simultaneously. Covering her ears was no use; the humming was not something heard, but something *felt*. It took all her energy to resist the urge to run.

The song grew louder as the trail led her down: down through the levels of Verre's House; down past the upper rooms, those that caught the light Casco and lesser engravers required for their work; down past the large workshops where the mixers of coloured silica plied their trade; then down further to the glassblowers' residences, where the golden glow from their lehrs and annealers kept the gloom at bay. Down the last set of stairs, past the guards who gave her cautious looks even while they let her pass.

The steps beneath her feet were not cool, as might be expected of flagstones implanted in the earth so far underground. Instead they were warm, so warm Casco could feel the heat through the soles of her boots; her heel spur gave off the smell of hot ossified hair.

The noise swelled now, its rhythm throbbing through her veins more insistently. A monumental iron door, which was weighted with mortar and banded with silver and bronze, confronted her at the end of the hallway. She knew what waited beyond it. Two more guards, stationed one to each side of the barred entrance, looked askance at her.

"Engraver?"

"Let me pass."

"It's too dangerous, Engraver Casco. Pater Claudio would have our heads if any ill came to you."

"The creatures are *chained*. They are all chained and channelled, for flints' sake. There is no danger to me." She smiled at their hesitation. "They never hurt me. They know my blood; they know what I am."

The men shrugged and shot the bolt on the only door that would keep the fire of the furnace dragons at bay.

Casco slipped through the opening.

The chamber seemed to spread across a width greater than the entire compound of Verre's House above, an effect that was enhanced by the tunnels leading off into the darkness of its far walls. An enormous central furnace rose from the floor and stretched to the vaulted ceiling high above; its embers bathed the room with a simmering orange glow. Casco's pale skin adopted a warm bronze sheen and her hair scales flickered with reflected tongues of fire.

At the four compass points were four huge cages, and in each one lay a dragon. Three were older creatures, their majestic scales now hoary with age. They faced arched apertures in the furnace's brick walls, though none of them were firing. The fourth was black, shiny, his musculature evident and beautiful under his plates. He was a robust young firedrake; his silver eyes locked on Casco's slender form as she approached. His tongue flicked out to snap up a mouthful of brimstone from the trough in front of his cage. Had she been two steps to the left, his glistening grey tongue would have wrapped around *her* instead. This thought echoed those inspired by the song too closely; she blushed, grew suddenly shy, and wondered where her breath had gone.

A snort like an abbreviated chuckle came from Casco's left. She caught the large emerald dragon winking at her. Her flush deepened. The emerald had been at Verre's House for decades, ancient long before an infant Casco first toddled past his crucible. He was from the greatest line of dragons in Sepphoris, and renowned for his keen eye. She nodded respectfully, her gaze steady, observing the traditional courtesies, which he returned.

Casco turned next to the northern dragon, a vermilion female well beyond breeding years. She had always been aloof, regal, but as the girl touched the bars of the firedrake's cage, the red rolled onto her side, exposing a soft underbelly. It was a gesture of trust, of acceptance. Without a second thought, Casco tilted her own head back, unbuttoned the neck of her tunic, and bared her pale throat.

In the southern cage, the yellow gave her a disdainful look. Something tightened in her stomach—it was the kind of look she'd seen on her father's face. The sort of look that said she was such a diluted creature that she was worth nothing.

The music from the firedrake's cage crescendoed. Made bold by this welcome, Casco reached through to rest a hand against his hide. The scales were strangely cool. She could feel the tremor of his humming.

She had watched, not many weeks since, when first the dragon-catchers had brought him to Verre's House, drugged and bound.

They had taken his freedom and his joy. Now he was channelled like the others and, barring an act of gods or accident, he would spend the rest of his life beneath the earth, a slave to the furnaces. She wondered if he missed the life they'd stolen from him; if he had a family that yearned for his return.

"Little half-thing." The voice sounded as soft thunder in her head, an edge of contempt brushing gently against her pride.

"What?" Casco looked around the furnace room, but there was only her and the dragons. She turned back to find the drake's eyes upon her. Inside them, a storm, a fire like nothing she'd ever seen. Inside his eyes, a universe, all colours and yet none; all life and all death. Love and hatred, pain and comfort, balm for sorrow and a talon to the heart. She wanted to fall into them, for there surely the ache would cease. She leaned closer to the bars, trying to defy their solidity.

"Half-thing, neither one nor the other, but blooded of both. How do you live?" There was mockery in the question. She pulled away.

"Who are you to ask me that? No one has chained me."

He laughed and sparks flew. "Your chains are not visible to the eye. I am Feus, prince among my kind."

"A prince in shackles. You are a tinderbox with scales," she spat. His candour rattled her; the truth of his words seared.

"Why did you call me here?" she asked.

There was a pause. "I could not *not* do it," he whispered.

"Feus," she said softly, her gaze sweeping around the room. The older dragons now slept, or at least feigned it. "Mighty Feus, reduced to a furnace feeder."

She turned away and was five paces from the door when his voice throbbed through her once more. "Don't go."

Casco lingered for a fraction of a second. *Flames on bare flesh—sinuous tongue lapping—claws tickling, pressing—she shook her head to clear it.* Feus' timbre filled the hollow inside her, it woke something, it made her *feel* new and bold. It made her feel different, maybe *too* different. She kept walking.

She opened the door, heaving its great weight slowly, then left it to clang shut behind her. It did not stop the sound of his song, merely dulled it.

OULD you like some lunch?"

Casco jumped. She hadn't heard Pater Claudio approach. She wondered how long he'd been standing behind her, clutching a bowl of soup. Watching her.

"Thank you." The pottery dish made a dull clunk as Claudio rested it on the workbench. Casco wasn't hungry, hadn't been since she'd spoken with Feus last week. The things he had said—the weight of his gaze! And that silver tongue... Her work-cell, the largest studio in the House, suddenly felt stifling.

"It's not very warm, I'm afraid."

"Pardon?"

"The soup." Pater Claudio drew closer to the Empire bottle, rested his hand on Casco's shoulder as he admired her handiwork.

No place in either world. Casco fumed silently. *But look at what I can create.* She wiped an invisible fleck of dust from the thing's smooth base. *Surely that's something.*

"Beautiful," said Pater Claudio. He was no longer looking at the bottle.

A sign that I belong here. She scraped her fingernail along a newly etched symbol, completing its curving stroke. With that, she finished detailing the trunk, two days ahead of schedule. She had only the base and stem left. It had taken all her concentration to keep working, to resist the pull of Feus' song. The effort exhausted her, not least because she was so short on sleep.

For six consecutive nights, her dreams had been unlike any she'd ever had—in these, she didn't feel alone. A presence, always hidden but undeniably *there*, shadowed her every move. She could sense him behind her, beneath her, around her as she floated from nonsensical fancy to fancy. One night, kittens tap-danced on an inverted canoe for her pleasure, waving miniature Empire Bottles in their gloved paws; but their purrs soon transformed into a sultry, familiar rhythm, and she felt her unseen lover press up against her as kittens became fire-breathing sirens. The next night, she swam the seas off the coast of Bandragoon; waves lapped at her naked skin, pulled her further away from her unknown goal, until a hydra surfaced to serve as her steed. And as it slid up beneath her, forcing her to straddle its slippery back, she awoke with a throbbing between her legs that had left her gasping. All week, over and over, it had been the same; the dreams, the insistent humming, the *reveille*—

"Just beautiful." Casco was shaken from her thoughts. She felt Claudio's breath against her cheek, the press of his thumbs kneading small circles into the firm muscles between her shoulder blades.

She stepped away from his grip. "I'm sorry, Pater," she stammered, remembering Mirko's warnings and horrified that the older man might now infiltrate her nocturnal sojourns. "I think I've left a scroll with the Incantors." She fumbled with her *porte-parchemin*, scraping its soft leather with her nails in her haste. "I really must go and collect it, immediately."

Pater Claudio sighed, then called for Mirko. "Go with her," he instructed. "Our deadline fast approaches."

*L*ET me take that," Casco said. "I'm going that way."

The courier paused, but did not relinquish the carefully wrapped package. He was new to Verre's House—she could tell by his boots, which were still shiny and looked stiff. His gait told her that his feet were pinched and blistered after hours of delivering the Guild's creations to buyers. Sweat ringed the cowl of his woollen tunic—he would learn, if he lasted long enough, that it was too hot to be worn in late spring. A saturated strap-mark ran diagonally across his chest where his messenger's *porte-livraison* had been hanging moments before.

"It's no trouble," she continued. It wasn't really a lie. She would have done anything to get out for a while; away from Claudio's advances, Mirko's watchful eye, Feus' unrelenting call. As she made to sneak through the vestibule she had heard the young courier being given his assignment. She had also heard his worn out sigh. If she could inveigle the boy, she would simply need to remember to bring something sweet back to placate Mirko. Then again, making the delivery would take no more than half an hour; he might not even notice her absence.

"I know where the Belluaire house is—it's right next to the arena, beyond the square with all the pigeons. The large one with the gables, right? I'm sure I've seen it before." Her voice was sweet and low; something of the dragon's song limned her tone. She could see it working: his shoulders slumped, the lines of his face relaxed and she knew she'd won even when he tried to argue.

"But, Engraver," he said, clutching the parcel close to his sodden chest, "this must be delivered to Sevante Belluaire himself. Do you know him?"

Casco grabbed the package and he did not fight her. She smiled. "Oh, yes, I know him very well."

She pushed the messenger toward the glass doors and told him to find himself lunch at the Dragon's Breath Inn down the street. She would meet him there and hand over the signed chit to say Belluaire received his parcel. In a flash of cunning, she told him to drop by the bakery and get the sesame pastries Mirko liked so much. The boy's face broke out in a dazed smile when she pressed first a tarnished silver coin into his palm for the breadman, then a crystal shilling for his trouble.

If only her thoughts were as easy to organise. Parcel in hand, her mind wandered as her feet travelled the familiar route to the Arena Quarter. The sun shone warm on Casco's face, easing the tension that had settled in her shoulders. Turning the corner at Lost Kraken's Shrine, Casco passed a troop of hunters gathering supplies for their next expedition. Their wagon was pulled by a pair of mangy dragons, both too small to do more than menial labour. The beasts' hides were dull, not just from a coating of dust. They looked unhealthy: their scales scarred, their wings clipped. They smelled sour, not musky; not virile, like—

Stop it, she told herself, but she still felt the ache at the base of her spine, the tingle left by an imagined talon. The citadel's clock chimed the hour; she hitched up the *porte-livraison*. It was midday, the perfect time to be out in Sepphoris. The streets teemed with people: guildsmen ran errands or scrambled at food carts for quick luncheons; gutterscoops bumped through crowds, saving boots from the mess transport dragons deposited in their travels; hawkers set up shop on the roadsides, selling everything from pontils to marvers. Casco's heel spurs clicked a merry rhythm as she picked up the pace, her hair scales streaming like quicksilver behind her.

For a moment, surrounded by the throng, she felt inconspicuous. With such a diverse mix of people and dragons about, nobody paid her any attention. As she ran toward her father's house she felt, however briefly, like a normal girl.

This is how it should always feel, she thought with a smile, *when you're going home.*

ASCO'S hands shook. Her palms were cool and dry on the package, but her heart raced. She knocked, quickly but insistently, then stepped back. When the heavily carved door swung open on well-oiled hinges, Casco's breath stopped.

Would he recognise her? What would he say? Did he think of her? Did he think of the day when he left her in the Dying Place? Did he regret what he'd done? Was he proud of her skill as an Engraver? Would he call her by name? Would he even remember her name?

"What can I do for you, miss?" The housemaid's raisin brown eyes, set in a shrivelled face, stared back at her.

Casco knew herself for a fool: Sevante Belluaire hadn't answered his own door in years. She said nothing, but held the chit out and the woman used a stub of pencil fished from her apron to scribble her sigil on the bottom of the paper. Casco handed the maid the parcel and the servant curtsied. Casco turned to make a quick exit.

She ran head-on into her father.

"Afternoon, sir," the maid greeted him.

He didn't seem to register Casco's presence. "Afternoon, Antonina."

Casco stared straight at Sevante. His skin was a deep golden brown, his wide eyes green and a scar bisected his left cheek, giving the permanent suggestion of a wink. His ruddy hair was peppered with white.

Her mood shattered, like a parison rolled too swiftly from the furnace. She couldn't quite understand why she was drawn back here. In the last year she had begun to gravitate to the house on Murano Street, surreptitiously watching Belluaire and his family (second wife, four new daughters, the youngest only three). She sipped at the dew of their lives like a moth drinking from a raindrop. Looking now at her father's striking face, Casco knew only longing and ache. Hatred overwhelmed her; hatred for the man who had cast her aside because she was different, because she reminded him that he had caused Priling's death with his arrogance. She shared nothing with Sevante Belluaire except blood. She glared at her father as he studiously avoided looking at her.

From inside the house a woman's voice called, "Who is it, Antonina? Send them away before Sevante returns, won't you?"

The maid opened her mouth to respond, but Casco's father cut her off with a brisk wave.

"It's nobody important," he replied, finally looking Casco full in the face. "It's no one."

Casco stumbled down the stairs, her heel-talons making a silent retreat impossible. It didn't matter: Sevante had already gone inside, closing the door noisily behind him.

CASCO? Engraver Casco?"

Casco did not slow down. The crowds parted in front of her. There was the sound of running and a hand caught at her arm. Casco did not like being manhandled; she swung about, her fingers splayed and her nails caught the sun.

"Engraver?" the young man said faintly. He was tall, handsome and muscular, but she could see he was terrified of her.

"Master Fourneau," she said. "Forgive me. You startled me."

He recovered his good grace, hooding his fear as quickly as one might snuff a candle. But she had already seen it; and she knew that hatred often sprang from such things. Forneau, son of the Master of Vitrine's House, Verre's greatest rival, made her uneasy. She had not forgotten his torments when they were children in the schoolroom.

"Easily forgiven and most understandable. My apologies for—mauling you, it was not seemly."

She gave a vague smile and waved his words away. "How may I help?"

"Oh, it's nothing particular. I simply wished to say hello. I have just returned from seeing Pater Claudio. Two of our dragons are almost at the end of their span. Nothing for them but the arena. Vitrine is sending its dragon-catchers out soon and wondered if Verre would like to join the expedition." He smiled.

Sometimes rivals joined a hunt together—the cost and risks of the dragon harvest were huge and not even Houses as rich as Verre or Vitrine liked to bear the expense alone.

"I understand you have only that young firedrake—the rest are, shall we say, superannuated? Barely fit for arena fodder."

"They've served our House well," she said defensively. "They deserve better than slaughter for petty amusement."

"The firedrake, though, would be a fine sight under Belluaire's instruction!" he said, more to himself than her.

"Thankfully Verre's House does not waste its finest resources," she said coldly.

"Of course not." He raised his hands to placate her. She wondered why he was going out of his way to be so agreeable. She backed away. He followed, drawing near enough that Casco could practically taste his breath. His face, pressed so close to her own, had lost its veneer of kindness; his jaw was set with a disdain that barely masked his hunger.

"You will forgive me, Master Forneau, I am very late and must return. They will be looking for me."

"Yes. Strange to see you without your guard-dog. Give the big man the slip?" he sneered.

"Good day." She turned on her heel and dived into the wash of the crowd, losing herself to his gaze as soon as she could.

*H*ow much trouble can you get yourself into?" Mirko asked as Casco handed him a sesame pastry, cold and rapidly stiffening. He closed the door to her work-cell.

"I was asked to make a delivery, Mirko. That's why I'm late." She stood in front of the Empire bottle, trying to gather her thoughts.

"You're certainly a popular girl. Suitors coming out of the cracks hither and yon," he said around the pastry. Casco frowned.

"Forneau was here, you know."

"I know. Saw the little weasel in the street and he told me so."

"Did he tell you why he was here?" Mirko keep talking and chewing at the same time. Casco knew that if she looked at him, she'd be treated to the sight of masticated pastry being tossed about in his mouth. She chose not to look.

"To see if we wanted in on their dragon hunt. He made fun of our dragons, by the way." *Not Feus though*, she thought, *his tone was quite envious of the firedrake.* She ignored the flutter this realisation caused in her belly.

"Least of his sins. Claudio yelled at him within five minutes. Fool had the gall to ask for your hand. As if Verre will give you up."

Casco felt cold.

"But, I don't want to marry *anyone*." It was true. She had never wanted it, had never felt an attraction to another person so strong as to warrant any action.

Mirko spoke gently. "Casco, everyone marries. It's the way all the guilds work. Glassblowers, engravers, incantors, all pair off with one another; the Houses stay populated; Sepphoris prospers. It's natural. You've been an exception this long because—well, Pater didn't want you to marry outside the House. He was... waiting."

"I won't marry anyone."

"Then they can appeal to our Guild. You know that. You know they can rule on marriages. If you really wanted to marry outside the House, you could put a case together, present it at the Assembly if it came to that. They might let you go." He shook his head. "But, in the end, you'd still have to marry *someone*, here or elsewhere." He popped the last bit of pastry into his mouth. "In case you haven't noticed, you're kind of unique. Any children you have will be valuable."

He could see her trembling, whether from grief or rage he wasn't sure. "Casco, your life doesn't belong to you, sweetheart."

She fled. Out of the room and down the stairs, down, down, down, to where the firedrake's hum was strongest. She had ignored him for so many, many days. It felt like months, but she wouldn't relax until she felt the deep rumble of his song in her bones, soothing her, calling her down. The fact that she noticed the dragon's absence so keenly told her, to her chagrin, how much she had come to need him.

Only Feus was in his cage. It wouldn't be long before the keepers came for him; the others had already been taken to their cells for the night. Casco stormed across the room. Feus raised one eyelid, kept his chin resting on the floor, his long tail curled around the great expanse of his body.

"Why did you call me?" she yelled. "Everything's gone wrong since then."

"I am not the catalyst, Casco. I'm merely at the confluence of events." He paused, then went on, less certainly. "My kind mate for life. When a dragon finds his equal, he knows. The song begins—it is a sound we cannot produce at any other time. For better or worse, little half-thing, you summoned my song."

Her hands pushed through the bars. She ran them over his scales; heat wafted from his open mouth as he sighed. Then she scratched, hard with her diamond nails, and left marks. He laughed, breathy, aroused. He hooked one claw through the bars, and caressed her neck, the talon sharp enough to sever her head in a heartbeat should he wish it. It felt nothing like when Pater Claudio touched her.

Fire raced through her veins as Feus traced the outline of her clavicle, her arm, her hand. Blue sparks struck from her fingertips as she scratched him more vigorously; she inhaled the heady steam of his breath and watched as curls of smoke escaped her lips. His tongue flicked at her torso, grazing her stomach, her breasts. Flames swirled in Casco's eyes; the dark scales of her hair stiffened, bristling up until a magnificent crest draped her head and shoulders like a queen's mantle. Feus wrapped his tongue around her wrist, drawing her closer; he gently nipped at her fingers. Casco pulled back, but didn't step away from the cage. A bead of warm blood welled from her index finger.

She stared at the crimson stain.

"My mother was in the arena," she whispered. "Dragon's blood killed her."

"It's poisonous, little half-thing. But you were very small, not fully formed. What killed your mother merely changed you: it made you what you are. But blood calls to blood, Casco. You've been a chrysalis for too long. Let go of your human flesh. Come home."

"I don't know how," she said, her voice trembling. His silvery tongue caressed her anew; its touch was dry and surprisingly smooth, intimate.

"Fire," he whispered. "It burns away the meat, leaving only the dragon."

"I'll die," she said.

"Trust me."

There was a rattle from one of the tunnels. The keepers were returning. Casco pulled away, her breath coming in ragged bursts, and shook her head.

CASCO stood alone before the wide expanse of the East Salon's windows, looking out over the sea. Floor to ceiling ran the strongest, thickest glass Verre's House could produce, strengthened by myriad incantations etched around the edges. They would last a thousand years against storms, attacking dragons, whatever might be thrown at the House's waterside facade. She was reflected against the dark glass. Out beyond her, lightning bolts threw themselves across the night sky, danced above the sea, writhed like serpents.

The girl concentrated on her reflection: the ghostly impression of her dragon self seemed to stretch higher and wider than the window could capture. Her scales, lapis lazuli in colour, were accented with starlight. She had a long tail, lovely wings, her eyes were lashless, slanted and silver, her limbs were muscular and sleek; she was monumental and beautiful and overwhelming. Never before had she seen this aspect of herself. It was breathtaking.

She was so absorbed that she did not hear anyone enter the room, nor did she see Pater Claudio until he seemed to materialise next to her in the glass. She started, focused on his image. His outline was not solid, a weak wavering line.

He rested his hands on her shoulders, tried a smile. Casco smiled back, a broken fleeting expression.

"Casco, it's time we had a talk." He directed her to one of the couches. "I'd wanted to leave this discussion a while longer, but circumstances have forced my hand."

"Pater—"

"No, let me finish. You know how fond I am of you, how we have always cared for you. You are important to us not merely for your exquisite craft, but also... in a personal sense. I know it isn't many months since my dear wife died, but I feel it is time to take another bride."

"Pater, I—"

"Casco, please! I have no children. There will be no further Claudians to follow unless I do. You are young, exceptional. I would be honoured if you would agree to be my wife." There was no question in his voice.

Casco tried to swallow her revulsion. "Pater, I have always thought of you as a father. This is a—great change."

"I know, I know," he said kindly. "But there is no blood between us and the Guild has given its consent."

"You have already been to the Guild?" There was an edge to her voice that he could not have missed.

"Of course, child. And they were only too happy to see us settled."

Casco rose, strode back to the window. Her reflection had withdrawn its wings, lost its vibrant blue glow, dwindled in size. Now she faced the version of herself she'd seen every day for eighteen years: a pale girl with fire smouldering in her eyes. Outside, winds whipped the seas into a fury. A clap of thunder muffled Casco's response.

"You'll have to speak up," Pater Claudio said, leaning forward, "I didn't quite catch that."

She didn't turn from the window. "I said, what if I decline?" Irritation flashed across Claudio's reflected features, and Casco heard him exhale sharply.

"Perhaps I've misled you," he said, standing. "By implying you had a choice. The proposal was merely a courtesy; a token of my affection."

Casco spun around. "Affection?" She laughed bitterly. "Is that what you call it? Tethering me to a workbench, treating me like a prisoner, punishing me if I steal a few precious moments for myself? Never caring about what I want—and then offering me a lifetime of the same? Spare me the joy of such *affection*, Pater. I'll have none of it."

"You won't deny me, child. Not after all I've done for you."

Casco's face flushed. Her eyes gleamed with unbridled rage and her incisors glinted as she growled, "I would rather you had left me to die."

"Of all the ungrateful, half-blood things to say—"

"Enough!" In the window, Casco's dragon reflection bloomed anew, rearing its head; her wings spread wide, and her tail lashed violently. Her voice filled the grand chamber. "I've had enough! Enough of being trapped in this House; enough of being neither one thing nor the other. Enough of you. Let me alone!"

Pater Claudio's head snapped back as if he'd been slapped. His face and shoulders sagged. Folding his hands carefully in his lap, he straightened, sitting as tall as his aging back would allow. He waited for the echoes of Casco's words to fade before he spoke.

"It appears, my love, that you've become overly agitated." He snapped his fingers; Mirko appeared from the antechamber. The bodyguard stood framed in the doorway while Claudio gave his instructions. "Escort Casco to her room now, Mirko. She's not fit for company this evening. We'll have to continue our conversation in the morning, when she's regained her composure."

Mirko slowly sidled up to his charge, a man obliged to act although he clearly had no taste for the task. Casco stood her ground. "There's nothing to talk about—don't touch me!" She wrenched her arm from her guard's meaty grasp. Glaring at Claudio, she repeated, "There is *nothing* further to discuss."

"Don't be ridiculous, Casco. We must make arrangements for our wedding. But it can wait for the morning. Until then, I bid you goodnight."

Lightning flared over the rough seas, briefly filling the salon with its harsh glare. In the window's reflection, a small girl was dragged from the room; an old man looked on, smiling, until darkness returned.

"ENGRAVER, good morning."

Forneau was at the door of her work-cell, Mirko close behind him. Her bodyguard's face was set in annoyance, but he knew his position was too low to speak rudely to Vitrine's heir, no matter how much he wanted to do so.

"Master Forneau," said Casco. "You are an early visitor."

"The dragons. I have come to speak with your keepers about the new dragons. Would you do the honour of escorting me? I cannot wander Verre's House unattended—who knows what secrets I might discover?" He grinned, looking past her at the half-completed Empire bottle.

"Very well," she said. "Keep an eye on the candles for me, Mirko. It seems such a waste to snuff them when I'll be back up in a matter of minutes."

"I should probably come with you, Casco," Mirko said.

Fourneau leaned toward Casco and barked once, like a watchdog, then tried to mask what he'd done by covering his mouth and coughing. She glared at him, and said, "That won't be necessary, Mirko. We really won't be long."

The furnace room was dimly lit; none of the dragons had yet been brought from their cells. There was only the low glow of the brazier, bronzing both Fourneau and his reluctant guide.

"When will you hunt?" asked Casco.

"Tomorrow. I still hope to convince Pater Claudio to sell me that firedrake."

"Feus is not for sale."

"Feus? You've given him a pet name?" Forneau laughed as if she was an amusing child.

"It's his name. He told me."

"Told you? My, my, you are a rare creature, Casco. Rare indeed." He grinned. "No wonder Pater Claudio wants you for himself."

"I will not marry Pater. I will not be mated with anyone against my will."

"He is very old. Perhaps you prefer younger flesh." He pushed her to the bars of Feus' cage and pressed himself against her. The metal bit into her back and Forneau's teeth bit into her tongue and lips. He was careful to imprison her hands and make sure she couldn't use her nails. She was so shocked she hadn't time to react. She flailed uselessly in his grasp.

From the mouth of one of the tunnels came an almighty roar and the shouts of the keepers as Feus broke free of them. They had become so used to the submission of channelled dragons they were unprepared for the fury of an outraged beast. Forneau released Casco and backed away from her, his face white as bone, his eyes large as terror seized him. He couldn't bring himself to turn his back on the dragon so he saw the fire as it came for him, the heat drying out his eyeballs before it even hit.

There was very little left after the first burst of flame. By that time, the keepers had rallied; they hung on the ends of the chains attached to Feus' collar and one of them jabbed the soft underside of his neck with a drug-dipped dart to tranquilise him. It took only moments to work, but it was too late for Forneau who lay smoking on the floor of the furnace chamber.

Casco looked in horror, not at Forneau, but at Feus, knowing he had just condemned himself to the arena.

*J*WILL marry you, Pater, but my bride price is the life of Feus."

"The firedrake? Stop this foolishness, Casco. Dragons don't have names, they are not pets!"

"They name themselves just as we do!" She took a deep breath to calm herself, knowing that aggravating him further would not advance her cause. She knelt before him, hating herself, put her hands on his knees, then slid them up to his thighs.

"Pater." She paused. "Claudio. This is the one thing I ask of you. Grant me this one small boon and I will belong to you and

Verre's House forever. I will give you sons to carry on your line. In this way I will give you immortality, if you just grant me this one thing in return."

He wavered, distracted by the stroking of her fingers and nails.

She smiled. "Besides, what kind of business sense does it make to waste a perfectly good firedrake? He saw me threatened and reacted. He has removed Vitrine's heir—done you a favour, really. Reward him with his life."

She leaned forward, lifted her face and offered her lips.

*M*IRKO gave her a pitying look. Casco was bent over the Empire bottle. The base had been completed; now she was preparing the bottle neck and stopper. He watched her, thinking she'd gotten thinner and paler in the weeks since Forneau's death; worse since she'd agreed to marry Claudio.

She looked up and smiled wearily at him. "Nearly finished." She gestured at the bottle. "The buyers are bound to offer a hefty price for this—"

"He lied," Mirko interrupted. She gave him an uncomprehending look. "Pater Claudio."

"Have the buyers withdrawn?" Casco stood. "Are there any buyers at all?"

"No, no. That's not it. It's just—the firedrake goes to the arena this evening."

She sagged, all the life gone from her.

Mirko had been ordered to keep his charge on a tight leash, to not let her out of his sight, to keep her away from news and people who might tell her anything. He had done his job, he had kept her in the dark; and she had not fought him, distracted as she was by her impending marriage and the demons she kept tightly inside her mind. Seeing her thus, working on the Empire bottle, about to become even more of a slave, he couldn't lie to her any longer. "What will you do?"

She began to weep.

"You are better than this, Casco. What are you going to do?"

*T*ONIGHT, you will witness a battle to the death!" Sevante Belluaire's deep voice boomed over the appreciative crowd.

He stood on a dais at the arena's south end, facing a series of tunnels, each of which led to the gladiators' subterranean chambers. Black and barred, the doorways looked like a row of rotten teeth held in place by rusty bands.

Casco watched her father's performance from the northernmost tunnel. A few choice whisperings in a young guard's ear and a handful of shiny coins in his palm had gained her this prime position.

Much as a king would from his elevated position, the beastmaster surveyed his audience, smiling condescendingly. The dais's wooden planks hovered over a filthy creature tethered to the arena floor. Belluaire was poised near the platform's edge; the crack of his whip punctuated each of his sentences with a stinging flick against Feus' hide. Weighed down by chains as thick as a strongman's thigh, the dragon could not retaliate.

"This devil," Belluaire boasted, "soaked up a century's heat from the Arnuvian deserts, where he feasted on boiling blood, flame-cactus and spitfire! Our bravest 'catchers tracked him along a perilous route—from roasting sands to Haverna's blackest volcanoes—until they finally caught him bathing in craters of bubbling lava. This devil—"

Sigils paraded through Casco's mind and she whispered the unbinding incantation she had found hidden away in one of the minor spell folios. Looking at the rapt faces in the crowd, each of them riveted by Belluaire's false words, Casco's lip curled in disgust. He had such power to charm; she could almost believe her father had a bit of the dragon in him.

"We've seen many a fire-breather in this arena." Belluaire paused for dramatic effect, lifted his eyes to the banners plastered against all of the building's vertical surfaces. Casco followed his gaze, taking in the variegated shreds of cloth and tinsel that commemorated the arena's fallen warriors. Her eyes caught on a gold and burgundy pennant, still rich in hue despite its age.

Priling.

Belluaire continued, "Many a fierce beast has torn human limb from limb before us, but none—" he raised his arm and spun it to gain momentum, "—none has caused as much damage as this one!" The whip lashed across Feus' flanks with skin-splitting force. The firedrake reared his head and loosed a spout of fury-driven flames.

"Lies!" Casco hissed, her dismay submerged in waves of the crowd's delight.

"Which of our brave gladiators will defeat this animal?" The sound of metal scraping across metal underscored the crescendos of Belluaire's rousing speech—the tunnels' heavy iron gates began to lift. Casco rattled the slow-moving barrier, urging it upward, still shaping the Incantors' sigils in her mind.

"Who will keep him from our children?" At this, the beastmaster turned away from the dragon and faced row upon row of seats ascending skyward at vertiginous angles. His youngest daughter waved down at him from the third row, her blonde ringlets bouncing as she proudly wiggled her plump arm for all to see that it was *her* daddy down there. "Shall we summon the gladiators?" The crowd cheered their assent. Casco heard the tramp of feet behind her. She dropped to the ground and wriggled beneath the gap. She strode across the arena floor as Belluaire continued his address.

"Strong Heracles, perhaps? Quick Induvio? The Incredible Serbonne? There are so many favourites—which of them will save my little Lapis from this—"

"I will."

She spoke loud and clearly, but had to repeat herself twice before the audience fell silent. Casco's boots crunched across the pebbles and bones littering the arena floor. Her breathing was calm, her posture assured. She inhaled the scent of sulphur and scorched earth, tasted salt with each step she took toward the dais. "Call off your killers, Father. Feus is mine."

A sharp hiss echoed around the stadium, a collective drawing in of breath; Casco wasn't sure whether it was because she had claimed her father or the dragon that crouched at his feet. One voice, coming from the stands behind Belluaire's platform, raised a more fervent protest than the rest:

"Casco!"

She kept walking. Pater Claudio stood and called again, his hands clenched at his sides, his face livid. "Stop right where you are." She ignored him. "Stop! Wife!"

"Wife?" Feus' voice resounded in Casco's mind. "I had hoped one day to call you that myself." The words warmed her, filled the empty space in her chest. "Then do so," she whispered. She drew as close to the dragon as she could without coming within range of her father's whip.

"Guards! Gladiators!" Pater Claudio's commands rang shrilly across the stadium. He had descended the stairs next to his seat, and was now leaning precariously over the protective barrier that kept the audience from falling twenty feet down to the sunken showground. "Get her out of there, Belluaire, or so help me you'll never see another one of our dragons!"

The portcullises had been fully raised and gladiators followed Casco to the foot of Belluaire's platform. Torchlight reflected off the points of their spears.

"He's mine," she repeated, staring up at her father, then switched her gaze to Pater. She held out the Empire bottle's incantation scroll; its edges were ragged where she'd torn it from the great book. It no longer mattered—the bottle itself lay in shards on the floor of her work-cell.

"Belluaire!" Pater Claudio paced along the barrier like a caged tiger. "Damn you—by all the gods—you can't do this!"

Casco thought she saw her father's eyes flick to Priling's banner and back before he said, under his breath, "This is no fault of mine. Let her stay if she's got a death-wish." An artificial smile spread across his face as turned his back on Pater Claudio's protestations and shouted, "A fight like none before! The beast faces the hybrid!"

The applause was deafening. Belluaire urged the gladiators back; then he sketched an elaborate bow, and tossed Casco his whip. "There's nothing else I can give you," he said. "You've brought this upon yourself."

Casco ignored the whip. She turned to face the dragon.

"Feus, I trust you: burn away the flesh."

"*Verba volant*, little half-blood: spoken words fly away. Prove yourself."

"I trust you," she repeated and knelt before him, placing the parchment on the ground. A woman in the audience screamed. Pater Claudio had negotiated his way through the rows of seats and began to lower himself down one of the many rope ladders ringing the arena's perimeter, quick exits for the Wranglers. Casco paid no attention and took brief moments to caress Feus' ravaged hide, her fingers glancing gently along the dull edges of his scales, eliciting a groan of pleasure from her mate. The long silver tongue flicked out and touched the back of her neck, whisper-soft. Casco swallowed hard and removed her hand, began inscribing the symbols of the unbinding incantation onto the dragon's chains with her nails.

"I trust you," she said, intent on her work. Eyes cast down, focused, she was unaware of her lover's fiery kiss until it had engulfed her. The scroll beside her became ashes.

The flames hurt less than she had thought, and more. She felt her human flesh drying out, then curling and finally burning away. New muscle grew, her body changed shape and scales sprouted all over. Her heartbeat slowed and the heat of her blood dropped. Wings stretched from her back, larger and more powerful than those she'd seen in her reflection. Her nails, grown thick with metamorphosis, sheared through Feus' remaining bonds.

Free, she thought, and the joy that shot through her was unlike anything she'd ever experienced. Every inch of her body tingled with it. Stretching her long neck, she nuzzled her lover's torso then nipped at his flanks, teasing him into action. She purred, expelling short bursts of steam from flared nostrils as she butted her sleek head gently against his muscular shoulder. Feus reared and roared. Casco caught the thrum of his humming, now rekindled and transcending to a victorious trumpeting; laughter bubbled in her throat. She opened her mouth and joined her song to his.

A storm of sand rose from the arena floor and blasted over the audience. The night sky was a satin backdrop as the two dragons stretched their wings and took flight.

GROWING SILENCE

MATT TIGHE

THE day before he went to town, Jeffrey walked to the top of the ridge. It was his favourite place. He loved to sit at the back of the house and watch the colours change as the sun slowly dipped below that line of stony earth. It was quiet up there. There were two trees on the ridge, and sometimes the leaves rustled in the wind, like whispers, but mostly it was quiet.

The larger of the trees was an Apple Box that he had helped his father plant, years ago, the day after his mother died. Digging that hole up on the ridge had been hard, for a lot of reasons. She had been young, and vibrant, and she had a beautiful voice that rose and fell like a landscape when she talked. But now, what he mostly remembered when he thought of her was the heat, and the sweat, and the quietness of his father digging beside him, his shovelling punctuated only by his soft crying. The much younger Jeffrey had been unimpressed by the spindly little tree that had resulted from their efforts. It did not seem like much of a trade. His father had seen his expression.

"She'll grow," he had said, his voice hoarse and dry. "It's a good spot for growing, this one."

His father had been right. The tree had sprung up over the last two decades, its trunk thickening and its branches bowing under their own weight. A tree now strolling sedately into middle age, like his mother never had. But its leaves rustled less and less in the wind as it grew, and the silence on the ridge had grown heavier.

Jeffrey had done the digging for the second tree himself. His father had been gone for ten years by then, his hulking, sombre presence first pared back by his own guilt, and then whittled away completely. Jeffrey had felt something close to relief as he pushed the stony soil back in around the new tree. His father wouldn't have approved of this new addition, an addition that had quickly developed into a wispy, pale-skinned adolescent of a White Gum, crowned with thin leaves that at first had rustled almost frantically in the smallest breeze. But then, his father wouldn't have approved of his relationship with Angela either.

Jeffrey placed one hand against the smooth white trunk. It had been too long, and when he tried to picture her alabaster skin and her teardrop face, he mostly saw only the tree now. And he heard almost nothing, even when the leaves did rustle.

"I'm alone," he said aloud, and he felt reassured when he realised it was true. It was okay. It had been a decade. The silence within him had grown as the silence on the ridge had.

"I'm alone, Angela," Jeffrey said again, with more conviction. "And it's too quiet out here."

JEFFREY hated town. Just big enough to accommodate one dingy pub-cum-nightclub and what seemed like a million gossiping hicks, it was a place that was most definitely not for him. Even at night, he felt too conspicuous walking the streets, awkward and gangly in a way that didn't matter at home. As he opened the pub door a whole mess of noises spilled out around him, a confusing cacophony of dated music, clinking glasses, and fragments of conversation. At least in there, you could hide in the swirl of activity and sounds, and choose how much of yourself to put on display.

He kept his eyes down until he got to the bar and ordered a beer, but he forced himself to sit right there, on a stool, and wait for his drink. He wanted to sit in the corner, but that didn't help with making any sort of contact. It had only been dumb luck that had brought him and Angela together, he knew that. The last time he had been in the pub he had made for the corner, almost panicking under the carefully blank gaze of the bartender and the studied indifference of the boisterous, posturing crowd. He had squashed down into himself at a table that was practically behind the door, watching with envy as the girls giggled under the attention of the hungry-eyed men. He had just gulped down his second beer and stood, resolved to leave, when the door had swung wide, clattering against the table with enough force to make him drop his glass. Several people glanced over, and he cursed his own awkwardness. It had been a mistake to come to town.

"Oh, I'm sorry!" a voice had exclaimed, as he bent to pick up the larger shards of glass.

He had sensed her near him, and he had glanced up to see her hiking up her sensible grey skirt right there in front of his face so she could kneel next to him. Her legs had been very white, smattered with dusty freckles. Jeffrey's nerves had kicked in at the sight, burning away the doughy feeling that had been his only gain from the two beers. And then he had looked at her face, which would become so familiar to him, and his nerves had stilled, and all he could hear was her voice.

"WELL, aren't you the quiet one?"

Jeffrey gave a start that sloshed his beer over the rim of his glass. She slid onto the stool next to his, and he found his eyes drawn down to her petite figure. She grinned under his gaze, and he blushed.

"Haven't seen you before," she smiled, just self-consciously enough to make it not a line. Jeffrey smiled in return. She looked nice in her little yellow dress, with her dark, short hair and deep tan. Hopefully the chatty type, but it was a bit early to tell. So unlike Angela. Jeffrey knew he wasn't great at reading the opposite sex. He hadn't had much practice.

"I don't come in to town much," he said, forcing himself not to look at her. It was too obvious. He ran a finger through his spilt beer.

"Oh, a farmer, eh?" He could hear the laughter in her voice, but it sounded kind-hearted.

"Well, maybe more of a gardener, I think. With a big garden."

For some reason she found this immensely funny, tilting her head back and laughing. It looked so beautiful that Jeffrey was sure it was a studied move, until she ended her laugh by snorting loudly.

"Oh my God!" she giggled, covering her face in embarrassment, and Jeffrey grinned, her laughter still sounding in his head.

"Well, don't we make the odd pair, Mr. Quiet?" she grinned back at him. "Everyone says I talk too much."

JEFFREY stood back on the ridge. There was still some time before sunset, and he wanted to be back down at the house where he could watch it and the ridge both, but still, he took a moment. The wind cooled the sweat on his face as it moved the leaves of the skinny White Gum. As they rubbed against each other they made a small sound that was quickly swallowed by the silence. He reached out and put his hand on the smooth trunk.

"It's too quiet up here, Angela. You don't speak to me much anymore." He turned to regard the Apple Box for a moment. "And she says even less."

Jeffrey looked away from them both and smiled down at the sapling. A Wattle, it would bloom into bright yellow flowers, and the many dark-skinned branches would move in the slightest breeze, chattering almost constantly. He bent down to carefully place this third seedling in the overly large hole he had dug, adjusting it carefully so it was on top of the large sack that was already there. As he pushed the soil in around the tree, he frowned. A Wattle was the right choice, he knew that, but they often did not live very long. They burnt out on their own frenetic energy. Jeffrey sat back from his work, his gaze wandering out across the ridge. It was mostly still bare, he realised with relief. There would be plenty more trees to plant, whenever the silence got too much.

The Hidden One

Astrid Cooper

C'THUNK. C'thunk. Screeitch.

In the midnight stillness of the museum, Tez's cleaning trolley skidded sideways as the back wheels locked. She kicked the wheels and just like a bloody supermarket trolley it refused to budge. Yesterday it had worked perfectly, but not now—thanks to the Pharaoh's Curse. Every mishap was blamed on "the Curse", but it was true that when the crowds had gone and the lights were dimmed, strange things happened, especially when there was a full moon. Like tonight.

Putting her weight behind the cart, she pushed forward and it flipped over, scattering bottles and rags across the floor.

"No!" Tez watched, horrified as the broom boomeranged against the wall, narrowly missing a Bust of Isis. Shaking at the horror of a near disaster, she knelt down to collect the equipment. Running footsteps sounded behind her.

"Teresa, I shall rescue you!"

Tez glanced over her shoulder as Zeljko strode towards her. He halted beside her and frowned down at the mess. The look he gave her said it all. He leant down and with one heave, righted the trolley.

"What're you doing here, Zeljko?"

"Securing."

Yeah right. She rolled her eyes as he grinned. Zeljko had taken it upon himself to be her minder. Theirs was an easy familiarity, a friendship forged over the last three months when he had replaced the previous security guard who had held a séance in the museum storeroom with two other night staff. Only he called her Teresa and only she called him Zeljko. The rest of the staff anglicised his name to Jake.

Teresa knelt to collect the cloths while he stuffed the bottles back into the trolley. His cologne wafted around her, musk and spice and man.

She stood up, pretending indifference to him. "The wheels got stuck."

His dark brow arched. "Pharaoh's Curse hits Adelaide Museum." Zeljko quoted the newspaper headline from three months ago.

"Do you think some Mummy's going to waste its time on a cleaning trolley?"

He laughed. "Who knows what a curse will target? *Quem deus vult perdere, dementat prius.*"

"Where's my Latin phrasebook?"

"Whom the gods would destroy, they first make mad."

"You think some spooky god is trying to make me mad by jinxing my trolley? I'd think a god would have better things to do!"

"Gods can be capricious, Teresa."

"Like Latin-quoting security guards."

"Touché!" He tried not to smile, but the light in his grey eyes gave him away. "Curses and spells exist, Teresa. This you know."

"Nope."

"You Westerners are difficult to convince."

"We're realists."

"It is your greatest failing."

"If you say so."

"I said just."

She glared at him. He returned her silent challenge. Zeljko often reverted to pidgin English when he wanted to tease, or play dumb with the other staff. "There's no mummy trailing a mouldering bandage along the corridors, terrorising staff, Zeljko. Just rats and mice and probably a possum in the roof."

"So, it is they who move the jewellery and amulets around in the locked glass cases?"

"I guess." She eyed him shrewdly. "How is the Security CCTV?"

"All static." He lifted his right shoulder. "You believe equipment failure. I say magic."

"What's magic in Bosnian?"

"*Magija.*"

"And you believe in all that hocus pocus?"

They'd had this conversation many times in the staff dining room, with the same result. A stalemate, if ever there was one.

Zeljko shrugged. "There are more things in heaven and earth than are dreamed of in your philosophy."

"So, in between spending ten years digging at the bottom of holes for pottery you read Shakespeare?"

"While sipping *rakia.*"

"It fried your brain, Zeljko."

"*Da.*" Laughing, he pushed the trolley into the Main Exhibition Room.

As always Tez paused at the entrance to admire the statue. Make that capital T, capital S: The Statue was an enigma. Carved from serpentine, it was life-size, almost as tall as Zeljko who stood six feet four. The Egyptian's muscular body was robed in a simple kilt. A bejewelled cummerbund encircled his hips, etched with glyphs that defied decipherment, despite the experts who had repeatedly examined it since its discovery in Thebes in the nineteen-twenties. Bracelets and amulets and ankle chains were all intricately carved with more spells—according to Zeljko.

"Good Evening, Ammon," Tez said walking forward. She saw Zeljko's smile.

"You call the statue Ammon? Yes, he is the hidden one. Why this name?"

"Well, it's better than being known as a catalogue number. I wonder what his real name was?" She ran her finger around the hollow where once a cartouche had been engraved. "To speak the name of the dead is to make him live forever, but this guy's lost his name and his chance at immortality."

Zeljko nodded. He had taught her a lot about Ancient Egypt. She could read a few hieroglyphs.

"The spells on the statue will allow him to live again," Zeljko said. "If the time is right."

"Magic and hokum. It's been proven—"

"Just because history books and experts say it is so, doesn't mean it is fact, Teresa." He spread his hands. "There are alternate histories and this man of the eighteenth dynasty belonged to a secret, ancient priesthood, wizards you would call them, who challenged the Pharaohs for control of the Duat, the pathway to immortality. Magic can open it."

"You told me this before."

"I tell you again. This time you believe?" He smiled.

She loved that smile. It lit up his face, his eyes, making him younger, handsomer, but then the moment passed and he was the usual Zeljko, sad and hurt and beyond her help. She watched his distracted look and knew, from past experience, that he was far from the museum, unaware of her.

When he spoke again it was in Bosnian. "History is written by the victors..." That phrase she knew by heart from their staffroom debates; other words were new, unfamiliar, but still, she understood on a spiritual level. Zeljko spoke of pain and hurt, things he would never tell her in English. Instinctively, she stroked the back of his hand.

They rarely touched. It would be an admission that more existed between them, and neither was prepared for that. He shook himself and smiled, his eyes focusing on her. Their gazes locked. "Ah, Teresa, what is history but one man's interpretation of facts to support the policies of the establishment?"

"You could write a book and challenge the establishment with your theories."

"They're not theories." His eyes danced mischief. "And I will leave the writing of books to you."

Tez flushed. Only he knew that she wrote novels. She had shown him the latest draft of her regency romance and he had read it with his typical intensity before returning the manuscript to her with some suggestions. "You want to make it erotic, I see this, and the characters lend themselves to it, so why do you not?"

"I... um..."

"Westerners are so... repressed."

"I'm not."

"Prove it."

"Right," she said snatching up the papers. Three days later she removed her revised manuscript from her satchel and set it down before him on the mummy case of Nefer-hetep—the place where she wrote when her work was done. Her laptop failed the first night, so she wrote longhand in a notebook. "There," she said ,pushing the book towards Zeljko. "Maybe that's better?"

He returned a few hours later and the look he gave her made Tez blush. She'd changed the story, making it a time travel reincarnation. The hero, who bore a striking resemblance to The Statue, and the modern heroine, bonked their brains out on the banks of the Nile.

"Much better," he said. "You have the nuance of the period perfectly. It will be best-seller!"

"You really think so?"

"I have said."

"You've got a crystal ball at home?"

In response came the ask-me-no-questions shrug. Mr Mystery, the secretaries in the office had dubbed him. Bob, the senior security officer told her that "bloody Kotic" probably had a wife and ten kids at home—in Bosnia or in Adelaide, maybe both. Tez refused to believe his sniping. The man was jealous. She was a prime target—twenty-two and single, and Bob decided she needed saving from herself. He'd made it clear what he wanted and until Zeljko had arrived Tez was considering resigning from her job, or reporting him for harassment. Zeljko realised what was happening and was always on patrol near where Tez worked. Bob changed tactics, trying to make Tez believe that the Bosnian was a fraud. "The guy's ten cents short. Doesn't speak unless it's to quote fucking Latin or poetry, or provoke a debate on some sorta philosophy that no one's heard of. I mean, the guy doesn't even like proper football."

Tez had laughed. Zeljko was doubly damned—he didn't follow Aussie rules. Must be a nutter. Few understood European intensity, but she much preferred it to Bob's cheap banter.

"Have you finished the final draft of your book?" Zeljko asked.

Tez glanced up at him. Since working at the museum she had become interested in alternate history and archaeology and the two had combined in her latest manuscript. She wrote as if possessed, as if she were living the story; when she slept she dreamed and when she awoke, she wrote the dream.

The radio on her hip crackled, cutting through her reverie. "Hey, Carrots, how's Mr Mummy?" Bob demanded. "All wrapped up an' nowhere to go?"

Zeljko swore in Bosnian.

"Don't worry about him, Zeljko. Anyone in Australia who has red hair gets called *Carrots*. I had worse at school." She snatched up her radio. "Bob... ?"

"Vaitch out for ze currrsse!" His accent was Hollywood Egyptian and Tez cringed. He finished his call with a yowl and ran his nails over the radio mouthpiece.

Tez stared at Zeljko. "If you tell me you believe in werewolves, I'll..."

"You'll what?"

"Slap you."

He laughed. "Is that a threat or a promise?"

Tez flushed, her mouth suddenly dry, her throat aching. "I've got work to do."

"Yes." His gaze rested on the statue.

"Just what part of the "do not touch" sign can't they understand?"

"The statue is irresistible." Jake's eyes sparked with amusement. "Even you, I think, are not immune. The hero of your story resembles the statue. In *all* aspects." Their gazes met and she looked away, a yearning between them that could not be acknowledged. Too much hurt, too much history, too many secrets to be overcome. She turned to Ammon.

Every night Tez had to clean the statue of the numerous hand prints, lipstick marks and bodily fluids smeared over the statue. On the few occasions when the Pharaoh's Curse did not interfere with the CCTV, Bob took bets with the staff as to which female would seduce the four thousand year old piece of rock. Occasionally someone performed fellatio on the statue—the contours of the carving were explicit. Bob had tried to show her the video of one of the women on her hands and knees in front of the statue. Zeljko and Bob had nearly come to blows over the incident. The statue had been measured for its own glass cabinet.

"Carrots?" Bob's voice cut through the static. "You seen Kotic?"

"Here," Zeljko replied.

"Go to the storeroom and get a box of books. Take 'em to the office. Now, matey. And Tez, you go to the Africa room. Rats—" The radio cut out. For once the Curse was working in her favour.

Tez glanced at Zeljko. "Why do you let him talk to you like that? Hell, Zeljko, you've got more academic qualifications than all the historians and archaeologists working in this place. You were curator of a museum in Bosnia—that place with the unpronounceable name."

"Why do you?"

"Why, what?"

"Work here. You write beautifully and—"

"That's why publishers reject me." She laughed scornfully. "I have a mortgage."

"I like working here, the scenery." His gaze was unwavering and her heart thudded in her ears.

As she went to speak, he shook his head. "I must go." Zeljko stalked to the door, and paused. "Teresa, do not fear the unknown."

Before she could reply he turned away, his footsteps fading along the length of the corridor. Now alone, the silence was thick, oppressive, the air charged as if a storm was building. She laughed to herself and brought out the artefact-friendly cleaning fluid from the trolley and sprayed it over the statue. She scrubbed every mark with a cloth, her fingers rippling, undulating over the perfect depiction of muscles. If she closed her eyes she could imagine that real flesh existed beneath her hands; except for the sleek coolness of the stone, the sculpture could be human, such was the artisan's skill.

She polished the stone with a new woollen pad and then stepped back to admire her work. Tez avoided looking at the face, too handsome by far, but it was the eyes that bewitched. It felt as if his gaze followed her around the room. She had told Zeljko that the statue gave her "the creeps" and one night he had put his sunglasses on the statue. Even though they both laughed at the sight of Ammon wearing Ray Bans, it had seemed disrespectful and she had removed the sunglasses.

$\mathcal{S}$HE gave Ammon another rub down. Stepping back, her sneakers crunched over something like glass. She knelt down and touched the fine layer of crystal dust on the floor. It wasn't the first night she had noticed the residue around the statue.

"If you're falling apart, I'd better tell the boss." That meant making an appointment with a secretary to see the acting curator. She didn't like Jordan Carter. Jordan Carter frequently implied that he was a relative of *the* Howard Carter of Tutankhamun fame. Probably why he had got the job when the real curator took extended leave due to a sudden illness. Nope, she wasn't going to approach Carter. She'd tell the CEO and to hell with the chain of command.

Tez ran her palm down the statue. As she touched the statue's hand, its fingers seemed to curl around hers. She squealed and leapt back, heart thudding against her ribs. She laughed nervously. It was only a bloody statue. She was spooking herself, thanks to Zeljko's talk of curses.

But the statue was watching her. Waiting. Her skin turned to gooseflesh. Her gut cramped.

She stared the statue down. The moonlight played over his full mouth. He smiled. She had freaked the first time she'd seen that smile, until she realised it was a trick of the light, not magic, as Zeljko had suggested.

Scratch. Scratch.

Tez started at the sound, turning full circle, trying to identify its origin. A rat maybe, or a possum in the old ceiling. She wasn't going to think ghost, let alone Curse.

The hair at her nape lifted as if smoothed away by a finger or lips. She shivered. From fear, from the *frisson* of pleasure. Perfume swirled around her: musk, myrrh, frankincense. She recognised the precious unguents, combined with the musty smell of museum.

From next door she heard the chink of metal against metal. She took up her broom and crept forward. Had someone broken into the museum again?

Peering into the room, she saw nothing. The chink came again, emanating from the glass cabinet closest to Nefer-hetep. Gripping her broom with fear-slippery fingers she tiptoed inside and gaped.

Undulating, as if fondled, she saw the jewelled, spell-inscribed collar of honour that had been found with Ammon. Dry-mouthed, she watched as it moved within the glass cabinet. Behind her she heard more scratching, then a sound like splintering rock.

She raced back to main room and halted. The statue was melting—*melting!*—and within it, something was moving. Curiosity overcoming terror, she crept closer. A skeletal hand like a snake emerged from the statue, fingers prising apart the stone, crumbling it to dust. She heard a man's deep voice invoking the Resurrection Spell Zeljko had recited to her the other night. The rock peeled away, like a skin discarded, dissolving into a billion pieces of golden-green dust that drifted to the floor. Tez blinked. A man stood in the centre of the room. He reached his arms high above his head, and stretched sinuously. He turned and stared at her.

Tez retreated a step and he held out his hand, palm up, his gaze capturing hers. Warmth flowed into her, familiarity.

"Fear not," he said, his accent crisp.

She lifted her broom to warn him off. He smiled, the light of it making his eyes glow golden. He raised his hands and the broom was wrenched from her fingers to hover before her. It sparkled with green and gold before bending in and around itself to form an Ankh. It vanished in a wisp of vapour that stank like burning circuitry.

Right, Tez thought. *Outta here.* But her legs were frozen. He stalked to her, around her, inspecting, as if she were some animal, he the predator, she the prey.

"You are Teresa." The timbre of his voice was smooth, deep, magical.

Only Zeljko called her that. Realisation dawned. "Zeljko put you up to this." She paused. "Tell him he had me going with the special effects. But where's the real statue? You can't go around playing with four thousand year old artefacts." She turned to go. His hand on her wrist restrained her.

He pulled her about to face him and she slammed into his chest. He cradled her head, his palms against her temples.

"You call me Ammon," he whispered.

"How do you know?"

"You name me thus every night when you come to clean me. Ammon was one of my names. I am the hidden one, yes, but I am much more. You know me, *mery*."

Tez swallowed: *mery* meant beloved.

He leaned closer, his hard body hot and she smelled sandalwood and man-spice and beneath it, the incorruptible aroma of the ancients. The unmistakable redolence of magic. *How'n the hell do I know that?* She bit her lip. He touched his mouth to hers. He tasted of gold and the power crackled through her. Memories coalesced, of nights spent in his embrace, of danger and passion and...

Tez tore her mouth free and raced to the door. It slammed shut in her face.

She confronted him, her back against the wall. "Who are you?"

"I am Ammon. I am your beloved returned to you. You are my beloved returned to me, though I find your latest incarnation somewhat strange."

She laughed at that. *He* was calling *her* strange? He strode forward and stood before her, his hand caressing her head. "Red hair was always considered special, the mark of the magic-priestess, feared because of it. Your eyes the colour of lapis. Your skin, like milk. You are beautiful, my beloved."

For a moment she was transfixed, then harsh reality dissipated the spell. "I am not your anything."

He smiled sadly. "He said you might be difficult."

"Who said?"

"Zeljko."

"Now why aren't I surprised he's in on this!"

"Of course he is involved. I revealed myself to him three months ago. He agreed to help me."

"Just like that?"

"He is a man of rare talents and rarer vision." He shrugged, lifting his right shoulder. "I need your help."

"That's an understatement. Let me get my coat. I'll take you to casualty and get you admitted to the psych ward."

"Madness is an affliction meted out by the gods. True, for the first one thousand years, I was demented by the horror of my incarceration. Dust by day and flesh by night, this, the curse I have endured for four thousand years. And in the first night of the full moon, I have the ability to walk as a man and search for the one who will free me from my prison. A creative punishment for a wizard who defied the gods." He paused. "My enemy placed me alive within the statue. I lived there, watched all, lived all, but couldn't move, could only think."

"That's inhuman."

"So my enemies were, from my perspective. Yet..." He smiled ruefully. "Four thousand years allows some time for reflection. I may have been wrong in the manner of my desires, but certainly not in their object." His gaze clashed with hers.

Tez stepped back. "Me?"

"This alarms you, *mery*? I have rejected the pursuit of power and immortality. These are inconsequential. Only love is eternal."

"How profound."

"You doubt it? You doubt me?" He smiled. "Your touch is as I remember. Every time. It was an agony, when you caressed and I could not respond."

"When I was polishing the statue? You felt me?"

"Of course, I'd have to be dead not to."

"Aren't you?"

"I need your help."

"How can I *help* you?"

He regarded her steadily. "I have only what remains of this night to undo the binding spell, or await the next full moon. Where are my jewels and amulets?"

"Next door."

"Please." He bowed to her and held out his hands, palms extended to the door. It swung open.

Tez drew in a deep breath. She walked forward and he strode beside her, his bare feet slapping the floorboards. Entering the Mummy Room, he halted beside the central display case and spread his hands over it. The glass melted. *Melted.* Light-headed with fear, Tez glanced up at him.

"This is all too much for me. I don't believe in it, or you. I... can't!" She backed away.

"That's unfortunate," he said dryly. "How you have changed."

"What changed?"

"We believed we could rule the worlds, you and I. We had only to reach out to the Imperishables and we could be as they, rulers of the Duat. You were once a visionary, but now you are so... reticent."

"Yeah, well, that's me, reticent. Ordinary Teresa Donovan. Museum cleaner and wannabe writer." Tears pricked the backs of her eyes.

"If you believe it, so shall you be. I have a different reality for you, if you dare it. If you have the courage."

She tossed her head, chin high. A tremor of power raced through her veins, tingling the ends of her fingers. She'd lived with ordinary all her life. Tonight was extraordinary. If she dared...

His smile was dark. "You have the essence of she whom I loved. This night will bring it forth. Like a lotus you will struggle past the mud and bloom into the light."

"You're a poet."

"Of course. A wizard has an affinity with words." He turned to the display case. "Yet, I must also have my amulets. Where is the heart scarab?"

Tez frowned, her mind racing through the inventory. The heart scarab was the most important ancient Egyptian symbol. Resurrection was impossible without it. "There's nothing like that here. Maybe it's been lost?"

He frowned and closed his eyes. "No, it is here. I can feel its vibrations. Beyond this room, but within this temple. I must find it. My enemy has hidden it."

"Your enemy is here?"

"Of course. We three, together for eternity. Bound by magic. We are part of the whole. Separate but together."

"You mean karma and reincarnation?"

He shrugged. "In your modern tongue, yes. I could discuss with you the Spells of Emergence, what you call "The Book of the Dead", the incantations to restore one's *ka* and *ba*, but reincarnation is a word you understand. It will suffice. Come." He held out his hand.

"I'm not going anywhere with you."

"Afraid, are you? Of me, or of yourself?" He laughed, a deep sound, full of amusement and layered beneath, the absolute dismissal of her protests. In that moment Tez knew he could do with her as he willed and she was powerless...

"Not powerless, *mery*, simply asleep. Tonight will see us both reborn." He held out his hands and the bracelets twirled around his wrists.

Within her was an excitement, an itching at her consciousness, a memory trying to resurface. "If there's anything kept out of the exhibition, it'd be in the curator's office."

"Ah, yes, Mr Carter."

"You know him?"

"I watched him engage in the negotiations with the family whose ancestor stole me from Egypt. I cursed the family. They were only too pleased to bequeath artefacts to the City of Adelaide. It took many years, but I am here and I have found you. Again." He bowed to her, his gaze holding hers as he straightened. "Take me to the curator's office."

Tez stalked ahead and he followed. Silently, they climbed the narrow spiral staircase at the end of the corridor, the gloom lifted by the shafts of moonlight through the slitted windows.

As Tez's foot touched the last step, her stomach lurched. Danger ahead. She stumbled and Ammon's warm hand steadied her.

"Sorry," she whispered. "This all feels so surreal. It's like I'm living a scene from a Bronte novel... No, this is more Edgar Allan Poe, because I have Mr. Mummy in tow."

Her laughter faded the moment she saw his frown.

"My name is Ammon."

Arriving at the curator's door, she grasped the handle. Pain lanced her fingers. Somehow, she sensed the wizard's barrier and paused. Now what? The memories awakening in her told her that the spell to counteract this binding was simple. Before Ammon could intervene, she put her palms against the door and concentrated. The wood shivered and grew warm. With the force of her own magic, the door swung open, slamming against the wall.

Ammon stepped past her and paced around the room, his arms widespread, fingers parted. A faint green light, the colour of resurrection, emanated from each fingertip.

"Here!" he said, halting before the far wall and a photograph of the great pyramid at Giza, with Carter on a camel in the foreground. A younger Carter. She'd never taken much notice of it before, but now as she peered closer, she saw that the other members of his party wore clothes straight out of the early nineteen twenties, complete with jodhpurs and pith helmets.

"That's only a picture, nothing magical about it. It's weird, though. Carter..."

"The man you know as the curator has lived many lifetimes, he is the guardian."

"The guardian of what?"

"Me. He is the originator of the curse," Ammon said.

"Were you so very wicked?"

"Depends on your perspective. I believed what I sought was my due; he disagreed. Who was right and who was wrong?" He smiled then and lifted his right shoulder in dismissal.

"History is written by the victor who has the absolute power of truth and falsehood." She gaped at her words. Now in place of Zeljko she was having the same debate with some resurrected Egyptian. *I'm crazy!*

Ammon smiled. "You speak like the priestess of old."

"I... what... ?"

"You served Isis and I, the older gods. The Imperishables—the starlords." He ran his fingers over the picture, then flicked up the frame to reveal a small wall safe. He reached out to the dial and reeled back with a yelp.

Tez smelled burning flesh and more. The deepest magic held an unmistakable odour—an acidic vinegar stench—and this room was imbued with it. She shook her head to try and clear her nose, her mind, against the whirling of emotions and memories—her own, from times past.

"Let me," she said and tentatively touched the dial, feeling the power, but it accepted her. She twisted the combination back and forth and then a clunk and she lifted the handle and opened the door. A flash of silver and something struck out and the fangs of the snake pierced the palm of her hand. She cried out, stumbling backwards, the blood welling from two puncture wounds.

The creature fell to the floor, shattering into shards of black crystal.

Ammon held Tez's hand between his own, concentrating on the wound. "For a time I can hold the poison at bay, but I must find the spell that my enemy used. Clever..."

"Poison?" Tez shivered. "I need a hospital."

"This was a demon's *shabti*, Teresa, an icon, not a flesh and blood animal. No doctor can save you, only a wizard. Only me." He reached into the safe and withdrew a box and flipped open the lid. The light danced over the fist-sized golden scarab. At its centre was an emerald, etched with resurrection symbols. Ammon closed his right hand around the amulet and placed Tez's injured hand over his.

The sickly sweet stench of Hekenu incense wafted about her. The room seemed to dissolve around her and she saw a temple, its walls painted with murals, with incantations to raise the dead, to lengthen life. Torchlight flickered over the stones, making the murals and the writing writhe, like thousands of asps. She heard voices intoning ancient magic, men and women, the tinkling of the sistrum bells, enforcing every word of power.

In that moment her mind touched his, a joining, an intimacy beyond flesh. She saw, she felt, she knew—as Ammon felt and knew: their life, their love. He touched the spell, buried deep, layers of bindings and hidden by millennia. The scarab pulsed with green light.

"We must return to the statue room."

"I'm not sure I can walk."

Ammon smiled. "What is it that Zeljko says to you? I will secure you." He swept her up in his arms and she felt the whipcord muscles and the softer skin—a contradiction, like the man. His warmth, his scent engulfed her. Pleasure-pain pulsed through her. She rested her cheek against his shoulder and breathed him in.

It seemed only moments later that he set her gently down on her feet. Going to the pile of green dust where the statue had once stood, he drew out the crystals with the big toe of his right foot and formed a circle on the floor. He beckoned.

"Remain within the circle, it will protect you."

Ammon departed and when he returned she saw that he carried every piece of jewellery from the display cases. He donned several amulets and then the collar of honour. He placed the scarab against his heart. When he withdrew his hand, remarkably the scarab remained attached to his chest. He smiled at her. "Heart to heart, *mery.*"

She watched as gold-green light flowed from the scarab, weaving a lattice around his body. He wrapped a lapis-lazuli girdle around her hips and pushed on bracelets and ankle chains. Their familiar weight comforted. How many times had she donned each piece as a prelude to her priestess invocations? The air around her pulsed with life, her nerves spiked. Her blood pounded like a drum. The poison thinned in her body as Ammon's spell gained ascendancy.

Ammon lifted his head, eyes narrowed. "Aapep comes."

Jordan Carter stood in the doorway. For a moment Tez saw him arrayed as a priest, his shoulders draped with a leopard skin. His great beauty was a mockery to the reeking corruption within him. Then his image wavered to become the wizened curator.

"You see, boss, I told ya they're crooks." Bob strode forward, his face alight with triumph. "I'll fire 'em immediately."

"Silence! Your usefulness is at an end." Aapep struck Bob across the neck. He crashed to the floor and lay unmoving. The curator raised his hands towards Tez and mumbled, intoning spells to sunder her heart and flesh. Screaming, she fell to the floor as his power imprisoned her. Fire burned through her. She screamed.

"Teresa!" Racing in from the corridor, Zeljko flung himself at the curator, fingers clawing, gouging. The two men went down to the floor in a tangle of legs and arms. But human-strength could not defeat demon-power. Aapep, the moon snake struck and Zeljko's chest ruptured as the curator-priest plunged his fingers into human flesh.

Horrified, she felt Zeljko's life-essence flow outwards. Aapep turned to her and struck a spell-bolt to her heart. She battled against it, drawing her own magic, lines of power forming vines and lotus flowers with glowing gems at their heart. Hers, the power of the lady, of life, of fecundity, was the antithesis of Aapep, whose power emanated from death. A man's power, to destroy.

She heard Ammon chanting, and the counterspells from Aapep; back and forth. Crackling energy coruscated over the walls, green light, golden, black, all entwining sinuously, battling for supremacy.

The scarab fell to the floor, skidding across the floorboards. She crawled towards it, every inch agonising, from the spells, from the poison that made her blood thick and cold.

Her fist fastened around the scarab and it seared her palm. Life flowed back into her. She directed the power outwards, towards Aapep.

The older wizard screamed, countered the spell, but too late. Ammon and she pounced and the death-spell imploded, returning to Aapep a thousand fold. He screamed again and fell to his knees.

"It is done, Aapep. I have prevailed. Let it be over between us." Ammon held back, his hands raised, green light eddying around him. "I do not want to be a destroyer of worlds, of lives. Too much has been unmade because of us. Let there be peace."

"You fool!" Aapep hissed, becoming his namesake, the Moon Snake. He transformed to a cobra, ten feet tall, a silver flared hood, red flicking tongue, and diamond eyes.

Ammon held his ground as the creature loomed over him, waving back and forth. Poison dripped from the cobra's fangs to the floor, burning the wood, leaving a rotting-sour stench. Ammon again cast his magic and it encased the snake, piercing its scales, like hundreds of tiny arrows, light destroying shadow. The room exploded with a golden brilliance.

When Tez could see again, three bodies lay on the floor: Carter-Aapep and Ammon and Zeljko. The wizard was now an eviscerated corpse. Zeljko was spreadeagled in a pool of blood. Ammon struggled to sit upright. His flesh was blistered where the poison had spattered him. He smiled at her, but the warmth did not touch his eyes. She saw his gaze harden.

Life battled death: the pain of it made her double over and she bit her lip to stifle the scream. The poison, like biting mouths, invaded her every cell. She had used her life-essence to defeat her enemy, to support Ammon and now his life would be born of her death. She crumpled to the ground, shivering.

"Beloved, no!" Ammon said cradling her in his arms. His tears fell onto her cheeks as he kissed her temple. His love flowed into her.

"Take the scarab, save yourself, Ammon."

"My life for yours?"

"I will return again. We'll find each other in another life... '

"That can never be," he said. "Such is the nature of the spell. My life begins and ends here. Give me your jewels." He removed the amulets and chains from his body and took hers and knelt, like Ma'at, his right hand and his left balancing the jewellery and the scarab. "Place your hands upon mine. Quickly."

With the last of her strength, she knelt before him. The jewellery melted, became a glowing cobweb of light over their entwined hands. Tez gasped as the puncture wounds in her palm pulsed, cold and sharp. Slowly, the pain ebbed. Her heart strengthened as he bent over her beginning the new spell, to bring her life.

Power erupted within the circle. The crystals flared and rose, enveloping them both like a second skin. She clawed at her throat. Choking. Suffocating, as she had died a hundred times before...

*T*RESA came awake with the thought that she needed to get a new mattress: the bed beneath her felt as hard as a rock. But then as her senses kicked in she realised she was lying on the floor of the main exhibition room.

Groaning, she pushed herself upright and stared about. Every artefact was upturned, the glass cabinets smashed. The mummy of Nefer-hetep, a charred husk in his shattered sarcophagus. Everything destroyed, as if a battle had been waged.

Ammon!

She knelt beside him. Horror made her retch. Where before Ammon was beautiful, as only a demi-god could be, now he was skeletal, strings of flesh on bones, a skin of stone in other places. His face was smashed. Only the eyes were alive and they pleaded with her to end it all.

Beside him lay the scarab, still potent, pulsing with magic. It could give him the peace he craved. There would be no resurrection, just empty eternity.

"Ammon, beloved." She bent forward and kissed his shattered mouth. Her lips found death and yet beneath the horror she tasted his life, his love, his gift. His one flesh-finger traced the tears on her cheek as she lifted her head from his.

"It is good, *mery*." He died between one breath and the next, a smile in his eyes. He crumpled to green powder.

No! Her cry shattered eternity.

A groan behind her, she turned. Zeljko was still alive! She dragged herself to him and touched his chest. His shirt was stained crimson. How could anyone lose that much blood and still live? She pressed her palms against the wound.

In that moment, in that touch, the touch she had never dared in life, in that moment, time, space, individuality peeled back and like a floodgate, emotions and experiences merged. His life: the betrayal by a wife and family, because he dared to denounce the war; his ordeal of weeks of hiding from patrols, fleeing, to be helped by his Serbian friends to reach sanctuary outside Bosnia... To find a new home in Australia. All he had hidden, she now saw. All too late. He died as she pressed her lips to his in farewell.

She crawled to Ammon and lay over the dust that had once been her beloved. She smelled smoke and heard the crackling of flames. She closed her eyes, her mind. Death here and now for them all. Darkness consumed.

Strong hands grabbed her, turned her, raising her to her feet. She blinked up at the familiar figure. Yet it was not the Zeljko she remembered. In his now-dark eyes she saw the ancient soul. The collar-length black hair was no longer grey-streaked, his face was softened. Where his uniform had been torn, blood-soaked, now it was whole. Like the man.

"Teresa, we have to go."

Flames leapt up the wall, igniting the wooden shutters. Hand in hand they raced forward. Beside the door, they stumbled over Bob's body. He groaned. Wordlessly, they lifted him, taking an arm and half dragged him along the corridor, desperately trying to outrace the flames and the acrid smoke. At last, they saw the exit.

Outside, fire engines were just arriving, their sirens piercing, lights turning night to day. They dropped Bob to the grass and he struggled to sit up, cradling his head in his hands. Crews plunged into the museum, as the snorkel was placed against the tower room.

The CEO raced up to them. "Have you seen Jordan? I was told he was inside with you."

"We couldn't save him," Tez said. It wasn't a lie. Carter died because he refused to set aside his enmity.

"Dear God!" The CEO paced back and forth. "But at least you're alive and... Bob. You got him out, too, but I don't understand—" A TV cameraman with a journalist shoved between them.

"Mr Turner, seems like the Pharaoh's Curse has struck again..."

Zeljko took Tez's arm and led her away, finding a quiet place amid the turmoil.

"Zeljko?" she whispered.

"Yes, and no. My *ba*, my *ka* entered the body of the man you called Zeljko, when the life of that one was extinguished. He died trying to save you, Teresa. Life for life and death for death." He smiled, holding out his hand to her.

She clasped his hand to her heart. "You are the hidden one," she whispered.

"Ammon, yes, I am he, but also another. I was sundered, my power broken, to live as parts of the whole, until one came to bind me together, with love, with the kiss of death and life. Such was the magic that destroyed me, such is the magic that saved me. You, *mery*. My beloved. And you, my *draga,* do you remember your past?"

"I am Tez, but also I have ancient memories." She blushed. "The heroine in my book..."

"I have always known you were the woman whose blood burns for her beloved, who defied the gods to take him to her bed. She, who made her man scream with pleasure."

She nodded, not looking at him. He cupped her chin and raised her face. "I will savour your passion, Teresa. We will find the knowledge we have lost, resurrect the memories, bring forth..." He frowned.

"It's gone," she said. "The power. We'll live, we'll die. Not Imperishables after all. This is what you gave up for me, to bring me back to life?"

"What life is there without you, without love, *draga?*"

"Am I your darling?" she whispered.

He smiled, his eyes alight. "You are my beloved, in every tongue I speak. Trust me, four thousand years entombed in a statue taught me that love is the most powerful force in the universe. And as Zeljko, I loved you from the first moment I saw you. But when I knew you were destined for the hidden one and I had promised to help him, I was honour bound to do so and not follow my heart."

"But do I call you Ammon or Zeljko?"

He raised her palm to his mouth, his tongue caressing. "In this new land I have been reborn. I am Jake. And as Jake I can love you as I have dreamed. Our joining will be more powerful than any damn spell." He grinned. "The scenes you wrote in your book were highly stimulating. Within you is a woman of passion. I want to be burned by your touch. Ammon remembers the way you caressed him when you cleaned the statue. I want to feel those hands and fingers upon my flesh. Tonight. Tomorrow. Forever."

"*Dragi,* my *dragi,* the poet."

"Yes." His gaze held hers. "When our minds merged, I know you saw part of the man in Bosnia, but I also saw things that you have hidden. No man will ever hurt you again, Tez. Never." His hands clenched over hers, emphasising his promise.

"We both need to relinquish the past."

"*Da.*"

"But how are we going to explain all of this? And Bob saw... They won't believe the truth, that a curse was responsible."

With narrowed eyes he studied the tower room. "I believe they will find the fire was caused by an electrical fault and all of the artefacts consequently destroyed. As for Bob, if he remembers anything, do you think he will admit to what transpired? You worry too much, *draga-mery*. It is your greatest failing." Pressing against her, his arm enfolded her. He bent his head to hers and Tez opened her mouth to his kiss, his questing tongue. She arched herself up into him, her contours moulding to his, a familiarity amid the unknown.

A Darker Shade of Pale

David Bofinger

"AND *the hospital said you need to come in for a battery change... Shara? It's very noisy, where are you?*"

Shara mentally inventoried her appearance. Makeup—check: no risk a paparazzo would get a nude-faced shot of the enigmatic Shara. Accessories—check: even the hands-free was designer. All in all, pretty good, except for the curves and the rosy good health blooming in her complexion. She hated that look and so did modelling agencies. "I'm in one of those places you don't like me going, Janice. It's filled with terrible people just itching to ravish me."

A man at the next table ogled Shara over his wife's shoulder. He wore an expensive tailored suit; his wife's frock was a frumpy off-the-peg. Shara snared the man with a look, ran a finger over her lips and slowly drew it down toward her breast. The way his eyes followed was a better check on her appearance than any mirror could have been. It wasn't just that he looked—she could have done that wearing a bin liner draped in kitchen peelings—but the smooth unthinking way his eyes travelled told her there were no distracting imperfections. When his wife turned to see what had her husband so fascinated, Shara was innocently turned in another direction and smirking only on the inside. Her good deed for the day: judging by the wife's furious tone his apology would cost one nice dress, at least.

"*Are you there? Do you want me to pick you up? Hello?*"

"Do you remember what I explained about the difference between a personal assistant and a mother? Oh my—Houston, we have a nibble." The man who'd walked in was definitely wearing tailored and it would have been a crime to give him anything else. Short dark hair framed an ageless face. "Janice, you should see what I see."

"*If it's a helpless male sucker melting in your hand then I've seen them before. It should be illegal to look as good as you do.*" Janice envied Shara her glamour, and sadly had cause to. In any sane world Janice's trim muscular body would have swept up eligible gentlemen like wind through autumn leaves. Instead it had abandoned her to an inexplicable manlessness.

The newcomer scanned the bar; for a moment his eyes met hers and Shara felt like she'd taken cocaine. She favoured him with a cool half-smile. It was rare Shara wasn't the most attractive woman in a room and in a minute their combined magnetism drew him to her side. She waited for his pickup line.

"*We could grab a quick bite, or I could drive you back to your place. Shara? Are you—*"

His palm gently cradled Shara's head, fingers slipping between the hands-free and her skin. Janice's voice hummed distantly, too faint to pick out words, as the hands-free lay abandoned on the bar. She felt her connection to the mundane world had been loosed, that she was adrift in stormy grey eyes. It had been done with such smooth assurance that anyone watching would have assumed they were lovers.

Shara said, "I was listening to that."

"And you were watching me." His voice was like cream liqueur poured over ice. He put his hand on hers and glanced down. "What an unusual ring."

"It's magnetic—" she blathered, then gathered together the self-possession to stop herself. She pulled her hand back but he held on gently, or she did. Their hands rested together over her heart then slid up to her lips. Suddenly her heart was pounding at half again its normal rate.

His hand slipped around the back of her head. The faintest upward pressure brought her to her feet as though she was weightless. As they walked out of the bar, she tried to say, "Where?" but her lips just quivered soundlessly. Their walks fell into synchrony, like a dance they'd practised so many times they no longer needed to think about it.

In the car park was a white stretch limousine with tinted windows. The door to the back hummed open as they approached and shut again when they were inside. The car rolled into motion.

The interior was dominated by a bed in shades of red. Shara lay back on silk sheets, gazing up into those wonderful eyes. A shred of her usual confidence reminded her she'd planned a seduction this evening, that his eyes were seeing what she'd wanted them to see, but most of her was past caring about anything but how they made her feel.

He tore off the brooch that held her dress together and most of her other clothes practically unpinned themselves—as she'd planned it, hours and a lifetime ago. Her boots were deliberately finicky to remove and he left them on.

She unbuttoned his shirt and pants, drawing him into arousal, but it was no real contest: his slightest touch made her whole body light up and within a minute she was lying back and moaning.

He brought her skilfully to the edge of orgasm. One finger traced the jugular vein down the side of her neck.

"Now," she begged: he lowered his mouth to her neck and needle-sharp fangs entered her. She felt like a butterfly in a collection, pinned to the ground through her body.

Shara wrapped her arms around his head. With her thumbs she closed off his carotid arteries: a vampire didn't need blood flowing to his brain to stay conscious, but as long as the arteries were blocked he'd remain thirsty no matter how much he drank. After half a minute he tried to pull away but he was fighting his instincts and the confusion made him weak: she held him close as she came, agony mixing exquisitely with orgasm. After a minute she felt weak too, her vision grey at the edges, but by then he had completely surrendered to the hunt and wasn't fighting her any more.

"More," she begged-commanded, then darkness claimed her.

BLACK hair framed a Chinese face: Janice kneeling over her. "Oh Shara," she half-whispered. "Can you stand?"

Shara's pulse felt rapid and thready. She tried to move her arm, trembled and shook her head. Janice took the magnetic ring from

Shara's finger and swiped it downward over the skin concealing Shara's artificial heart so it resumed its normal pace.

Janice bent down and scooped Shara from the cold ground. Shara felt helpless and safe, like a baby. She imagined she could count Janice's wiry muscles individually through her skin.

She sat like a sack of flour in the passenger seat of Janice's car. The needle slipped into her arm with hardly a prick. Janice attached the intravenous drip bag to the handle above the window. Shara drifted in and out of consciousness while Janice drove. Streetlights flashed past hypnotically.

By the time they got to Shara's home she was strong enough to walk with a little assistance, and to insist Janice pull out the needle. She tried to say "thank you" as she fell asleep holding Janice's hand.

*J*ANICE'S alarm, set for half an hour before Shara's, woke them simultaneously. Shara lay on one side of her king-sized bed, feeling sharp and predacious, while Janice stretched out in a reclining chair beside it. "Doesn't my assistant rate a bed?" asked Shara, shedding sleep-rumpled clothing on her way to the shower. "I'm sure I've seen it in the other room. It's far too hard and uncomfortable to be mine."

Janice looked embarrassed but determined. "I was worried. You looked awfully pale—like you'd been drained dry."

"And the bastard left my hands-free in the bar. There's no excuse for that; it's just uncivilised."

"He must have been a very handsome barbarian. I'll collect it today." Shara could tell from Janice's voice that she was scrawling a note in Chinese.

"He wasn't really a barbarian." Shara smiled at the memory. "But he was wonderfully decadent." Emerging from the shower she spun on the spot, nude and dripping. "How do I look?"

Janice shrugged helplessly. "Like the world's most beautiful tapeworm host."

"No pink?" Her skin looked satisfactorily milky but she liked Janice to check the bits she couldn't see. They were mostly places the fashion columnists never saw either, but Janice, bless her heart, never said so.

"After how much blood he took? You're pale as ermine and twice as expensive. Now sit—you have to strut a runway in a few hours." Janice applied thick layers of foundation to Shara's face, much more skilfully than Janice ever put on makeup for herself. The final layer would be added by a professional at the fashion show, but Shara didn't go out with nude skin, ever. "You're sure you'll be OK? I've got a unit and a half of whole blood in the chiller, if you need it—"

"Don't fuss."

Janice looked stricken.

"What's wrong?"

"What's wrong?" Janice laughed, a little hysterically. "Only you would ask that. You could have died—he probably thought you were dying when he dumped you. What if he'd decided to dispose of the body by throwing it in an incinerator? What if he'd taken your boots, or found the phone you had hidden in them, or left you somewhere without coverage, and I couldn't find you in time?"

Shara took Janice's hand. "It's fun to pretend I'm human." It came out flip and devil-may-care and Shara immediately wished she could take it back, and not dismiss the fears of a woman she loved like a favourite niece.

Janice squared her little jaw in determination. "Only it's not really a pretence, is it? When you hide your strength of will, when you fake an inability to resist, you really do become weak—as weak as you want him to think." She was shaking and looked ready to cry. "You take these insane risks and you say not to fuss—"

Shara slipped slender arms around Janice's compact body, moved that this infinitely competent woman could be frightened for her, and relaxed into the warm comfort of hugging a friend. Janice's breath tickled her ear; Shara moved her head so Janice's lips brushed across the point of her jaw in what could almost have been a kiss.

Suddenly there was no almost about it. Janice's strong arm was gently supporting her as she fell back onto the bed; Janice's eyes shone into hers; Janice's finger drew hardness from a nipple. Pleasure and confusion chased each other round Shara's mind.

For a moment pleasure won, then Shara rolled away. "But—" *But you're Janice.* "I didn't know you were... "

Janice laughed sadly. "The genuine 'don't ask, don't tell' employer. I figured out you didn't know when you kept introducing me to men."

"You could have said."

"My employer had just revealed she was a vampire. Announcing I was a lesbian felt like anticlimax." Janice curled her fingers in Shara's. "I've felt this way about you... well, a while. I know it's unprofessional, but it feels good to finally say it."

"But... me?" The last word came out as a squeak. "You know what I am."

"I know you better than anyone. You dominate everyone you meet, but you fantasise submission. When you drink you're careful not to take too much, not to hurt the donor too badly—but you take stupid risks with your own life. You're a creature strange and beautiful beyond my understanding and yet you have never, ever suggested or implied I was less special than you." She spread her hands. "Of course I love you. I couldn't understand anyone who didn't."

They sat looking at each other: Janice obviously thinking it was Shara's turn to speak, Shara with no idea what she should say. After a long half-minute Janice picked up the makeup kit again. Shara sat very still and did nothing while Janice with professional care helped Shara conceal herself from the world.

FEELING sexy?" Shara's agent always asked that before she went on. It wasn't exactly rhetorical—she occasionally improvised routines that had been in nobody's choreography. But he knew she was too professional to turn in less than a superb performance. That she didn't come back with a flip reply was enough to make him come into her dressing room and close the door behind him. "Shara? Is everything OK?"

"Can you help me find a new assistant?" The stylist put the finishing touches on her hair.

"Things not working out with Janice? I thought you were joined at the hip." Shara stared at the screw holes in the wall, where the mirror had been removed. She tried to imagine working with Janice, knowing how Janice felt, and couldn't. She tried to imagine not having Janice to help her and found it just as impossible. Her agent said, "I'll find someone. Don't worry about it," and left.

They walked up to the stage together. Shara felt nervous, for the first time in she couldn't remember how many showings, and then someone said, "Shara, three, two, one," and everything else was forgotten.

She strode the catwalk like a panther eyeing sheep. The audience was full of fashion editors and TV personalities, jaded by years of exposure to extraordinary beauty. But every single one caught their breath a little at Shara's entrance. She glowed with the glamour she'd not been able to use the night before when she'd pretended to be human, a mesmerism more polished and potent than the one that had enchanted her. Women walked ahead and behind who were more beautiful, whose names commanded higher prices, whose images could glue a man's feet to the floor of a newsagency until he'd guiltily leafed through a whole magazine. But when the reviews of this night were written they would mainly focus on the outfits Shara modelled, because those who wrote them would struggle to remember anyone else.

Quick change and her cue for the second time around. She was calmer this time and used her power more subtly, allowing the audience to surrender themselves rather than carving through their defences with unsheathed charisma.

Tucked away in corners were the hangers-on, including Janice. Notably missing were photographers. Shara had been offered fortunes for a shoot but turned them down for the usual vampire reason—it would only take one makeup malfunction to gain some very unwelcome attention. Instead she haunted the rare eyes-only events, where designers tried out new concepts without the risk of permanent humiliation if they failed.

She caught a face that made her strike the next two poses on automatic. Standing near the back, his arm wrapped by a glassy-eyed starlet, was her partner of the night before. He watched uncertainly, unsure whether this majestic creature was the helpless prey he remembered, unable to conceive the transformation.

Third time out and she made the model's strut a message just for him. She danced his humiliation, the greatness of his vanity and the smallness of his reality. Women around the room nodded approvingly while men shrank in their chairs. He lasted for about half her display before he broke and ran. He missed the bit that made male legs cross all around the audience.

Her last outfit of the show was the least explicitly erotic. On impulse she took the sex out of her performance completely, making it a story of how love grew out of friendship. A man and woman in the front row had argued then not spoken through the whole showing: now their hands reached out and clasped. Janice's eyes shone through tears.

*I*N the dressing room, Shara waited for Janice. They would spend the evening at home together. Perhaps that would end in bed, and perhaps not.

Tomorrow night, perhaps Shara would take a safe half-litre from each of a dozen entranced humans, and waddle home bloated with blood, red-faced and curvaceous. The night after, perhaps, she would seek out another innocent vampire, deceive him with an artificial pulse into thinking she was human, and have him drain that blood away to restore her fashionable emaciation and pallor.

Or perhaps she would not be doing any of those things. Shara knew only that she was looking forward, very much, to hearing Janice's voice again.

THE VALLEY

MARTIN LIVINGS

His name is Nowhere, and he is alone.

See him? He stands atop his hill, barely breaking the grey acrid mist that fills the valley below. He can hear the muffled screams that fight their way clear of the stench, torn from throats that barely sound human or even alive. He knows that what lies hidden in the fog is more terrible than he could even imagine, let alone endure. He knows he should stay on his hill, where there is enough food and water to survive, albeit barely.

But in the distance is another hill. It looks green and beautiful to Nowhere's eye, an island paradise in a smoky sea of troubles. And on this hill is another person.

His name is Nowhere, and he is lonely.

He raises his hand to the distant figure and waves. The person waves back. He knows the person is not real; so many times he has ventured into the fog-shrouded valley below, questing for the other hill. So many times he has tried, and so many times he has ended up exactly where he started, a little more scared, a little more scarred. But still he hopes that this time, just this once, it could be different.

So, once again, like a thousand times before, Nowhere takes a deep breath, pulls the rough pack with some rations and warm blankets in it onto his shoulder, and starts down the slope.

The mist is not as thick as it looks from above. It is as if there is a skin on the surface, like milk that has been left out too long. Nowhere looks around anxiously, as every shadow seems alive, every movement in the corner of his eyes seems threatening. Something brushes past his left sleeve and he cries out in terror, shying away, nearly losing his footing. He blinks.

There is a roiling mass of man-shaped shadows all around him. It is a whirlpool of faceless people, all going about their unknowable tasks, all aware of each other yet seemingly blissfully ignorant of Nowhere. And although they are shadows, they have enough physical form to knock Nowhere back and forth, disorienting him terribly. As they pass, nudging and elbowing him as they go, he can make out snatches of faint conversation, whispers of whispers, nonsensical to his ears.

... and the bus didn't arrive until...

... never heard of such...

... it sucks, man, it really...

Nowhere tries to block them out, ignore these shades, but the further down the slope he goes, the more insistent and incessant they become, until he is running downhill, hands clasped over his ears, screaming for them to leave him alone. But they cannot hear him; they are in a different world to him, like a man kicking over anthills without ever noticing the destruction he leaves behind.

... did you see...

... did you hear...

... did you know...

Slowly the words change, seeping between his fingers and into his ears like black oil, filling his head.

... you are useless...

... you are worthless...

... you are nothing to us...

The sentiments are nothing new to Nowhere. They are as familiar as the jagged white furrows on his forearms, the pains in his head at night. Nonetheless, they sap his strength, his will, leaving him weakened and discouraged. Only gravity and momentum continues to propel him down the slope.

... you are useless...

... you are worthless...

... you are nothing to us...

... no.

He pauses in his descent. That was something new. Nowhere cocks his head, trying to catch it again.

... you are useless...

... you...

... no.

There it is again, clear in the muddled maelstrom of noise and movement, like a diamond suspended in a roiling ocean of pitch, occasionally breaking the surface.

... you are nothing to...

... NO!

This time it is loud enough to hurt Nowhere's head. He cries out, his fists against his temples, and stumbles to his knees. His backpack pulls him over, and he begins to tumble down the slope.

His fall comes to an abrupt end, as his shoulder jars against something solid, leaving him still and on his back.

... worthless...

... NO!!!!!!!!!!!!

The sound still hurts him, but somewhere in his head he wants it to continue. It drowns out the other voices, overwhelming them. And when they come back, they seem weaker, tentative, uncertain. Still, his instinct is to escape, and he looks up to see the solid thing that stopped his descent.

A house, again as familiar to him as the voices. He knows what to expect. Nowhere gets to his knees, reaches up with one shaking hand, and opens the wooden door, letting himself fall inside, the door closing behind him of its own accord.

He lies curled up on the stone, the echoes of the voices still ringing in his ears even though the sounds have stopped. But they slowly fade, until he is no longer sure if what he is hearing are the voices or just the memory of them. Eventually he dares to remove his hands from his ears, and sits up.

There is no light in the room. His eyes begin to invent shapes in the darkness, walls and ceilings and furniture which he knows are not really there. His ears strain to hear a noise, any noise save his own breathing or heartbeat, but there is nothing here but himself.

So why is he so afraid?

He becomes increasingly aware of the sounds his own body makes. His stomach growls and churns, and his swallowing seems ridiculously loud and grotesque. Every noise that comes from him sounds amplified. At first it is just distracting, but soon it begins to sicken him. Then the smell of himself assails his nose, sweat and food and fear vying for attention. Nowhere can feel his flesh creep, the awkward way he is sitting, hand on hand, the clammy skin making him shudder. And the taste of his own saliva causes a periodic tide of bile to climb his throat, which makes him feel even more nauseated.

He is disgusting.

He whimpers, caught in a suffocating blanket of sensations. Even that tiny sound hurts his ears, as it adds to this miasma of self-awareness. Alone in this environment of absolute darkness and profound silence, Nowhere can at last understand the very essence of his being.

He is pathetic.

You are pathetic.

The whisper in his left ear shocks him, his body spasms involuntarily. He spins, still trying to see without light, attempting to fix on where the sound came from.

You are disgusting.

The right ear this time. He turns violently again, lashing out blindly with his arms, finding nothing but air. His heart is pounding, loud as thunder, his breathing a vicious gale. He turns his head back and forth, giving up on his sight now, trying to hear whoever is in the room with him.

You are useless.

You are worthless.

The same venomous assertions as he had heard outside, but not the same voice. No, this voice is different. Familiar.

You are nothing to them.

To them.

The voice is his own.

He screams, the noise absolutely deafening and shocking. Part of him, a small calm portion of his soul, recognises the scream, the inhuman terror. His scream continues, becomes one not only of horror but of remorse and loss, of leaving behind his comfortable existence in the pursuit of something better, only to find himself in the dark, trapped, alone with the creature that hates him the most.

Himself.

His scream finally dies, cracking like old wood and becoming an almost inaudible hiss, just dead air escaping his throat. Then even that passes, and he is left lying on the floor, curled up again like a beaten dog, sobbing silently.

How long has he been here? It feels like years, but it must have only been minutes.

You are useless.

He tries to block the voice out, his hands held so tightly over his ears that his head hurts. But it is not coming from outside his head.

You are worthless.

And then something in him gives way, and he is filled with a sense of relief, of a great weight being lifted from him. His body relaxes, his hands falling from his head. If there was light in the room, you could see that he is smiling.

You are nothing to them.

There is a greater light than a lack of darkness, Nowhere realises. And that light is known as truth.

He *is* useless. He *is* worthless. He *is* nothing to them. He does not even know who 'they' are, but he knows that it is true. Truth has a clarity, a pitch, a purity. It identifies itself, unmistakable. At last he knows the absolute truth. He is repugnant and repellent and revolting. He is useless and worthless. He is nothing. He is disgusting.

You are not disgusting.

Nowhere nods, accepting the echoed sentiment... then stops, shocked. Did it say...?

You are not useless.

You are not worthless.

Nowhere lies very still, unsure of what to do. He has no idea how to react to this.

You are something to her.

He doesn't know what it means, but he begins to cry anyway. Then there is light, and his tears stop as he blinks them away.

He finds himself in a room he knows all too well. The room is made of stone, and is featureless save for the four doors in each of the four walls. As always, Nowhere has no idea which one he came in through. In the middle of the room is a table. On the table are four wooden boxes, each around the size of his head. He stands shakily, feeling as if he has been on the floor for a lifetime, his legs having to remember how to hold him up, and stumbles over to the table to examine the boxes, each one so familiar to him.

Each of the boxes has a word carved into its lid.

LOVE

HATE

LIFE

DEATH

Nowhere looks around himself at the doors of the room. They also have words carved into them, at eye-level.

SATISFACTION

OBLIVION

HAPPINESS

FREEDOM

He knows these boxes, doesn't need to open them, though he also knows that he will, he always does. The first, the one marked "LOVE", will contain what appears to be a human heart, the size of a clenched fist, rotting and long dead, filled with a writhing mass of maggots eating at the flesh and each other, clamouring inside its hollowed chambers. He knows that the other boxes are equally cruel; "HATE" conceals a vicious snake, "LIFE" a flesh-piercing array of hooks. And "DEATH", the worst, most seductive box of all, has a knife, stained with his own blood from countless times before. The scars on his wrist throb at the thought of it.

This time he doesn't hesitate. He knows what is expected of him, knows what is in the box marked *LOVE*, having opened it so many times before, yet he reaches for it nonetheless. The lid swings back, and Nowhere gasps.

Inside is not the putrid heart he was expecting. Instead there is a red velvet cushion, dark as blood, and on it rests a glass bell, intricately crafted, swirls of delicate fibres spun around one another in translucent swirls. It seems implausibly fragile, impossibly beautiful.

Reaching out, both his hands shaking slightly, he slides his fingers beneath the bell, cradling it gently, then raises it out of the box. As it leaves the shadow of the box, it lights up with all the colours of the rainbow, and many more besides, as the light of the room refracts and diffuses within its finely blown glass.

He is almost afraid to ring it, it looks so delicate. He is terrified that it will break under his touch. But somewhere in his head, he knows that it's stronger than it looks, stronger than he could ever imagine. Only his fear could ever break it.

Carefully, he grasps the top of the bell and shakes it softly.

The sound is the most beautiful thing he has ever heard in his existence, high and clear. It reverberates through him, head to foot, and he feels things falling away from him inside, like caked-on mud crumbling in the sun. Again his eyes fill with tears without his bidding, and his heart feels like it's going to burst. He can barely breathe. Yet he is completely unafraid.

The sound fades, and the door marked *HAPPINESS* opens for the first time.

Finding his breath again, Nowhere steps through.

He is on the slope of a hill. Behind him, the door of the stone house has closed once more, perhaps forever. He wonders where the shadows have gone. He sees nobody, hears nobody.

His name is Nowhere, and he is alone.

Then he remembers why he is here. He has almost made it. All he needs to do is climb the hill, and he will be there. Then he will not be alone any more.

Somehow he finds the energy to move. Still on his hands and knees, he crawls up the slope, cutting himself on the sharp rocks and broken branches that litter the ground. A number of times he slips and tumbles back down the hill a bit, tearing his clothes and bruising himself, but he is determined and continues. He can see the roof of the mist just a few body lengths above him.

Then, almost without noticing, he passes through the skin of the fog and into the pale sunlight. He blinks, unaccustomed to the light, and looks around.

He knows what he will see; he's seen it so many times before. There before him will be his house, the rough structure made of gnarled wood and woven grass. Behind it his vegetable patch, and just past that the well. His footprints heading down the slope,

But something doesn't seem quite right. The shanty is built differently, the vegetables laid out in a different pattern. He looks around at this hill, so much like his own and yet so very different. He feels strange, like he's in a familiar place yet seeing it for the first time.

"You came."

Nowhere whirls, shocked at the sound. It is the first voice he's ever heard, outside of his own head. He stares at the person standing beside him on the hill, *her* hill. She is tall and slim, dressed in much the same kind of rags as himself. She is covered in the scars of countless wanderings in the valley beneath the hill, as is he, and her eyes betray a sadness and pain that he knows all too well, but something else is there as well. Something more.

He wonders if it's in his eyes as well.

"You came," she says again, quiet astonishment in her voice.

"You called me," Nowhere replies, his face feeling strange, tight. It takes him a few seconds to realise why.

See him? He is smiling.

His name was Nowhere, and he was lonely.

His name is Here, and he is not alone.

CURSEBREAKER:
THE WELSH WIDOW AND THE
WANDERING WOOER

KYLA WARD

IN all my time as a cursebreaker, this is the single most appalling mess I have ever laid eyes on."

"It was their wedding! Oh, my poor daughter!"

"I think it was her husband who got the blunt end of the—what hit him?"

"The altarpiece went first."

"I might say, oh my God."

"You might say who you are."

"I did: a cursebreaker. You summoned me."

"Don't think so... "

"Well, someone did. Oh, that noise! He should be dead what, three, four times over?"

"I wasn't counting."

"The impact damage would be within the power of the average curse of undeath. But here, it looks like... did someone try beheading him?"

"Something had to be done!"

"Well, never mind it now. Your daughter, is she alright?"

"What do you think?"

"I'll need to talk with her. That's the third thing; first is to get a doctor up here."

"If I thought for one moment a doctor would *help*—"

"You didn't think of morphine, did you? Or opium, laudanum; whatever's standard for this period. Call the doctor and get him to bring, oh, everything."

"I'll send Hywel to the village."

"Well, it's a start."

"You... you really think you can redeem this situation?"

"Put it this way, I'm here until I do."

"I'll take you to Merideth, she's in the tower."

"No, that's the third thing."

"What's the second?"

"Dinner. The best you can provide."

AND so it was that Dr Phineas Maunders found himself in the Marimort family trap, driven by a Marimort family servant towards the estate some time in the small hours. The trap rattled alarmingly along the causeway, the surrounding peat bog scarcely illuminated by the single lantern. What it did illuminate was Hywel's face: pocked, grimy and seeming vaguely familiar, despite the owl's talons plaited into his beard.

He could have left the pounding at his door unanswered. He was already in bed with the candle snuffed: he could have pretended to be asleep or away and hidden in the attic if really necessary. But even as he bumped and jumped along, to the great disturbance of last night's mutton hash, curiosity maintained its grip on him. There had been some grand affair at the estate today and if his services were required as a result, that would be no less than local legend demanded.

The Marimorts had a reputation. It had been established long before his arrival six months ago, a graduate without the connections to help him to anything better than this godforsaken corner of Wales. With unseemly relish, his new patients had informed him that the local gentry—who refused his call, made without introduction but all due courtesy—were cursed. Most talk concerned the Lord Marimort, long since dead in a variety of peculiar ways, and his seldom-seen widow and daughter. But the story proper embraced a host of former lords, suitors and gentlemen friends, all fated to meet a gruesome, untimely end. They said it was witches. Witches caused a lot of things around here. Hywel's choice of personal adornment was simply typical of the lengths people would go to ward off their attentions.

Light danced through the trees ahead. Hywel made a guttural sound and touched leather to the horses. He had been articulate enough when demanding Phinney bring his entire supply of laudanum, although refusing to explain why. Taking his cue from the opiates, Phinney had also packed his precious few ampoules of nitrous oxide. Cases of French wine had gone up to the house this week past and oysters packed in ice. He wanted to make a good showing.

A sharp bend and the Marimort fief was revealed in as much glory as might be on a moonless night with a slight fog. Much of the desperately asymmetrical construct was dark, but light blazed from the main entrance and the windows of the east wing. A reddish glow emanated from a tower towards the rear. Hywel sent the trap careening directly across the lawn, or whatever was presently squishing beneath their wheels, while Phinney clung to his seat and grappled with a bizarrely insubstantial dread. It seemed to him that he could hear the building screaming.

When the trap halted at the last possible moment before running up the front steps, Phinney realised his mistake. The screaming was real and coming from within.

"Mau lady waits yon," grunted Hywel, vaulting from his seat with the doctor's bag.

"Wait—I say!" Phinney shuddered as the ghastly sound scraped his ears. "What is that noise?"

"The young master." Hywel glared at him from his place on the steps and Phinney saw little choice but to follow.

An ancestral hall where suits of armour alternated with pallid domestics gave way to a dining room surpassing his wildest expectations. The heavy beams were draped and garlanded for a festival, including further good luck charms making use of the local wildfowl. Below, in the light of numberless candles and a good fire lay grouse and pheasant, glazed racks of venison, suckling pig and stuffed fish, roast and roulade, tureens of soup and sauce and platters of pastry, all of it stone cold and flecked here and there with wax.

The terrible screaming had not ceased, not for one moment. It undid his stomach, even as the aromas mingled deliciously around him. He licked his lips and reached for his bag, taking in his first sight of the Lady Marimort.

"Doctor." She rose from her chair, rustling in acres of candle-burnished silk. Red does not fare well in candlelight and the Lady was red: hair, costume and complexion. In all fairness, she appeared to have been weeping. Jewels winked on her enormous bosom and on the plump hand she extended.

"My Lady," he said, giving it a nervous peck.

"So good of you to come, Doctor..."

"Maunders. Phineas Maunders."

"So very good." She glanced back at the table where a slighter figure was tearing into a plate of quail.

"Mmm, doctor... right, just a sec." The contents of a goblet followed the quail and she stood.

She? The pale face with its frame of dark hair had seemed feminine, if sharp. But those eyes belonged on the battlefield and it was now obvious the figure wore the scarlet jacket and high boots of Her Majesty's cavalry. The younger brother? cousin? approached, pouring wine into a fresh goblet which he thrust at Phinney. "Drink. Go on!" He gestured emphatically. "You are *so* going to need it!"

*A*LMIGHTY *God*!"
"I don't think so, actually," said his companion, between bites of a sugared crosier. "I mean, this bears some of the hallmarks of a deity's wrath, but interrupting a wedding at the crucial moment feels more human to me."

The scene in the chapel was not to be contemplated. It annihilated reason and seized him like a vice through the guts and eyes. He could not form another word, he could not turn away, although some fragment of his will begged it. And that would not stop the screams or the stench of drying blood. There were still white petals upon the floor, mingled with splinters and a considerable amount of flaked gilt. The majority of candles had perished in the chill sweeping through the broken window; it was by a crimson votive that he saw the ruined altar and the impossibly mangled human body writhing and voicing its agony.

Perhaps a surgeon in the armed services might see such a thing, for an instant after the ball had hit. This went on and on—*how long had it been already?*

"Okay, what have you got?" said the strange young man. "If it's laudanum, I suggest we get a bath brought in here."

His fingers were already digging through his bag. Shaking, he held out the leather case.

"What's this?"

"N—n—"

"Nitrous oxide!" It was swept from his grasp. "So this *is* the nineteenth century! Come here, Doctor, and help me find a lung."

The operation was an eventual success. Phinney could not be sure, after, how long it took him to repair the partly-severed neck so the vapour would stay inside. But at the end he was kneeling on the sticky carpet, staring into dreaming, dilated eyes. The young master had been extremely handsome. His face, bled white and contorted even under the drug, was finely boned and possessed of a devastating chin. His hair was long, the golden strands blackly clotted. The velvet wedding coat had been torn to ribbons and the remainder soaked with blood, despite what looked like an attempt at bandaging around the ribs.

The silence in the chapel was deafening. Their breaths and the rattling as the pierced chest rose and fell seemed only to scratch at the edges.

"That's the problem with magic," his companion whispered and the voice did not sound masculine, nor young. "The moment people accept it exists, they forget about all the little things. Like painkillers. And dessert."

The cavalry jacket had fallen open and Phinney realised his companion was female after all. "Um. Yes," he said.

"He was standing here, opposite the bride." Her gaze roamed the vaulting. "First, the altarpiece—oh dear, a triptych. Then the rose window exploded and pretty much every fragment..." She looked down once more, at the sight. "He's not regenerating. Shit, this could be a wish."

"Um, Madam." Phinney managed. She looked at him, her expression unchanging. "They say that the Marimorts are... cursed."

"Not familiar with the wish-curse dynamic? Let's go have a word with Miss Merideth; that's bound to be educational." She sprang up: Phinney glanced back down at what he supposed was now his patient.

If this was magic—and no other explanation really offered— then the sensible thing to do was run as fast as he could, as far as he could. Away from this benighted bog and back to England; maybe even as far back as Mother.

Instead, he patted the man's hand very, very carefully and followed his new tutor.

*M*ERIDETH Marimort lay across the bridal bed like a wrecked ship with sails still flying. Although she had scarce a quarter of her mother's fleshy bulk, the volumes of lace, gauze and white satin more than made up for it.

"Is he dead?" Her face, framed by dark tendrils, was as white as the rest. Apart from the bloodstains.

"He is not dead but sleepeth," said the cursebreaker gently.

Merideth considered this for six of Phinney's heartbeats. Then she began to howl.

"Oh dear, oh my dear!" Lady Marimort pushed past them and began wading against the intervening material.

"Strange décor for a bridal suite, wouldn't you say?" In her mannish clothes, the cursebreaker wandered in the Lady's wake, eyes busy about the black drapery, the repeated skull motif and the bearskin coverlet.

"Never married, myself," Phinney hazarded. Recalling his view approaching the manor, he thought that the tower windows were stained red.

"If I may ask," said the cursebreaker, "are either of you ladies practising witches?"

"*What* did you say?" said Lady Marimort.

"Just want to get things clear, about the..." She indicated the further garnish of bird charms and the distinct ribcage design of the fireplace.

"No," the Lady said stiffly. "And for three centuries Marimorts have spent their wedding night in this chamber. It is a family tradition!" With a mighty sweep of her arms, she clasped her daughter to her. "There, there, my dear, it will be alright."

"How the *blazes* can it be alright?" Meredith's voice came somewhat muffled.

"These people have come to help."

At the cost of some beading, Merideth slipped her mother's grasp. "I am beyond help," she declaimed, extending a lily arm. "Even death has abandoned me." With that, she fell back against the bearskin.

"And why would that be, exactly?" The cursebreaker steepled her fingers.

"The man who loves a Marimort in agony shall die."

"Oh hush now," said her mother. "That's just silly."

"Then what happened to Father?"

"I've told you a thousand times, that was an accident." The lady smiled, rubicund, at her guests.

"Nonetheless." The cursebreaker smiled back.

"He died three days after I was born," Merideth said, in a manner well-rehearsed. "He went hunting on the mountain, for the day was fine and clear. But a storm blew up from nowhere and the horse startled at the lightning. He was flung from the saddle and impaled upon a stag."

With that, her gaze met Phinney's. Her eyes were black yet somehow luminous.

"I'm... very, deeply..." he mumbled. "Condolences."

"Impaled, you say?" said the cursebreaker.

"Now listen here," said the Lady. "Miss—Madam—"

"Mark will do."

"Miss *Mark*. I have accepted your story at face value, that you are an expert in unnatural events."

"You'd better believe it."

"But ours is an old family and a noble name. I will not have aspersions cast upon it."

"So the fact your name means "death of husbands" in French—"

"Really, I must *insist*!" The Lady rose but came to grief on the train.

"Merideth." Mark leant over the prone girl. "*Were you expecting this?*"

Merideth seemed to partially deliquesce. "Yes," she gulped. "No. I mean, not like this!"

"But you expected him to die?"

"Not right there! Mother and Father were married six years!"

Mark turned to the floundering Lady. "You're a Marimort by marriage?"

"I was born to the name! I wed my cousin!"

"Ah, I see!" Mark seated herself on the edge of the bearskin. "And your mother?"

"A Teasel, from Shropshire."

"And father?"

"Both are still quite alive." The Lady regained her footing with an air of triumph.

"Where is Grandpa?" Merideth said plaintively.

"Grandma felt faint, so they went outside. He said they were taking a turn about the garden. I... I haven't seen them since. I think Cousin Geraint is in the wine cellar."

"Alright," said Mark. "The ceremony. Would you be so kind as to tell me exactly what happened?"

"Oh, to think of it!" The Lady resumed use of her handkerchief. "He looked so beautiful—and you too, my dear."

"He swore to love and cherish me, so long as we both should..." Meredith nearly broke down again, but recovered. "Then the priest asked if there was any here who knew why we should not be joined in holy matrimony. I saw Louis glance back and I thought how silly he was. But then..."

"Yes, I think I've got that part."

"Cousin Geraint said he would end it. He cut Louis' throat with his cavalry sabre." Phinney winced as Merideth sobbed. "But that didn't stop it. Then Mother tried to smother him."

"It seemed appropriate," said the Lady faintly.

"But that didn't stop it. He was still lying there, looking up at her. The priest wouldn't go near him so I said..."

"What?" Mark leaned closer. "Did it start with "I wish"?"

"I said, 'Please, won't somebody help me break this terrible curse?'"

Mark sighed. "The summoning. So much for the wish theory."

"What do you mean?" demanded the Lady.

"If she had wished with all her heart that he not die, that he stay with her forever—well, that might have done it. And proved once again that the only difference between a wish and a curse is whether it's you or them."

"It's a curse," said Merideth blankly. "The villagers all say so."

"The Marimort curse involves women bearing the name bringing death to their menfolk in circumstances yet to be precisely determined. It explains the shrapnel, but not why he in fact *failed* to die."

"There is no Marimort curse," said the Lady.

"What about your grandfather?" said Mark, "did he hold the title?"

"No. He was Mr. Glendeagle and my grandmother the Lady Marimort."

"So what happened to him?"

The Lady paused. "Died on his wedding night. In this very room. There used to be a chandelier."

Phinney clutched his bag and affected to study the ceiling, which indeed bore attachments for a central lamp.

"Doctor," said Meredith. It took Phinney a moment to realise she was addressing him.

"Miss Marimort?"

"You seem a kind man. Have you any laudanum?"

Mark clapped her hands together. "Anomalies are good," she pronounced. "Seek out anomalies is the third rule of cursebreaking."

"Third rule," said Phinney. "So... what's the first?"

Mark stared at the Marimorts. "Don't make things worse."

At that moment, a severely inebriated chuckle floated through the door, amplified by its journey up the stairs.

"Whoever that is," said Lady Marimort, "I shall see flogged. Even if it is Cousin Geraint."

"Um," said Phinney. "I think that it may... in fact... be Monsieur LePerdue. The nitrous," he added in the face of Merideth's incomprehension. "It takes some people this way."

"You mean he's awake now?" Mark sprang off the bed.

"Still quite numb, I would think. I have witnessed people laughing at their own surgery."

"He laughs?" Merideth's eyes were pleading. "Does he forgive me?"

"Come on," Mark tagged Phinney. "We've got to try."

As they left, that sad, black gaze brushed him like a velvet glove.

"So what's the second rule?" asked Phinney, as they tramped downstairs into the growing hilarity.

"Establish parameters. So, you're from the village: give me the story."

"I'm not from the village, I'm from Oxford."

"But you know the local legend, obviously. How did it all start?"

"*Je voir mon estomac! Hee hee!*"

"Um, Gwyllam ap Gwyllam fought for the English at Agincourt and was knighted," said Phinney, trying to remember the story and not his schoolboy French. "He fell in love with a French noblewoman and brought her back with him to his new estate, but died horribly. It was witches."

"Which witches?"

"Does it matter?"

"Yes, it does! A curse is, above all, personal. A regular spell can be empowered by worship, sex, pain; anything that can build up the necessary psychic charge. A wish requires an overwhelming desire and nothing suffices for cursing but sheer hatred, which you might take as an overwhelming desire to see someone suffer."

He considered this. "But these men have been dying for centuries."

"Circumstance plays its part. Look, the initial curse punches a—a little, round hole in reality. If that hole isn't repaired, it just sits there and any round peg has had it."

"*Ou est mon peepee?*"

"So le Monsieur and Miss Merideth are—" Not pegs. "Stand-ins?"

"For the first Marimort and the man who, your legend says, loved her. She didn't love him, obviously."

"Oh, she did really; that's what made it so tragic. It's only that he killed her entire family when they tried to keep them apart, so she couldn't accept his love but he was going to marry her anyway, so she cursed him."

"Tragic? I call it pathetic. An open-ended curse like that? Anyway, if you're right and the trigger is love, it's not good news. Unattainable yet unavoidable, intangible yet unshakeable; as triggers go, love's a real bitch."

"HEE HEE HEE!"

Several servants clustered at the front door, holding trunks and little bundles. Hywel blocked their way, beard raised threateningly in one hand. Catching sight of Phinney, he gave him another ferocious glare.

"A Welshman fights at Agincourt." Mark led the way towards the dining room. "He comes home knighted with a name meaning "the death of husbands". I think your legend is missing some salient details."

"Uh," Phinney was still looking at Hywel. The owl claws had distracted him, but now he was sure that Hywel had been lurking around outside his surgery. He'd assumed the man must have an especially embarrassing personal problem and be working up the courage. "Shouldn't we attend to Monsieur LePerdue?"

"Do you know the last thing I had to eat before coming here?" Mark walked straight across the room to the desserts. "Partially decomposed whale blubber and mead. Way too much mead. The temperature was ten below and no one had washed in months."

"Whale what? Where?"

"Forget it, I was working. When I wasn't drinking. Was I drunk enough to shag a skinchanger, that's the question; though obviously *something* cracked it. Next thing I know I'm in a wine cellar."

"You travel," he said. "You repair these—holes."

"That's it, essentially."

"Are you a witch?"

"No. Nor a magician, necromancer, saint, *hougan, itako, goçs, volkhv, walcyrie, garadyigan, ker heb* or any other kind of sorcerer, medium or priest." She selected a Napoleon pastry. "Now. You should never mix alcohol with nitrous oxide, right?"

THE brandy did not vanquish the laughter entirely, but gasps of *mon Dieu* became frequent, together with heavy sighs. Phinney winced as the spirit seeped through his stitching. Still, as Mark had said, he supposed it wasn't going to kill him. They had brought a lamp from the dining room and in the increased illumination, Mark looked down upon the handsome face and frowned.

"Louis the Lost," she mused. "Interesting name. Not your original, I assume." There was no response. *Surely,* thought

Phinney, *the man would have lost his reason long since.* "My name's Mark," she continued, "which is also quite interesting and this here is Phinney. So Louis, why aren't you dead?" The man groaned, the sound passing visibly through the cartilage and flapping skin.

"Here," Phinney said. "Perhaps I should put a dressing on that?"

"*Non.*" The cartilage quivered and the chest swelled. "No, please. But bury me so deep I may forget to live."

"Oh, that's never a good idea," said Mark. "Louis, you need to tell us what happened."

"I saw her in the garden early and made myself known to her, before I sought her kin. I spoke with her, walked with her and bent all my thoughts upon her. In truth I desired her, yet love is its own master!"

"She is a most charming girl," Phinney said softly. Here in the circle of light, it was starting to seem quite warm.

"I loved. Once more I loved and once more I betrayed. Is that why, even now, I may not die?" He groaned deeply. "And if t'is true you love me, I make you this reply..."

"The man who loves a Marimort," Phinney took up the verse. "In agony shall die."

"You knew?" Mark's eyes were sharp. "You courted a Marimort and you knew?"

"I sought only an end to my wandering." Fluid seeped from Louis's eyes. "So long it has been, unceasing, unforgiven..."

"Undying." Mark exhaled the word and bent her head. She stayed like that while Louis sobbed and giggled and Phinney sat, aware of a certain impropriety. *I shouldn't say such things of Merideth—Miss Marimort,* he thought. *This is her nearly-husband. I am his doctor. Why can't I feel my nose?*

"Diametrically opposed," Mark murmured. "Neither able to fulfil... by the Kindly Ones, what a mess!"

"*Mon Dieu, mon Dieu,*" moaned Louis.

"Err," Phinney said. "I mean... euw. You just said... eee."

Mark looked up curiously. "Are you alright?"

Phinney took an enormous breath and blurted, "So why didn't he die?"

"Because he was *already* cursed, to live."

"Eee. Hee. Hee hee."

"Phinney, I think you need some fresh air."

"Oh God, not here; everything stinks of bog!"

"Then at least stop leaning over Louis's abdomen and inhaling."

*P*HINNEY turned his face into the freezing draught through the rose window, that indeed stank of peat. He had been sitting there, inhaling second-hand nitrous through Louis's perforations and there was simply no way to palliate the fact. Against the darkness, he envisaged loops of artery and vein twisting towards infinity like some crazy mathematical diagram, as Louis's impossible tale unfolded.

Slightly over a hundred years ago in 1757, he had been a dashing young captain in his father's company. His was a family of note, but he refused them the details; only that while awaiting mobilisation at Paris, he fell madly in love with a girl named Justine. She returned his passion, to the extent that when the order to march arrived, she insisted upon disguising herself as a boy and joining his company.

"What sweet madness, to conceal her rich hair beneath a tricorn and her lush curves beneath a soldier's coat!"

"Yes, but did she curse you?"

"No. Merely damned me." He heaved a mighty sigh. "We faced the Prussians at Rossbach."

"Oh dear," said Phinney, despite himself.

"I gather things did not go well," said Mark.

"If I remember my history it, um, wasn't the best day the French ever had."

"We were routed," said Louis flatly. "And I played my own, small part.

"I had placed Justine in the baggage train, in keeping with her role as a boy. She should have been safe. But when the Prussians overran our lines and I saw smoke go up behind, I abandoned my men to go to her rescue. My men abandoned their position, my father's flank collapsed. And yes, I saved Justine and brought her to shelter. Where my father lay dying."

"Ah." Mark set down the sacramental wine.

"All concealment was at an end. I faced my father's judgment, held by men who had served him better than I. And all the while,

Justine wept. When they placed a pistol to my head, she threw herself forward and begged my father not to let me die, to have pity that we were so young.

"Finally, my father spoke. His life blood soaked the piled cloaks that were all his bed and he said, 'Live then, my son, and be young, but as my injury cannot heal, nor shall yours! Forever shall you suffer for what you did this day; never again shall you know rest or peace—unless such a woman can give it you! By this white sky and this black earth, by this *red*, I curse you and turn you forth!'

"He died and I felt it in every fibre of my being. I turned on Justine, would have killed her, I think, but those fellows threw me out. I do not know her fate." He drew a ragged breath. "Three days later, riding at the rear, I took a musket ball in my left side. I was off my horse in agony, unable to breathe. A week I lay in the forest, without water, food or succour of any kind, but I did not die."

Phinney moved forward. A kind of light was glowing in his mind.

"He probably didn't mean any of it literally," said Mark. "But his last words, magnified by all the deaths at Rossbach. Now, *that's* a psychic charge."

"But if you can't die," said Phinney, "why, we can take this in stages! I can't say how long it will take to heal, but by your leave, I'll start with the infarction." He reached for the punctured breast.

"Heal?" said Louis. A stained bubble appeared at his lips, then burst with the ghost of a chuckle. "Did you not hear what my father said?"

"Yes. But, we have to start somewhere."

"Try my left side."

Phinney's hands froze. He looked at the bandages he had noticed before.

"In the end," said Louis, "I dug the ball out with my own bayonet and plugged the hole with wax. That got me to a surgeon, who fixed the ribs in place with wire and shot himself shortly after. I keep the damn thing stitched but it still bleeds. Even," another bubble welled and popped. "On my wedding day."

Phinney turned aside, all his nausea flooding back.

"You don't age," said Mark, "but you don't heal either. That's almost classy."

"Do you know," burbled Louis. "That the majority of Europe was at war from 1756 to 1815?"

"You fought?" Mark queried.

"For a time. I hoped to gain absolution. But as I realised just what I was risking—after that time I fell overboard in the Channel and it took three weeks to—I fled the battlefield, trying only to find safety. But to avoid accidents over any real length of time, *c'est impossible*! I joined a monastery at one point—"

This is not happening, Phinney told himself, *not happening. I am asleep in bed after too much self-medication -*

"—the scriptorium and I got a paper cut! Right in there, between my thumb and finger! I know it doesn't sound much compared to the other but I've had the damned thing for thirty-two years and every time I open my hand—"

—I will write to my mother, I swear.

"Whether it be cowardice or no, I can stand it no longer! When I heard the legend of the Marimorts, I thought that surely, this was the rest my father spoke of!"

"Enough," Mark said crisply. "Phinney, dose him."

"*Oui, s'il vous plaît.*"

"And be careful there are no more leaks.

He broke the ampoule in Louis' mouth and watched as it took effect. He examined the abdomen and applied another layer of bandage. Then he sat back. "There's only one more dose."

"Mm."

"When that's gone, what do we do?"

She shrugged. "Onto the laudanum?"

"Damn the laudanum!" He waved the case at Louis, "*I can't help him*! And if you're not a witch, how can you do any more?"

Mark sighed. "You understood what I said about curses being holes?"

"Yes, I suppose." After a moment's indecision, he slid the case into his jacket pocket.

"Well, they're totally rigid. What fits fits, what doesn't doesn't. Each curse has its own definition of death and love. The Lord and Lady Marimort were married for six years before he died, three days after Merideth was born."

"What does that mean?"

"I'm working on it." Suddenly, she was looking at him. "You like Meredith, don't you?"

"Ah... "

But she said nothing further. Slowly, he stood. He nearly jumped out of his skin when he saw Hywel. The man had contrived to enter silently during their conclave and was working his way around the circumference of the chapel, bending at intervals to pick up whatever it was he considered worth salvaging. He glimpsed something glitter as it dropped through his fingers. It was none of his concern. He had thought he might learn from this dreadful woman and what had he learnt? That there were fates worse than he had ever imagined; he, a weedy little bookworm who had rather go to Wales than into the armed service...

Hywel passed behind the altar. Phinney picked up his bag and glanced at Mark. "Laudanum's mostly alcohol. It'll go further if I get the brandy."

"Good idea," she nodded. "And bring some of those chocolate almonds."

As the chapel door closed behind him, Phinney breathed a sigh of relief. He could see the trap standing outside the door, surrounded by a slight mist, but there were no more servants. So far, so good.

"Doctor Maunders?"

"At your service," he said automatically, then jolted against the door with heart hammering and his blood whispering mad things in his ears. At the base of the tower steps stood Merideth Marimort, having shed the veil and most of her train. White as a ghost, with the scarlet stains still on her breast, she trembled uncontrollably in the draught.

"Has he said anything?" she whispered.

"Miss Marimort, you are freezing! Here, allow me to escort you—"

She stamped her foot and those wellspring eyes flashed. "Has he said anything about me?"

"Um..." Although his reminiscences of Justine had been copious and detailed, Louis had not so much as mentioned his current fiancée. "He said, 'love is its own master.'"

"That certainly sounds like him." But it seemed not to please her, as she crossed her arms and glared at the suits of armour.

"We've been able to make him more comfortable. I'm sure... I'm sure all will be well in time."

"We should have eloped. That's what I suggested! But he sided with Mama: oh no, think of your dignity, what about the family name? All I wanted was to be *shot* of my family name!" This last was addressed to a particularly elaborate set of full plate.

"Still, wouldn't you have been sad to leave your home?" Phinney ventured.

"I hate it here! There's nothing to do except read papers which are weeks old, memorise the new plays and shop by catalogue. I never get to go anywhere; I'm not even allowed to go down to the village!"

"I don't know why you'd want to," he said.

"I'd have met you sooner, at least! You've been to London, haven't you?"

"Um, I've been through it."

"There now, I knew it! Oh, I do so crave the streets of London! All the people, the theatres, the excitement! We see so few new people: sometimes I think Mama gets Hywel to chase them away. Louis was the first visitor in ages: Mama really liked him. She likes men who are old-fashioned; you know, walks and poetry and ever so many cups of tea with her. I don't think she would have ever forgiven me if I hadn't accepted him." A fresh fit of shivers seized her.

"Miss Marimort, please. I think you should sit down in the dining room and have a little brandy."

"Is that what you think?"

"Yes, as a doctor."

"Well, tell me, doctor." She came towards him, her ornamented bosom heaving. "Would it not be advisable for me to get absolutely stinking drunk, given that I'm alone on my wedding night?"

"Um. Perhaps a little laudanum?"

But at the last moment she stopped before him, staring at the chapel door. "Is that woman still in there?"

"Yes. But you don't want—"

"Is she a witch?"

"No. I'm not sure what she is."

"You know," she said, once more addressing the armour, "I don't think my ancestress was one either. I mean, if she had been, why would she have let Gwyllam kill her family and drag her out here?"

"That... that does make sense. Monsieur's father was certainly no witch—"

"His father! Louis never talks about his people!"

"I'm really quite certain you don't want to—"

"Oh, but I do!" She was at him again, all eyes and bulging beadwork. "I want to know which witch is responsible for ruining my life!"

"You know what?" His knees trembled. "I don't think there are any witches in this all."

"*Tylluan a tharw, arth a charw, rwy'n rhwymo d'ysbryd!*"

Through the door behind them came a blinding flash and Phinney had a distinct impression of owls, white and gold-taloned, streaming past him and out into the night.

"Shit," he heard Mark say.

Then he realised Meredith was clinging to him. Her skin was surprisingly hot. "What the *blazes* was that?"

Phinney made a noise he meant to imply that it was nothing to worry about, or that he'd go and see, or possibly that they should both go into the dining room and have a little lie down. But then the door opened behind him and he pitched backwards. Meredith released him with a squeak and he saw her standing against the light as he fell. Then the bog-stink welled up and pain burst in his head, sending everything black.

*Y*OU'D bury us in peat? Oh, that's just sick!"

Phinney realised he had passed out. Louis must have been leaking after all. He felt ill.

He felt like he was outside. He was cold all over and the surface beneath his cheek was spongy.

"It won't achieve anything, you realise. Except the death of your village doctor."

"That damn boy! Thirty years I've been the village witch and then he comes along saying those charms are na good! Take pills and lotions, practice hygiene! Never mind reading the omens and performing the old rites!"

"Or making the offerings that went with them, I'm sure."

There was a seepage of light. Phinney tried to raise himself but his hands were caught behind his back and his feet, too, were bound. Mark had said something about his death.

"Owl and bull, stag and bear. What kind of a witch are you, anyway?"

"One who knows well enough how to bind the likes o' ye!"

There was an inarticulate gurgle. Phinney realised it was Hywel and that he was probably laughing.

"Yeah, yeah: I'm summoned so I can be bound. Doesn't take a genius."

"I know thy nature, *ysbryd*!"

"Actually, I'm not so much a spirit as a—"

"Were I to destroy your body, ye would only reform. The earth will trap ye, the peat will preserve ye. Ye'll trouble mau Lady na more."

"I'm here to help her. Can't you hear through that bird's nest you're wearing?"

"I'm he that helps mau Lady." Was that sound a shovel? Phinney flipped like a fish to face the black sky and screamed at the top of his lungs.

"That'll do ye na good." Hywel's ghastly face heaved into view. "They'll think it the young master."

"And you're going to bury him as well?" The light was Mark, by tilting his head he could see her. "Miss Merideth's husband-to-be?"

"Well he *should* be buried! If he's na dead by noe, he's stubborn sure."

Louis lay beyond Mark, in a mercifully silent heap. Had the crazy Welshman carried them out here on his own? And what had happened to Merideth? Had the villain harmed her? He struggled against his bonds, but it was useless.

Mark had been speaking. "... the local witch, you must know all about the curse."

"It is part of their dignity! They are of the ancient blood of Cymru, never minding the French bitch."

"The one courted by Gwyllam ap Gwyllam?"

"If that's what ye want to call it."

"What would you call it?"

"A spoil of war."

"Ah, I suspected as much. Not as pretty as the song, but makes more sense and I'm sure he killed all her family anyway."

"Gwyllam's cunning secured his land. When he slew her husband, he claimed it was in duel for her love. Amongst those English fools with their chivalry, this gave him standing and so he were knighted, after ceding *her* lands to the king. So what if she cursed him? Three sons she bore. An English King, a French name, but Welsh land and blood!"

"Doesn't it bother you that he and countless other men have died for it and countless women made miserable?"

"Who minds a curse? In the old days, a king wasn't a king without a *geas* or two. The great Math could only rest with his head in the lap of a virgin—"

"Which obviously wasn't Gwyllam's problem. Look, Hywel. You know you could always just banish me."

"Don't see why. Mayhap they'll dig ye up in a hundred years and burn ye for fuel."

"Well, what about Phinney here? If you set him free, all he'll do is run back to England, defeated and humiliated."

"Yes, utterly!" Phinney squeaked.

"An enemy defeated is worth power to me. I'll take his hand for a talisman."

"Then what about..." She sighed. "Actually, this might be the best thing for Louis."

"Bloody Frenchie." The shovelling ceased, replaced by the squishy sound of Hywel's steps. "Poncing around after that chit while mau Lady sighs after him."

"All the same. There's no reason for him to suffer any more than he has."

From yet further back in the mist came the nervous whicker of a horse. *The trap*, thought Phinney, *if I could only reach it... then what would I do?* If only he had a scalpel in his pocket instead of the case of nitrous and his keys. Perhaps the keys would do.

"Steady now, Phinney," Mark whispered, then shouted, "Are you sure that hole's deep enough to hold a body?"

"I've been digging peat all mau life!"

"Just if he pops up in a year or two, there'll be Hell to pay! I'd take it down another foot—" Another growl, followed by squishing. "Okay, okay, then you'd better stake him in place."

"I were going to!" There was an ominous *schick* of steel against wood.

"Good, good. Now, all I ask is that you keep him sedated. There's more of the drug, it's in the doctor's pocket. Come on, you don't want him thrashing around now, do you? And to torture him, a man whose only crime is to love a Marimort. Do this and even once the effects wear off, he'll sleep. Underground, he'll sleep."

Now I really will be sick, Phinney thought, then convulsed as the steps came towards him.

"Pathetic, ye." Hywel took the case and left him lying in his own vomit. Dimly, he heard Mark giving instructions.

"Pop it in his mouth and crack it. Now hold his lips together, that's right. Okay, you're set to go. Need a hand?" There was a thud. "Ow! Just asking."

A slow slither joined the squelching. Phinney knew that if he turned his head he'd see Hywel dragging Louis into his living grave. He tried not to listen to the successive thuds and the final shallow splash.

Now or never. Phinney forced his fingers into his pocket and against the ridged metal.

With an almighty grunt, Hywel drove the stake home. There was a hiss as of escaping gas, followed by splashing and a spluttering, choking sound.

"Alright there, Hywel?" said Mark.

"Heh... heh heh... "

"How are you going with that rope, Phinney?"

"I, ah..."

"Wheeee!"

"I think we have some time."

After a few minutes, Phinney pushed himself to a sitting position and shuffled on his buttocks over to where Hywel's knife lay abandoned on the moss. Hywel, partially interred, found this hilarious.

"Right now, Phinney." Mark was still glowing. "Somewhere on Hywel you'll find a little loop of rope or leather or something. I need you to break it, okay?"

"Heh heh hoo! Heh heh hoo!"

"Stay still you old bastard," said Phinney. "Oh God, don't step on him!"

"Hoo! I'm an owl! I can fly!"

After undoing a belt and a number of pouches, Phinney looked at the beard and braced himself. As the old man tried to peck his ear, he took a grip around the talons and yanked.

Flash! But succeeded, this time, by a darkness less painful.

"By the three—gentle—ladies!" Mark was, by the sound, standing up and brushing herself down. Phinney punched Hywel soundly in the head, knocking him backwards out of the grave.

— 151 —

The trap's lantern revealed the scene in grotesque detail. A two foot stake of roughly hewn wood had shattered Louis' chest and thick, black water was oozing inside the cavity. Of his face, only the chin protruded. Mark wrenched out the stake with an expression of extreme distaste and seized his arms. But it took both of them and some fiddling to get him out in one piece.

"Put him in the trap," Mark puffed. Hywel was crawling haphazardly around the pit. Phinney took Louis under both arms, being careful not to inhale. "Hywel! Hywel, you old goat-kisser— oh bugger it." She strode over and hauled him upright. By the time they reached the trap, he had been noosed with his own belt.

THEIR return to the manor occasioned no particular fuss. He could hear Merideth's voice, high and upset, coming through the dining room door. There was a stark naked man with red hair in the hallway, but he spared them not a second glance as he belched and staggered through it.

"Geraint, you are a DISGRACE!" cried the Lady Marimort. "Mama, you're not listening to me! I tell you, Hywel took everyone—"

"Don't be silly, dear. Geraint is certainly still with us."

"Right," said Mark. "Tell the ladies that everything's fine and bring them to the chapel."

"You can break the curse?"

"I can break both curses. And I have *you*," she clapped him firmly on the shoulder, "and *him*—" she jerked Hywel's leash, "to thank for it!"

Feeling a certain trepidation, Phinney turned back to the dining room.

"I'm not marrying *him*!" Merideth shrilled. "He's old and drunk and has hair everywhere."

"I know, dear." The object of their discussion was fixing himself a scotch, apparently oblivious. "But your marriage has been announced. If news of your husband's death gets out, just think of what people will say!"

Mother and daughter faced each other across the fireplace. Merideth had the brandy decanter in hand. "I won't do it!"

"It is your duty!" the Lady said sternly. "Now, where did that priest get to?"

"I told you, it was Hywel—oh! Doctor Maunders, thank goodness!"

"Why Doctor," Lady Marimort stared. "What happened to you?"

Phinney became belatedly aware of the mud, blood and no little vomit encrusting him. "Um... deepest apologies..."

"You look like someone tried... to bury you in the peat bog."

"Ah, very deeply..."

"I told you, Mama, but you never listen!"

"Ah, the cursebreaker requests your attendance in the chapel."

"The cursebreaker? What does she want now?"

"She believes she knows how to end this, my Lady." He waited, in an awkward half-bow, as the Lady considered.

"Very well," she said finally.

"Is Louis still in there?" said Meredith, "I can't look at him; I just can't."

"Come along and don't snivel," said her mother, starting towards the door. Meredith stared after her, eyes smouldering, then slowly gathered up her skirts. But at the first step, she swayed dangerously. Phinney found himself at her side, offering his arm.

"Thank you," she said, taking a firm grip.

"Any service," he said, "that I can ever do."

MARK had not wasted any time nor, presumably, Hywel's assistance. The light of a dozen or more lamps revealed Louis lying upon a platform made of the broken altarpiece and a number of pews. When Meredith saw him, she gasped and buried her face in Phinney's shoulder.

"So beautiful," her mother said. As a woman walking in her sleep, she advanced towards the bier.

"It seems," said Mark, "that any man who loves you has to die."

"I know," she said. Carefully, she leaned across the bier and wiped Louis' face with the edge of her sleeve. "All my life I've tried to keep going and hold things together, for appearance's sake. But it's always been there, the knowledge."

Mark nodded. "Mortally wounded, bled dry, eviscerated—" Meredith squealed and Phinney patted her on the back. "Just doesn't cut it. Now," she stepped up to the head of the bier. "Louis here can tick all of the above and not die. That's his curse."

The Lady snivelled. "Oh, it's just not fair."

"But he's got an escape clause. He shall never know rest unless such a woman can give it to him. He thought he knew what that meant and he was close, he was very close. But close breaks no curse. Come here, Meredith."

"Go on," whispered Phinney and gently nudged her.

She moved forward like a satin lamb to the slaughter. Whether her gaze was fixed on that wretched form or on Mark's gleaming eyes, Phinney could not tell, but when she took her place opposite her mother, she was weeping.

"What... what do I have to do?" she gulped.

"For the moment, just stand there and listen to your own history. Gwyllam ap Gwyllam didn't fall in love in France. He got himself knighted by pledging his love to a woman whose husband he had killed. Your family name was probably Henry the Fifth's idea of a joke."

"I must protest," said Lady Marimort automatically.

"So, picture a young widow brutalised and used as a political pawn, cursing the man who had the gall to claim he loved her. Now, how did Gwyllam actually die?"

"Maypole dancing during a joust," said three voices.

"Is that in the song? How quaint. Well, anyway, that didn't happen until after they had three sons. Now picture this. Four centuries later, a man is out hunting, just like he does every day. Then suddenly it occurs to him that this isn't just another day. His wife, whom he married for form's sake, has given him a daughter. He has a family now. Then before he knows it, an antler in the liver."

"You're saying my father died because of me?" Merideth's face consisted of three round holes.

"I'm saying that the Marimort curse defines love as commitment. The moment the man accepts he is part of a family and wants nothing more than to stay here with his women in their home. Which, given the situation of the first Lady Marimort, is both reasonable and very sad."

"With the very words of marriage!" whispered Lady Marimort. "Oh, what a noble heart!"

"She never meant to doom her descendants to loveless marriages and tragic affairs. That's why she almost certainly wasn't a witch:

it's just not professional. Which brings us to Hywel and his startling suggestion that someone might burn me for fuel."

"Hywel." With a hasty wipe of her eyes, the Lady swung round to confront her servant. "What exactly did you do?"

"Ye said the word mustn't get out. I were only trying to help."

A strangeness came over the lady's features. "I don't suppose you know anything about the priest? Or my parents?"

"My lady, I drove them to Caerphilly." Hywel looked shocked. "The priest is tied up in the wine cellar."

"Very good. Now." She turned on Mark with arms akimbo. "Can you break his curse or not?"

"Louis," said Mark, bending over him. "Wakey-wakey."

His eyes focused somewhat, on her face. Then they dipped towards his chest cavity.

"No Louis, don't—"

"HEE HEE HEE!"

"*Louis LePerdue, by this white sky, by this black earth, by this red I command thee.* You have been shot, hacked at, smothered, broken and drowned. But have you ever, in all your years of wandering, been burned?"

"No!" Phinney shouted, starting up the aisle. He arrived just in time to see Louis's chin tip up, then down.

"He understands," said Mark, a smile curving her lips.

"You can't!"

"He won't feel a thing, if we're quick about it."

"Oh. My." Lady Marimort sank down upon a pew.

"You're going to burn him up," said Meredith. "Like the heathens." Perhaps it was the brandy, but she didn't seem as shocked as her mother. "That's how you break his curse?"

"Actually, no." Mark's smile grew wider, showing unbelievably white teeth. "Someone else's."

"What if you're wrong?" Phinney grabbed Louis's shoulders protectively and felt the bones come loose.

"Then at least things will be quieter. Okay Hywel, your magic circle still up? That was pretty smooth by the way, creeping round me like that. I didn't realise what you were doing until the last moment."

Hywel looked at her stonily. She came to within inches of his face as she undid the belt. "Come, son of Math. I need fire."

The faintest smile, as if in reflection. Then he stepped forward.

"Hywel, what are you doing?" Lady Marimort sat up.

"*Tânau!*"

The bier became pyre. Flames shot upwards, embracing Louis in the same way the light had embraced Mark, only beneath it his skin began to split and peel as Meredith shrieked and Phinney wrestled her back, away from the inferno where Louis's body was already charring. He lost so much fluid, thought Phinney, his tissue is bound to be dehydrated. Then he vomited again.

The fire died. Meredith trembled in his arms. He smelt ash and wine and somewhere across the aisle the Lady was sobbing.

"Ssh," he said. "It's over."

"Is it?" Another voice resounded through the chapel. A new voice, richly masculine with a French accent. "There's... no pain."

The Lady gasped and Meredith shrieked. Phinney may have shrieked a little himself, at the second naked man to appear that night.

"Whoa, baby," said Mark.

Louis LePerdue, completely whole and flawless down to the least golden curl, unfolded from his nest of ashes to face his bride.

"The fourth rule of cursebreaking," said Mark, "Is push it on over the edge. The hole can't be filled by a pile of charcoal."

"Hywel, a robe," said the Lady, "and we'll speak of this no more." He leapt to obey.

Meredith was absolutely frozen in place. "Oh my... goodness."

Then Mark turned to the Lady Marimort. "You must tell him you will let him rest," she said. "That's all it is. That you will let him bear scars, grow old and die, even though you love him."

"What?" said Merideth.

"I will let you rest." The Lady's voice was soft. "Oh my love, I will love you scarred, or old and even dead, but I would not have you know a moment's pain."

Something changed. Phinney felt it quite distinctly, but couldn't put a finger on what. Certainly, Louis looked as handsome as before.

"But, the Marimort curse?" The Lady's bosom heaved.

"Has been fulfilled. There was certainly enough agony beforehand."

Louis turned around and fell into her arms.

"What. Are. You. Doing. Mama." said Merideth.

"When the curse struck, Louis wasn't looking at you." Mark reached for the wine again. "He had his head turned, looking at the woman he loved in the right way, however that pans out."

"But... what about me?" Meredith stood there in her bloodstained dress. A slight flush tinged her skin, which Phinney thought was the least the circumstances were due.

"What about you?"

"If he loves Mama, does that break my curse?"

"No."

"So any man who actually *does* love me is still going to get furniture jumping at him?" The look she threw Phinney was almost accusatory. "I have to marry Cousin Geraint? I'll be a Marimort forever!"

"Oh no, no! Sweet Furies, you've got an easy way out! It's so simple I can hardly believe no one in the family has taken it before." Mark tipped the bottle, not taking her eyes off Louis' rear. "Mind you, look how long it took for someone to call for help."

"Um," said Phinney, "I think she means, that if you don't like being a Marimort... you shouldn't be."

Mark nodded. "Very good, Phinney."

"You mean, not marry anyone?" Merideth said slowly. "Run away to London, change my name to Teasel and go on the stage? Do exactly as I please and disgrace myself in every way possible?"

"Um, I expect so."

Merideth's skin was definitely flushed. "Right," she said. Before Phinney knew what was happening, she had seized him by the cravat. "I'm just *craving* medical attention. You'll examine me won't you, doctor? Look in my eyes and listen to my heart?"

"Um," said Phinney.

GIVE the Marimort name a week," said Mark. "And that's only because the fastest transportation round here is a goat."

She was sitting on the steps of the manor house with a half-demolished trifle, watching the dawn. As Phinney emerged, she turned to him, waving a spoon. "I've never understood why people make such a fuss about this sort of thing. I mean, in reality the age gap is all on his side and now he's mortal again it won't really matter. How's Merideth doing?"

"She's sleeping," he said. "She and I... um."

"It's fine," Mark said. "You know that was my second clue, that you seemed immune. If you love her, it's in entirely the wrong way."

"Oh. Good," he said. "I'm going back to the village now to pack. Then we're going to Caerphilly and leaving this place behind forever."

"Which will make Hywel happy. And I untied the priest, so a pretty good result all round." She took another scoop of cream.

"Thank you," said Phinney.

For the first time her smile seemed genuinely human. "I guess you're welcome."

"Will you be staying on with the Marimorts? Or can I possibly give you a lift to the station?"

"Oh, I'll be leaving before you, I'm afraid," she said. Above the mist, the sky was kindling pink and gold.

"Where are you going?"

"I have not the slightest idea. Wherever I'm summoned, there I shall be."

"But surely you don't have to leave right away." He chuckled nervously but did not know why. "After a night like that, you must need a rest."

"Rest; oh, by the Three." Her shoulders slumped beneath the scarlet jacket. "What I would give to rest."

"Then, why not—"

"Oh Phinney," she said. "Don't you see? I'm cursed."

"What... how?"

"It was the twenty-first century, I'm nearly sure. Everything's confused now: I've no idea how much time has passed, always in different times and places. Fortunately, I specified true immortality and a knowledge of all languages as prerequisites for the task; otherwise I just don't dare imagine."

"You volunteered for this?"

"Ha! No, I thought it was all a joke. If I'd had any idea that magic was real, I'd have been a lot more polite, I can tell you. But I was the professor. I was teaching Euripides' *Orestes* and I wasn't going to let some stranger wander into my class and challenge what I said. Which was, that any curse in history or mythology could be undone by the proper application of logic. There was no such thing as an eternal doom."

"You're a classicist, then?" said Phinney. The gold was spindling down through the mist, turning the bog into an enchanted garden.

"Not any more. I'm marked, the cursebreaker, and that's all I am."

"But surely, just seeing what you did here—"

"Don't you get it, even now? I'm cursed to break curses."

And then he did understand. Something, perhaps just a glimpse of it. "I'm sorry," he said and could think of nothing more to add.

"Never curse," she said wearily. "Never wish. And above all, don't tempt Fate."

"What do you mean by fate?" Cresting the horizon, the sunlight speared his eyes.

"Any of three! The kindly ones. The gentle ladies. To change yours, I sealed mine."

He blinked and turned to face her, but she was gone.

HEAT

DONNA MAREE HANSON

A SQUARE of dark and quiet amid a city of lights and sounds. A park not so different from others. Parks are her favourite place. She waits, her body swaying, making the hem of her crimson-coloured, satin dress caress the acorns beneath her feet. Strapless, the bodice clasps her breasts, easing them up and cradling them. Her bare arms are white and cold and so too is the column of her throat. Overhead the limb of an oaktree groans, its heavy burden of leaves tousled by the wind. All around tufts of breeze rustle the trees and sweep the leaves along the well-worn paths. Among the scents of damp and rot, she can detect rain approaching, yet it is far enough away as to not spoil her plans.

Closing her eyes, she reaches out with her mind. In amongst the general hum of the city, she can feel his approach. There is something in the way his mind hums, the way his craving calls to her. He moves closer, turns the corner. Licking her lips, she makes them shine. Then he steps onto the curb, far on the park's edge. Purpose infuses him and she can track him as he moves swiftly, surely. He is so close now she can sense the blood pulsing beneath his skin and the warm wave of heat spreading out like a bow wave in front of him as he strides eagerly toward her.

A cloud breaks and cool moonlight floods the park, exposing the rustling leaves dark olive and damp and then she can hear him, the crispy crunch of his heels on the red gravel path. Turning her head, she searches for that first glimpse of him, the shape of his shoulders, the glide of his slim thighs, the desire in his eyes. Suddenly, the recollection of when she walked that same path, through a park such as this, descends. She remembers the desire thumping through her veins and the complete surrender that drove her body and her mind and her heart. She hopes his surrender will be as deep and as binding. She remembers...

Walking.

Walking through Gaten Park. I was taking a short cut a few weeks before my seventeenth birthday. The night was hot and damp and I wanted to go home to bed and be accounted for before the folks came home. I entered the park, a place I had never ventured into after dark. It was very gothic, tall trees, clumps of unkempt grass in the depressions, a swing grating rustily in the playground. A wind seemed to spring up as I trod across the first section, past the gardener's shed and into the shadow of the oak glade. Ahead the willow fronds waved hula-like and I felt the urge to walk through them, letting them trail over my body, letting the dew cool my heated skin. It was within the veil of willow leaves I saw him.

I froze—first from the fright at encountering someone and then from fascination at what he was doing. I had never seen someone having sex before. Never caught my parents at it. They slept in separate beds. He was behind her and I could see his white penis thrusting into her and out again, his mouth anchored at the junction of her neck. She was caught like a kitten in its mother's jaw, moaning, bleating and the sound of her ecstasy washed over me, wove around me and punched me in the gut. His hands clasped her breast, which trickled blood. I thought he had long nails because she moaned louder when he lifted them higher and dark fluid trickled down onto her ribs. Then he lifted her off her feet for that final thrust, and she sighed, pale and flaccid. They stayed in that pose for a few seconds and then he let her body ooze down his front to puddle in the grass. The expression on her face mesmerised me. It bespoke pure joy, pure ecstasy. It made me want to feel that way, even though I knew that she was dead. That he had killed her.

As he moved, I saw the carved muscles of his back and buttocks. I saw his head turn along the line of his shoulder, angling in my direction. His eyes blazed, sending an arrow of fright down my throat and into my heart. I ran. It was like a switch had been flicked on, powering my legs as I ran all the way home. In the dark, clinging to my blankets, I was shivering cold and hot at the same time. Every time I closed my eyes, I saw that body of his, felt that look and craved that touch.

It took a few nights of fevered fascination to draw me back to the park, back to where I saw him. I don't remember if it was surety or hope that guided my steps. I dressed in jeans and a t-shirt and tried to calm the racing of my heart. What drew me to him? He was handsome, alluring and full of sex. To me, a young virgin, obsessed with my body, obsessed with ending my childhood chastity, obsessed with wanting to be loved, he was a beacon, a means to answer my desires. Did I love him? Not then, but the seeds were there. I was infatuated with him. From that glimpse of him, I supposed many things about him. My nights were filled with visions of me running my hands over those carved and perfect muscles, of feeling his mouth on my skin, on my neck. I wanted to make those sounds that woman made, I wanted to feel the ecstasy that I had only read about in romance novels. I wanted to feel what that woman felt when he fucked her to death.

He was there under a tree, leaning against it as if he wasn't expecting anyone, just standing, eyes half closed, lips slightly parted. His muscles were hiding in a black shirt with a high collar and dark, skin-hugging pants. By the sheen from the streetlight, I thought they were leather. I stood there saying nothing just looking. My eyes travelled up his legs, the mound sculpted by his pants, up the firm torso that flared out to the shoulders. Then I saw his eyes, piercing blue beneath the halo of dark hair that swept below his ears to curl around his neck.

"Hello," he said. I felt a thrill when he spoke. His voice stirred me, made me moist and warm between my legs. I liked how that felt.

"Hello." I walked toward him.

"I was hoping you would come back. I've been waiting for you, pretty one. My name is Vincent. You?"

My breath stopped; so did my heart. "Waiting for me? Josie. My name's Josie." I had not been called pretty before. Looking back, I can see that I was nothing of the sort. I was an ignorant, horny girl, flirting with danger.

Before I knew it, I was close to him. Heat radiated from me and I closed my eyes, not wanting him to see how much I trembled, how much I wanted him. My nearness seemed to animate him. Carefully he touched my chin, lifted it to the light and with his other hand he ran two fingers down my neck. The feel of him was electric. I moaned and shivered. His lips brushed against mine. I opened my mouth, letting him explore me. He caressed my back, held me hard against him. Soon his hands fondled my breast, while his lips travelled along my throat.

The first bite filled me with terror. I squirmed and cried out. He bit harder and then I couldn't move. I hung there in his arms until the pain turned to something else. I don't remember how long it was, but later, when I was aware again, my t-shirt was on the ground next to me and he was sucking my breasts while I throbbed with desire.

I blinked and pulled away from him, aware of how cold I was, even though the night was warm. He helped me put my t-shirt back on. "There you go little girl. Best you go home now."

I felt bad leaving. The tears were burning in my eyes. I was frightened and intoxicated by him. "Can I see you again, Vincent?"

"Maybe... if you are good."

"Good?"

He smiled then. "As long as you think about me all the time. As long as you are sure because next time, sweet, I'll take more, I'll want more. Are you ready to become a woman?"

With a sick sense of relief, I nodded. Why wouldn't I spend my time thinking about him? He made me feel so good, so loved. He desired me.

I was awash with desire.

Desire.

Her smile is triumphant when she can make out his expression. That look on his face reveals all that was hidden and all that she anticipated. Desire burns beneath his skin. He is hers to control, to consume. His smile is sexy when he approaches her. "I was hoping to see you here again, Josie," he says, reaching out a tentative hand to brush his index finger down her forearm.

She moans softly, feeling the heat of him rush up through her arm and kick starting her heart beat. She smiles, showing no teeth, and moves her shoulders just so. "I was expecting you." Her voice is low, pitched to snare and entangle. She sees his eyes flash with lust, and his tongue as he swipes along his neat white teeth.

At her confession, he becomes bolder and moves his arm around her waist, draws her close. The heat rushes into her, making her back arch and her breath suck down deep. Her heart beats again, satisfyingly strong. Kaboom, kaboom, kaboom. His right hand trails along her bare shoulder and then down past her bodice to capture her waist. The rich fabric of her dress crinkles and swooshes, making her sigh. She so likes that sound. Her back curves, lifting her rounded breasts perched in the bodice within the purview of his hungry gaze. His hot lips brush against the swelling creamy mounds. A groan escapes her throat. So much heat next to her cold heart. It rushes into her, making her head spin. How she missed the warmth, the pulse, the breath. She seeks it always. It is her need. Josie hates the cold so much.

He eases her back into the sweet summer grass. Her dress lies in a pool around her head. His naked body is oiled with sweat as it rubs against hers. Suddenly, she turns him over, making him lie face down, pressing his face into the satin of her dress. She licks up his spine, liking the salt and the moisture, sucking up his heat with her tongue. Crying out, he turns again, head haloed in her dress, and she leans over him. His cock is pink and hard. Trailing her hand along it, she wants to take the warmth from there too. She opens her mouth and aims for his erection. Again he cries out, inarticulate, desire laden, when her lips enclose him.

Her teeth gently tap into the vein of his penis and a small trickle tantalises her tongue. He is calling out now, calling for more. She sucks, she draws in his heat. But it is not enough. She needs more. She needs it all. Gently she pushes at his shoulders and makes him lie back. Mounting him, she catches the wash of ecstasy that escapes his lips and bucks, fevered and hard. She is taking in all of him, all of his heat, and then she lowers her mouth to his neck stretched tight in his climax, taking his blood.

She sees her dress like a puddle of crimson around his head.
Blood.

The second time I went to the park, Vincent was not there. I cried against the oak tree and punched at the bark. It was not fair. Where had he gone? Was he fucking someone else? I was insanely jealous at the thought. A voice in my head told me that what choice did he have. I was a young virgin, inexperienced. The next night I was there again waiting. This time I was wearing a halter neck sundress. The fever inside me made me burn. I willed him to me and he came.

"So you came back. Missed me?"

"Oh yes. I missed you so much." I launched myself at him, burying my face in his chest. At first he gasped and then he laughed.

"So you did miss me."

I pushed back off his chest and stood on my tiptoes to offer my lips to him. He kissed me deeply, hands straying to my breasts. He kept on kissing me, pushing me up against the tree, exploring my wetness while I moaned so loudly I thought they could hear me out on the street. While he bit me on the neck again, he fondled me until I came, my body shaking, the pain immobilising me. I passed out as my body shuddered, orgasm raking over me, down to my toes. I was alone when I woke up that time. I had been propped up against the tree, legs splayed, my dress tugged neatly into place. I called out for him but there was no answer, only the damp, trees waving in the wind and the howl of dog in someone's yard. I was angry that he had left. I was angry that he hadn't fucked me. So angry that I never wanted to see him again.

I stayed away for a whole week, but every waking moment I thought about him, remembered his touch. I burned for him at nights, touching myself where he had touched me, wanting to feel his hard white cock inside of me.

My mother had bought me a dark, red satin dress for my seventeenth birthday and she had organised a surprise party at the local community hall. I curled my hair and placed it to hide the bruising on my neck. I wore make up and high heels. My Dad cried and said I looked all grown up. At the party, we played spin the bottle in a corner out of view of the parents. I French-kissed Toby Reagan and made his eyes widen. I bet he didn't know I had it in me. I smiled at him, letting him know that if he wanted, I would, and inclined my head toward the door. He nodded back, a slight smile on his face, uncertainty and desire in his dark gaze. I went to the door and looked around. I saw someone move behind a tree, caught a glimpse of black leather in the porch light. It was him—Vincent.

Immediately my anger died away and desire swamped me. I ran to where he was but he was gone. I ran further on, holding the skirt of my dark red satin dress. I knew where I was heading, knew where he was leading me. I pushed aside the willow fronds and faced him.

For a full minute, I drank him in, feeling my desire, my love and my heat anchor on him. I wanted to drown in him; my surrender was complete. I heard the swish of my gown as he peeled it off me. I felt his cock sever me and felt the heat leave me, sucked into his mouth with my blood. It was more than I imagined it would be. He drove me harder, he sucked deeper and I felt my surrender.

As I felt myself float, I knew that what had kept me warm and alive now lived in him. But something happened, like it sometimes does.

I came back. I remember the cold, white cock sliding out of me and I saw my body ooze down his to pool in the grass. I remember the ache inside me when I woke up. I remember the craving. I remember the need, for heat and for blood.

"Vincent?"

He turned toward me, shock evident on his face. "What? How... ?"

I stared at him "I don't know. I am cold, so cold."

Vincent smiled. "Really? I'll warm you."

I STAYED with Vincent for a few years, but he could never warm me. I left him to search for heat. Blood was secondary. I was forever the seventeen year old. I kept buying red satin dresses and wearing them to lure my prey.

Her prey.

She watches his pale penis slide out of her, still hard and virile. She licks the trail of blood on his neck, and runs her tongue over his now cold lips, as she lifts off him. She is warm. Her blood pulses and she can hear a faint heartbeat as his blood and warmth swim inside of her, inhabit her. She will miss his devotion, his slavish desire, but she revels in his surrender. It was sweet. It was delicious. She slides back into her dark red satin dress and smooths out the creases. If she hurries she will make the party. Someone there caught her eye.

As she watches the pale form lying in the grass, bathed only in moonlight, she is startled by a voice.

"Josie?"

She spins around and there he is, her love. She smiles, because she is warm and she wants more to sate her. She wonders why Vincent is here. Was it accident or design?

"Good to see you, Vincent." Her voice floats around her, pregnant with desire.

"I see you haven't changed your routine. Red dress, party dress, party hair." He walks toward her, black leathers gleaming in the moonlight.

Josie glances again at the man, a smile lifting the corners of her mouth. "It works."

Vincent walks around her prey then inhales. "There is still blood in him. What a waste."

Josie laughs lightly. "Help yourself. You know it is the heat I crave."

Vincent leans closer and snatches at the throat of the man, drinks deep of the blood now cooling in the man's veins. He stands up, wipes his lips with the back of his hand.

"Miss you," he says.

"Really?" Josie gazes at him blankly. "What do you really want, Vincent?"

He comes close to her, walks behind her, trailing his fingers through her hair, picking out a stray piece of grass. At his touch, she feels desire kindle. She remembers how well he fucks.

His breath caresses her ear as he whispers. "I want you, Josie."

Josie inclines her head, watching him, assessing him. "What do you want from me?"

He smiles a slow, sexy smile. She reaches out with her senses, sees that he has a heartbeat and radiates heat. He had been feeding often lately. "Well, if you must know. There is this girl. She's curious. I thought you could... "

"Take her heat?" Her eyebrow arches.

He grins and nods. "I get her blood."

Josie casts a glance down at the body now empty of blood and heat. She considers the party and its possibilities and then studies Vincent for a moment or two. "I suppose so. But afterwards I want you. Solo. You have enough heat to satisfy me for a while."

"Sure thing."

The man in black and the woman in red walk out of the park hand in hand. Under the streetlight a woman waits, with a slowly blossoming smile.

$\mathcal{P}$HAEDRA

$\mathcal{B}$RUCE $\mathcal{G}$OLDEN

$\mathcal{O}$KAY, I admit it. I had this... this affair with a cartoon... I mean an animated babe. I don't mean she was hyper, I mean she was a drawing, an illustration—you know, not real. No, that's wrong. She was real all right, but she was a real cartoon, like Mickey Mouse or Roger Rabbit.

I don't expect you to believe me. I wouldn't believe it myself, if she wasn't the best thing that ever happened to me. But she was more than that. She was this vibrant, tough, intelligent woman. She may have been a cartoon, but she was still a woman. A woman I fell in love with.

You can choose to believe me or you can laugh it off as one man's perverted fantasy. I don't really care what you think, because I lived it. I know it happened.

That first time it was late, like most of my nights were. I had the TV on, and I was a little drunk and a little stoned. Hell, there wasn't even a decent old movie on, so I was flicking the remote like I was getting paid by the channel. On top of my boredom I was feeling a little lonely, and more than a little horny. It had been a while.

I was flipping from station to station when this one program catches my eye. Something I hadn't seen before, a whimsical mixture of science fiction and fantasy. I didn't know if it was a regular series or some obscure animated film. I'm about to zap the remote again when *she* swings into my picture. I mean literally swung in on some cable right into a cluster of Brand X bad guys.

She had high cheekbones and long hair as deep, dark red as the Merlot I'd been drinking. A thin silver headband kept it out of her tempestuous green eyes. The black leather strips she wore were just enough for the modesty of the censors, and the flesh it did expose was every comic book artist's ideal of sinewy, supple perfection. In other words, she had it all.

Her boots pounded the head of yet another generically depraved minion as she drew her rapier from its ebony scabbard and began dealing death to and fro. She'd feint to the left as her blade licked out like a serpent's tongue to the right. Leap and parry, roll and thrust. Her battle dance was as deadly as it was seductive.

Waging war with my own lethargy, I found myself imagining what it would be like to get naked and do the nasty with this voluptuous heroine darting across my TV screen.

This, of course, is where you're going to think I've totally lost touch with reality. You'll probably write it off as drug-induced, or maybe severe manic depression. I know I did... at least at first.

I was still fantasising about what it would be like to be deep inside such a powerful woman, tempering her pleasure with every stroke, when she comes flying boots-first through the television screen and lands with a distinct *thud* on my living room carpet.

What did I do? Well I did what any red-blooded American male would do in that situation. I froze. I sat there with my mouth hanging open and my hand clutching the remote as if it were a high-tech crucifix that would ward off televised apparitions. For the first time in my life, I thought I'd blown a fuse.

There was something odd about her that added to my understandable amazement. She no longer looked like—well, like a drawing. In becoming three-dimensional, her flesh tones had taken on depth, her emerald eyes the spark of life. But there was still something not quite right about her colour—about the corporeality of her presence. It was as if she were only part human, and still part the pen and ink of someone's imagination. At that moment, however, with her standing there flashing the look of a trapped panther, blood dripping off her sword onto my coffee table, I had no doubt of her existence.

"What wizardry is this?" she demanded as both the look in her eyes and her blade threatened my very existence. "Who are... ?"

She scanned the room as if she'd just gotten off the bus in Bizarreville. My black and white photo of Leonard Nimoy seemed to intrigue her, but she didn't know what to make of the stuffed Alf doll. Then she saw the television and almost freaked. The show, *her* show, was still on. She recognised the villainous hordes she'd been doing battle with and spun into a fighting stance, knocking over my Tony Gwynn-autographed baseball. The bad guys were searching for her, looking everywhere. But it wouldn't do them any good, because *she* was in my living room.

"It's all right," I found myself saying. "Nobody's going to hurt you here."

"Where is this?"

"You're in my house. I don't know how you got here, but you're obviously here."

"Where is this house? What strange world is this?"

"Well, until a minute ago, I thought this was the *real* world. Now I'm not sure what's real. But you can put your sword down. I swear no one is going to hurt you here. Please."

She regained some of her regal composure, surveying the room and deciding there was no immediate danger. One look at me cowering against the cushions of my couch made it obvious I was no threat. She sheathed her sword and turned her attention back to what was on the TV screen.

"That's... my world?" It was part statement, part question.

"That's where I was watching you, until you popped in unexpectedly."

"This is a window between worlds?"

"Yeah, I guess it is. Actually, it's a window to many worlds. Watch this."

I aimed the remote at the TV and changed the channel to CNN, which was airing a report on a new electric car.

That, as I discovered, was a mistake.

As I watched her watching the television, she began to change. Her colours weren't as bright, her presence not as imposing. She was dwindling away, becoming transparent. When I finally realised was happening, she had all the substance of a ghost.

As fast as I could fumble with the remote, I switched back to her show. But it was too late. She had vanished—at least from my living room. I saw her there, back on the screen. She looked disoriented for a moment, and that moment was enough for the bad guys to drop a wire-mesh net over her.

That was it. That's where the episode ended. They rolled credits over scenes from previous shows and I dove for my *TV Guide*. The name of the show was *Phaedra, The Warrior Princess*, and it was on Channel 3 five nights a week.

*I*COULDN'T get to my TV quickly enough the next night. I left it on Channel 3 more than an hour before the show was due, just in case. Instead of working, I had spent the day worrying. Worrying what might happen to her in the hands of the villain—though I told myself she was the show's star, and nothing really bad could happen to her. I also worried I'd never see her again, except on television. And, I worried plenty about my sanity. Who wouldn't after what I'd seen?

So I waited. But this time I didn't have anything to drink or smoke. I didn't even want to eat. I was damn sure going to be in my right mind if it happened again, even though I'd convinced myself it wouldn't.

When the show started I learned she was indeed the title character, and that she now lay at the mercy of the grotesque Dark Prince, who intended to use an odd amalgamation of science and magic to make her his love slave. She had been stripped naked and strapped to a table somewhere deep in the bowels of his citadel. The straps, of course, were strategically placed to cover her more feminine parts.

As the episode progressed, there appeared to be no rescue for Phaedra. The Dark Prince was only minutes away from reshaping her mind, and I didn't see any way for her to escape. I couldn't help but wonder if it was all my fault. If I hadn't started fantasising about her and sucked her into my world, she probably never would have been captured.

Yeah, I know, it was schizoid reasoning at best. On one hand I was sure I'd imagined the whole thing, and on the other I felt guilty. There was only one way to find out for sure, and only one way to rescue her.

I stood, closed my eyes, and began thinking about her as hard as I could think. I thought about her straps coming untied... I thought about her cutting the Prince's throat and escaping... I even thought about her beaming into my living room like something out of *Star Trek*. But nothing worked. I was such a dismal failure I couldn't even hallucinate properly. She was doomed to become the mindless bride of that villain now.

I tried to remember exactly what I had thought of the night before. That was easy—the same thing I was usually thinking about—sex, of course. So I envisioned making love to Phaedra—the passion of her kisses, the power of her thighs, the deep dark red of her—and *wham*! I felt a rush of cold air that nearly knocked me back and suddenly I felt her. I opened my eyes and she was there, *right there* in my arms, as naked as she'd been on that table.

"You," she said, actually sounding relieved.

I, of course, was my usual eloquent self. Standing there with this incredibly beautiful, naked woman in my arms, I replied, "Hi."

"You have saved me from the clutches of the Dark Prince," she said.

"It, uh, was the least I could do."

That's when she kissed me. And it wasn't just any kiss. At least, it wasn't like any kiss I'd ever had from a *real* woman. It was a kiss that seared my lips, assaulted my insides, and rendered my legs immobile. It was a TKO.

Have you ever been in a situation like that? Of course not exactly like that. But a situation where you thought, *this is too good to be true*. Well at that moment that's what I thought, and I wasn't about to waste a second of it.

I kissed her back. One thing led to another and we proceeded with the most passionate, most ferocious lovemaking I have ever, or *will* ever, experience. On the floor, across the couch, in the shower, over the kitchen sink—she couldn't get enough. And who was I to argue?

Somewhere between unbridled lust and rubbed raw passion, she wore me down. We were lying there on the couch and I realised the TV had been on all this time. I let go of her to sit up and check out what was on. Her show was long over with now, and some infomercial had usurped the channel. When I turned back to look at her, she'd already begun to dissipate.

"Phaedra!"

She opened her eyes and sprang to her feet like an adrenalised cat, then realised what was happening. I tried to grab her, but it was too late. She faded from my arms like a misty day and vanished.

ROM then on, I was by my television set every night, five nights a week. My weekends were one long holding pattern, waiting for the arrival of her show late on Monday.

Though she was staying with me longer and longer after her show ended, we discovered the only sure way to keep her from dematerialising was continuous lovemaking. That led to some marathon sessions I will not elaborate on here. She relished escaping from her violent, barbaric world into mine, and I relished her—the feel of her, the sound of her, the scent of her.

It was the perfect love affair. Perfect, that is, if you fail to consider the fact she was the figment of someone's imagination. But I no longer worried I was losing my mind. I didn't care. I was immersed in a cascading pool of bliss. Every night with her was ecstasy, and reality, whatever that was, be damned. Hell, she called me her hero. What more could a guy want?

Then, one Monday night, after a particularly long and boring weekend, I turned on my TV and waited for her. I had a bottle of semi-expensive champagne and a new kind of chocolate for her. In the few weeks we'd been together, she was always wanting to try something different from my world.

I no longer had to concoct elaborate sexual fantasies to make her appear. We had established some kind of preternatural link. One quick thought was all it took now. And you could see it in her face. No matter what the creators of her show had her doing in a particular episode, her heart wasn't in it. I could tell she was waiting for the moment when I would whisk her away from the fighting and into my arms. I never waited long, and the more she disappeared, the more the show's minor characters began to take centre stage. In fact, her mysterious disappearances had become part of the plotline, with both her allies and her enemies left to wonder where she had vanished to, and what magical powers she had acquired. In the opening of one show, I actually watched as Phaedra confided to her maidservant that when she disappeared, she flew into her lover's arms.

So there I was, waiting for her, when I see the opening sequence to an episode of *Gilligan's Island*. I started messing with the remote, figuring I've got the wrong channel. But I don't.

Now I like Ginger and Mary Ann as much as the next guy, but at that moment pure panic clutched my throat. I flashed through the TV listings and there it was, *Gilligan's Island*, right where *Phaedra* should've been. I spent the rest of the night looking at every single show in that week's listings; maybe she'd been moved to a different time-slot. I frantically stabbed at the remote until my fingers grew numb. Finally, I drank myself into oblivion with the champagne I'd bought for her.

The next day I called the station and found out *Phaedra* had been cancelled. I'm sure I sounded desperate. But I guess they get a lot of crazies calling about their favourite shows, so the woman on the other end took it in stride. I asked if the show had only been cancelled locally, and whether it might still be on other stations around the country. Even before she answered, I was contemplating what I'd have to do if I relocated to a new city.

No, she had said, the show was an independent that had ceased production, and as far as she knew, there would be no new episodes. I asked her about reruns. Yes, in time, some station somewhere might pick up the show for reruns. Would her station? She sincerely doubted it. It seemed viewers had been complaining about the show's change in focus from its heroine to other characters. Its ratings had plummeted. Could she give me the address of the production company? Sure.

FOR a long time after that, I wrote letters to the company that had distributed *Phaedra, The Warrior Princess*, and then to the creators of the show. I begged, I pleaded, and in one particularly deranged moment, I even threatened. They thanked me for my interest and my praise, empathised with me, and eventually told me, in so many words, to get a life.

After the third letter they did send me a DVD copy of one episode, but there was no magic in it. No matter how much I fantasised, no matter how much I conjured up images of the nights we had spent together, Phaedra no longer left her world for mine.

Like any great love affair, I'm left with wonderful memories, memories that widen the cracks in my heart when I dwell on them.

Of course, if you're reading this, you're most likely thinking I'm cracked in other places. That's all right. I don't care. I know it was real. I know *she* was real. I know I touched her, kissed her, and, on occasion, even transformed that stoic warrior look of hers into a childlike smile. She was real all right. She was the love of my life.

DATE WITH A VAMPIRE

ANNETTE BACKSHALL

LOOKING back at Umbra's profile it's hard to see how I could have missed 'Vampire Seeks Victim' glaring at me from between the lines. Not that I'm saying every male on MatchU.com could be assumed so simply as Man Looking for Love. In fact, deciphering the true meaning of what's written is all part of the long and dreary process of trying to find someone worth sending a 'kiss' to. My friend Christine thinks women approach the whole vetting thing like snipers; carefully perusing each profile, identifying the types, searching out one worthwhile candidate to aim that kiss at. Whereas men take more of a machine gunners approach, spraying the site with kisses to see how many responses they get.

The types? There's hundreds. Your chief one is of course Man Seeks Wife. He's slightly different to Man Seeks Incubator, who's the same as Man Seeks Wife *but* said wife must be under 40. At the other end of the spectrum there's Man Seeks Anything with a Pulse—keen to meet women between 18 and a 100, no photo necessary—and has a typical profile name like, lonelyguy437 or lookingforlove972318. There are also not surprisingly types like Man Needs Sex, opposite to Man Looking for Friend; closet-gays Chris says, but I think they're just another version of Man Needs

Sex, who's really Man Incapable of Emotional Intimacy but isn't yet a Total Loss to Humanity.

My knowledge of types, if not a 100% accurate, was in identifying the various *human* male varieties and their subtle complexities. I had no awareness of any supernatural beings amongst us and therefore no template to work from. Six months ago I thought vampires were at best mythical creatures, and at worst, a subculture of weirdos who drank blood to get off, keep young or whatever. So on that seemingly normal night when I sat down to check my emails, a kiss from a gorgeous vampire was the furthest thing from my mind.

The credits of the last BBC instalment of *Jane Eyre* were rolling as I switched off the telly and sighed. It had somehow revived my flagging interest in the whole internet dating game. What if I threw it all in and *my* Mr Rochester was only a virtual kiss away?

Mind you, a 21st century version of Edward R could have turned up wearing all but a rose between his teeth a few days prior and I would likely have slammed the door in his face. But that was after a somewhat disappointing first encounter from the site the Thursday before.

In a nutshell some yet unidentified type had stood me up. I hopped on the computer after I got home that night wondering if there was a message explaining why he'd left me to endure the clumsy passes from an array of drunken sleazes while I waited alone for a date that never came. I logged on and found he'd disappeared into the icy oblivion of cyber space. I'd tried his phone earlier and got, "Sorry, the number you are calling is temporarily out of range or switched off... ." So I don't know what I was expecting from the computer. I suppose there is that underlying faith in humanity that's hard to extinguish. "I'm sorry Hannah, my car broke down, and I'd dropped my phone down the toilet in my haste to get out to meet you on time so I couldn't call..." Something, anything that says that society hasn't really gotten to the point where we feel we can treat strangers so disdainfully because we have technology to hide behind. I didn't know it at the time but in a lot of ways this had uncanny similarities to what was to come. If I were to categorise the likes of HotRod—stander-upper extraordinaire—it would have to be something vampiric in nature. He took something unnameable from me to feed his own selfish needs and was no doubt satisfied.

But then, as Christine put it, "In all honesty, what did you expect from a family law court lawyer?"

As I made my way through the latest list of maybes that following Sunday I found it hard to cling to the delusional hope that only one of the Bronte's tales could imbue in the failing heart of a cynic. As usual, a disheartening assortment of emails awaited my rejection. There was LionTamer—he asked if I'd been tamed lately, wrote that he was "a intelagent guy," and thought we had a lot in common. QuickMike and Weenie sent kisses—no incentive for a girl to look much further there. AManCalledHorse and HandyAndy69 were obviously mates with Powercord who I guessed spent a lot of time with his hand on his tool. TheRealOutbackJack turned out to live within 10 kilometres of the CBD. Delete, delete, delete. And so at last, Umbra.

Thirty-six years old, lived locally, he worked night shift, an atheist, liked people watching, red wine, star gazing. He seemed to me a little quirky, definitely interesting. So the odd comment like, "I'm a sucker for a pretty face", "I like to get my teeth into juicy subjects" and "I've always been a rapacious devourer of knowledge..." simply went straight over my head.

He provided me with the password for his photo gallery. I logged on and typed in *Batman*. A moment's suspense and then, there he was.

Umbra was simply beautiful. I studied his features minutely trying to create a three dimensional image in my mind. He had lush medium length swept back black hair, accentuating a slight widow's peak in the centre of his brow and retro shaped side burns. He had lovely eyes to match, piercing ebony points contrasted by porcelain white skin. His nose looked aquiline. I wondered if it was very hooked or just a slight curve. His chin seemed pointed, but not so much as to lose its masculine line. His lips: lovely cupid bows. I was guessing they were full and soft, *very* kissable. He was a little on the slim side, but not unmanly. I remember thinking at the time that he could do with a good feed.

There was certainly something about him, something compelling. So, when the banner below his photo flashed, "Like Him? Yes? Then send him a kiss!" I did just that.

Events happened rather quickly from then. He wrote me the next day, an exquisite email. Umbra's real name was André. His command of the written word was perfect, his spelling and grammar faultless. He even knew how to use parenthesis properly. Being an English teacher I tended to be impressed by things like that. His expression was almost poetic. He was flattering, noting that he found my Eastern European looks alluring. We exchanged numbers. He rang me the next night.

I picked up the phone after letting it ring Christine's suggested five times—"You can't seem too eager, darling."

André had a deep melodic voice with a hint of an accent. My skin tingled when he said hello. We spoke for hours. He had a profound knowledge of the world: history, religion and politics. We discussed his job; he was a social worker who helped the homeless.

"I take people off the street at night," he explained.

He was married once. In a stilted voice he explained that she had died some years ago and had not found anyone since.

"My nocturnal activities tend to restrict my ability to form any lasting bonds," was how he put it. He didn't have any family either. He'd been an only child and his parents were gone—it seemed to him like centuries since they'd passed.

"And what about your family, Hannah?"

"Oh, well, my parents were from Hungary. They migrated here after the revolution, in '59."

"Ah!" he exclaimed, "How wonderful. My parents were born in Romania, though we are Szekler in ethnicity, who still identify as Hungarian."

"Wow! Really? That's amazing."

I told him, as it happened, my grandfather was Szekler, from Transylvania originally I thought.

It was around 11.45pm when I relieved my ear and set the phone to rest in its cradle. André had assured me I was most enchanting, but it was getting late and he had to go out to find something to eat. Speaking of which, he'd love to have me for dinner one night, should I wish to grace him with my presence.

I know. I should have heard alarm bells clanging. I probably would have if my mind wasn't screaming, *yes, yes, yes!*

He left me with his address and a time, and assurances that it would be the most illuminating evening I'd ever have—he was prepared to stake his life on it. I told him I was dying to meet him. He seemed exceptionally pleased with that.

*I*MUST have changed outfits five times until I came to like my reflection in a conservative grey fitted woollen tunic, spiced up with fishnet stockings and a pair of black leather knee-high boots. Well balanced: sexy but not tarty, classy without being stuffy. Teeth brushed twice, tongue once, hair done, makeup just right, a dab of rich, musky perfume, Gucci watch and diamond earrings; I was ready.

As I stepped from the taxi I couldn't help but notice how the still night air was, bright with the glow of a rising full moon. André's home was a funky sub-penthouse in an apartment block that sat on the fringe of the foreshore park along Mill Point Road in South Perth. Not bad digs for a non-government organisation worker I'd thought. Family had probably left him money.

His place had huge glass windows that revealed the city's skyline in panoramic splendour across the river. I'm not sure how I came to be standing before this beautiful sight. One moment I was on the sidewalk, the cold making my nose tickle and my cheeks smart, the next I was in his home, admiring how the town lights stretched out to me, like fingers across the surface of the Swan. There was a smell of spice. I had a glass of aromatic mulled wine in my hand. Just the thing for a cold, clear night.

It seemed as though I was there but not, aware but asleep, dreamlike. I sipped. A tantalising tingle ran along my tongue and down my throat. Warmth infused my body and slowly sharpened my senses, as though I had lived my life just off station and only in that instance was I being tuned in. I turned my head and there was André, watching me. He had a strange almost wistful smile on his face.

"Hello," I whispered. By God he was beautiful.

"Hello, at last."

He took my free hand, turned it up and kissed the middle of my palm with soft cool lips. My body quivered with pleasure. My knees almost buckled. I locked them straight. It was all I could do to stand still for fear that if I moved I'd pounce on him like some deranged sex fiend. The thought surprised—and pleased me.

He gazed into my eyes. He was seeing into me, knowing me. I was mesmerised. He tilted his head slightly to one side as though listening. He held me by some dark, pleasurable compulsion. He smiled broadly. It was then I knew he was a vampire.

No, it wasn't that his parted lips revealed a pair of exceptionally pointed canines. That was secondary, almost a confirmation. It was more an innate knowing that flowered within me and with it a sense of destiny, as though this meeting was always going to happen, that in my deepest heart I had secretly yearned for it. Part of me rejected that notion out off-hand with bemused cynicism. What did I know of the vampires?

I remembered having a conversation in the staff room over lunch once when discussing a vampire story one of my students had written. He'd had them sucking blood with their mouth. I'd thought they drew blood through their fangs, so I asked a couple of colleagues what they thought. Gino, from Science, was of the standard opinion that they just drank blood from the wounds.

"But surely once the initial blood pressure dropped and coagulants went to work it would be hard sucking someone dry through a couple of small puncture wounds. How could they keep going?" I'd argued.

"Maybe they inject a blood thinner with the fangs?" was all Gino could offer.

John Mathews from Manual Arts, in his usual languid way, threw in, "Maybe they put a straw in one of the punctures to keep it open—pop an umbrella and a piece of fruit in the other—there you go, human cocktail. Beautiful."

Keith the 24 year old party animal from Phys. Ed chuckled then said, "Nah, I reckon they stick a finger over one hole and blow air into the other, then quickly move their mouth over both to give themselves a kind of blood shottie."

I looked back to Gino. "My sucking through fangs is looking stronger all the time, I think."

"Are you going to suck my blood—make me a vampire?" I asked André. It sounded lame once it was out of my mouth I'll admit. He laughed.

"Oh, but my dear, I don't need to."

I tried to make sense of that. I looked down at the glass of rich red wine in my hand. My insides went to jelly. Had I been drinking blood? His blood? What did it mean to drink a vampire's blood? Wasn't it some kind of horrible virus thingy? Had he infected me?

This wasn't how it happened in the movies. He was supposed to drink *my* blood, and depending on what he wanted from me, he would either kill me or allow me to morph into one of the hideous living dead, destined to become a parasite on humanity for the rest of time. Maybe he'd have me as one of his harem of sex-mad vampettes, all big hair, lip licking, hissing and cleavage.

"That's all a little dramatic, Hannah."

I looked up at him. Could he read my thoughts?

Of course I can came to me not as words but as that same innate knowing I had experienced before.

"But I don't want to be a vampire."

"Don't look so crestfallen, beloved. Don't you know you've always been one?"

"I think you've made a mistake. I can't be a vampire. I'm a vegetarian for God's sake!"

He didn't have to use further words. I understood the meaning. I just didn't want to acknowledge it. And he was right. I recognised my vampirism. It had started before I was born, in the womb, stealing sustenance from my mother to sustain my life. In fact when I thought about the state of the world, it was clear just how vampiric humanity on the whole really was, sucking the planet dry with its insatiable appetite for more, not giving anything back. There used to be a balance, there was supposed to be a balance.

"Yes, Hannah. And what happens when Nature herself cannot counteract the tip? What happens when the takers develop ways of surviving disease and famine and drought? Is it then that something *super*-natural comes into being?"

The depth and complexity of André's question staggered me. Could it be that vampires-proper were the superheroes of nature?

Nah, it would never sell. Superfluous to nature, maybe. Though, the thought of vampires acting as something good for the world was intriguing.

"Why me?" was all I could think of saying.

"Your blood my dear. It's all about the blood."

So he *was* going to suck my blood. I knew it.

"Couldn't we get to know each other a little first?" I stammered.

"Of course."

He smiled, stepped forward, folded me into his arms and kissed me.

I fell into him. His being was my being. His aura impressed itself upon my heart. I knew him absolutely and loved him totally in that moment. I knew that he had waited for me for more than two hundred years. He had known me when he first saw my photo, knew me for the one. My face was a reflection of a bloodline thought lost. I saw a woman with a stake through her heart: a heart that had belonged to him—her loss a metaphoric stake in his own heart. The fictional love of Charlotte's heroines seemed all of a sudden adolescent, even trite in comparison. Pain, loneliness and time pulled him away from me. I reached to take him, own him. I stretched hungrily out, needing him to give that love to me.

He pushed me gently away from him, his lips no longer an extension of mine.

"What happened?" I was lost, devastated by the broken connection. An intense need to have this man, body and soul screamed in me.

"I gave you my life force, Hannah, my prana, the very essence of my being."

"The wine?"

"Yes."

"It made me love you?"

"No, it made you know me. It is you who saw fit to love."

That put a whole new spin on the meaning of speed dating.

"To complete the connection, will you offer your blood to me freely?"

"You *do* want to drink my blood."

He wanted more than that I knew. He wanted me to offer my throat—reciprocation in the form of total surrender, physical and emotional.

I pictured myself stepping forward and leaning my head to one side. I imagined his fangs piercing skin and artery. Would he siphon or suck? My thumping heart pumped lava around my body with such pressure it seemed as though it would burst from my veins. Desire, white hot, flooded me. Yet I couldn't take that step. I would be leaping into an abyss. Everything was pushing me towards him with the unspoken promise I could fly. But something deeper still was saying I would fall.

He would know me completely, every nook and cranny of my being, my soul laid bare before him. Love was not enough for a vampire. I inwardly shrank. Shutters came down on my heart. His lips pressed together, his eyes left my face and he turned from me.

"André, please. I can't." I grabbed his arm pulling him back to me.

He gently released my grip. "I'm hungry," he said and walked from the lounge into the hall. I looked to the front door but followed him.

I found him in the dining room. He was standing across from a naked woman sitting at a table set for two—white linen, fine china, silver and candles. I stopped in the doorway unwilling to enter.

André moved round to where the woman was seated. Her full breasts rose and fell with a quickening of breath as he came close to her. He ran his hands through her fine fair hair. He moved his fingers over her pretty face, traced her little nose and full lips. She kissed them as they passed. He swept the table setting aside with one arm and motioned her up. She lay upon the table and stretched her body in supplication before him.

"Do you like her, Hannah? Do you want her?"

"I'm not that way inclined."

I knew it wasn't what he meant, but I said it anyway.

He licked her breast, gently following its curve down and around. She groaned. I gritted my teeth. He ran one hand down her body and the other up her thigh. She panted, moaned and arched her back. His hands skimmed her contours, but his eyes never left mine. He brushed her breasts, between her legs and she writhed beneath his teasing touch.

I could feel what rose in him, not lust or love, though it was those in her that fed The Hunger in him.

My mouth watered, but I was repulsed. I couldn't take my eyes from him either, unable to turn away from the scene unfolding before me. A date with LionTamer didn't seem such a bad idea all of a sudden.

The woman's breath was quickening. Her moans increased in volume as his lips deftly played upon her body. I could smell her arousal, sweet and intoxicating.

André's mouth moved to her throat. She bent her head to one side exposing her neck. She gasped, open-mouthed.

I lunged forward yelling, "No!"

At the same time, she screamed, "Yesssss!"

She died with a smile on her face. Some girls will do anything for the big O, was all that passed through my mind as I watched her life ebb. I wondered in disgust if it was worth the price, giving him everything? From the look of frozen ecstasy on her face one would have guessed, probably.

If the shocking truth be known I was glad she was dead. André had known her, been closer to her in that moment of vampire-victim communion than any man could be to a woman, closer than I was to him. Now she was out of his reach in death and that's all I cared about. I disgusted myself.

"You would never have to worry about another, Hannah. I would be wholly yours."

My attention returned to him. For an objective moment I took in the tableau. There before me was a vampire, complete with blood stained mouth, holding the body of a naked young woman who's life had ended in a cheap thrill on a candlelit sacrificial altar. The reality or *un*reality of the situation slammed into me.

I was supposed to turn up, have dinner, be bored to death listening to yet another man go on about his ex and how she was screwing him out of everything, even his superannuation, after all he'd done for her, the ungrateful cow. And then I would have gone home disappointed as always to live another day of singledom. Instead, I found I was supposedly related to his last wife, he ended up boring someone else to death, literally, and I wasn't going anywhere by the looks except straight to hell. And for what? Him and his selfish wants.

"You manipulative bastard," I said in a slow flat voice that contained my rage to a manageable level.

"You want a soul mate. You talk of equal soul-baring love given of one's free will. But you *tricked* me into bonding with you and that's pretty much buggered my choices somewhat, hasn't it? You peddled your 'humans are really all vampires anyway' pitch, but I'm not buying it. I'm not buying a thing, you hypocritical prat. Despite the fact that I now find myself crazy in love with you, I'm not going to be manoeuvred into something I wouldn't otherwise have wanted to do naturally. That's not how I wanted the love of my life to happen. So you can just go and, and get sucked! You MAN!"

André didn't move to stop me from walking out. He stood there, still cradling the dead woman in cold comfort.

I sat for a long time on the banks of the river. The cold should have been what made me shiver, but I was immune to the elements now. What shook my body was anger and fear. I hugged myself for comfort and watched the moon set behind the city. I discovered that the night had songs that could sooth the darkest of souls. I walked home humming a dirge.

SCHOOL holidays were never long enough in life, and not much changed in death. I'm sure given the seven weeks of Christmas holidays I might have succeeded in killing the vampire in myself. But the two week, third term break wasn't quite long enough.

Only patches of that time remain in my memory. I knew it was imperative that I didn't see anyone, so the first thing I did when I walked in my front door was record a message on my phone in the cheeriest voice I could muster. "Hi! Sorry I'm not home at the moment. I've gone hiking a section of the Bibbulmun with John and Julie and won't be back until Saturday, the one before school starts. If this is a robber, I've got CCTV and an alarm and I've taken all my valuables over to my mum's. Don't forget to leave a message." It sounded convincing, I thought.

I went to bed, curled up and slept. That night the first full pangs of The Hunger attacked me. I half heated some left over pumpkin curry, but it tasted like papier-mâché and ended up in the compost bin. I bit off some cheese; it was like chewing pasty vomit. I tried some chocolate but it tasted like, well, bad. Milk curdled in my mouth. Water helped a little, even though it stank of chemicals and had a copper tang. I knew what I really wanted, something plump, sweet and juicy and it wasn't an orange.

Giving in to it was not an option. I couldn't kill a mouse for heaven's sake. How could I hunt down and kill one of my own kind? *But they aren't your kind anymore* said a voice in my head. I pulled at my hair and covered my ears, but it didn't help. I dead-locked the doors and windows and flushed the keys as insurance. I was never good at diets. I think the only thing that got me through was the fact that I had spent the last twelve years practicing a traditional form of Karate in the hope that one day it might save my life. I shook my head more than a few times at the paradox of using that long cultivated self discipline to help save myself from becoming a vampire by starving myself to death. Eat your heart out, Buffy.

I spent the days lolling about in restless exhaustion, wondering why I found myself written into some demented kind of Kafka tale when I should have been bumbling my way along in a good clean romantic comedy.

The nights were spent pacing my room trying to run down my rising agitation. Even as my strength diminished I was forced to move, crawling back and forth along the length of my room, panting and growling like a caged animal, whining as the pain of The Hunger gnawed at my will. I would lift my nose every now and again and sniff the air. I could smell people as they walked past my villa. Their scent was as delicious as hot waffles used to be. I don't know exactly when that terrible hunger finally abated, but I remember feeling relief that I could crawl at last under the bed where it felt secure enough to sleep forever.

SHE seems to be responding very well Doctor. Blood pressure is up, colour is better."

"Give her an IV of fluids after the blood is done and I'll reassess her then."

"Right, will do."

Blood! I shot up in bed. I looked up to see an almost empty bag hanging from a hook. I followed the tube to my arm and yanked the needle out.

The doctor and nurse dove in unison to stop me. It was too late. I was up and out of bed, sweeping them both aside. I couldn't believe they'd given me blood. *All the agony was for nothing.* I screamed my frustration at them.

"You gave me blood, you idiots. You gave me blood!"

I'm not sure what they were thinking. Probably wondering if anyone had checked to see if I was a Jehovah.

"Do you feel okay, Hannah?" was all the stupid doctor could say. She looked pale, her eyes wide. She'd be a hell of a lot paler if she realised that she'd just created a full-blown vampire.

"Of course I feel okay, I feel bloody fantastic and that's the bloody problem, you bloody idiot!"

I broke down then. I couldn't say any more as a fit of crying got hold of me. I didn't resist when they steered me back to bed and gave me a sedative. In fact, once I realised what it meant, a sense of simple, calm acceptance settled within me. I will admit I was even kind of relieved that it had finally all come to some kind of conclusion. Now there was no human option at all, only living or dying a vampire. It seemed there was no free will when it came to vampires. I lay back and closed my eyes and tried to pretend that the sedative they'd given me had an effect. *I am a vampire*, I thought. Was that so bad? A centred certainty of place in the scheme of things that wasn't present in my human life seemed to take root, grow then bloom. I wanted to go home, to rearrange my life. But, I thought, I didn't have to go just that minute. The doctor had said something about another dose of blood. I could think on things a little longer over a free dinner.

GOING home didn't turn out to be as simple as getting up, getting dressed and walking out. There were forms to fill out, a social worker and a dietician to see, and an appointment with a group of specialists to endure.

They said, "You've been a very sick young lady, Hannah." As if I hadn't noticed.

I had developed cutaneous porphyria. I liked their confidence. The symptoms of which included, receding gums, excess hair growth, anaemia and photosensitivity. Wow, what a coincidence.

"You shouldn't be concerned," one of the specialists said. "It isn't life threatening and it can be managed primarily by staying out of direct sunlight and regular RBC transfusions."

"RBC?"

"Red blood cell transfusions."

"Ah!" I said, and assured them I thought I could bring myself to manage that if it meant I stayed healthy.

They said that there wasn't anything much they could do about the excess hair growth that had already started to bring my hairline down into a widow's peak. I think they were being sincere when they said it actually suited me.

I concurred. It was only slight and I thought it broke up my high forehead and gave my face more of a heart shape.

My receding gum line made my teeth look a little longer, especially my canines, "making them look a little, err, vampiric," one, Mr Something winced.

I smiled and ran my tongue over my new fangs. I gave them my best vampire impersonation, hissing and looking hungrily at the particularly delicious male nurse who was taking my blood pressure at the time.

"I vont to suck yorr blurd."

He froze, his fingers still gently pressing against my quickening pulse. I realised with sudden pleasure that I had captured him in my gaze. I could smell his pheromones pumping perfume into the air. The Hunger stirred. He bent ever so slowly towards me. My doctor, the silly one, coughed and informed me that there was lot that could be done these days with cosmetic dentistry. I looked at her and stopped smiling. The Hunger growled. My nurse dropped my wrist and stepped back into the blood pressure trolley, almost upending it.

They all seemed to disappear rather quickly after that. Yes, I was certainly feeling a lot better.

*I*FINISHED my story for Noel McBride with the usual, "And I suppose it was all downhill from there. Needless to say I am no longer a vegetarian."

He had asked me how I'd come to be a vampire and I was more that happy to tell him. We were at the top to the DNA tower in Kings Park. The tower was named because of its resemblance to the DNA molecule—the controller to the development of life. I thought it was a fitting place to kill.

Noel was wrapped in my glamour, but not yet begging me to take him. The night was clear and still and I was in no particular hurry. My victim was quiet, digesting my story. He looked at me and asked if I was going to make him a vampire. I laughed, saying that as much as I liked the Irish it was impossible, even though he had spent most of his life successfully living as one.

"You've been gorging yourself, Noel—sucking the marrow from the bones of existence until you're almost bursting. Your want never stops, especially your lust for power. You stink of it, you know. *And* you intend to go into politics. We can't have that now, can we?"

He shook his head. The Want had almost totally drowned any logical thought in him.

"You've tipped the balance, Noel. There needs to be a balance."

"You didn't tell me," he said in a quiet, reflective voice. "Are vampire fangs hollow or not?"

I could see his smiling hazel eyes glint. His breathing was

shallow and fast. The higher tones of his desire cut through the base notes of beer, Gucci—Pour Homme and cigars to caress my nose.

"Well, Noel," I motioned him forward with my finger. "There's only one way a human can find that out."

I WAS at the foot of the tower, inspecting my victim's 'fall' when I smelt André. Noel's handsome head had smashed nicely on the pavement. I'd left just enough blood in him to make a good and gory splatter after his drunken slip down the darkened stairs.

I breathed deeply. I'd found in the passing months that I could sense André most of the time, even from across town. When he was close though, I could smell him like spring pollen on the breeze. I ignored him as usual, thinking he would meld back into the night when he was sure I was safe. I smiled. I loved that he checked up on me, loved the feel of him near. But I would never let him know it, even though his absence continued to feel like a gaping hole in my body.

"Still using the old, 'blind date stood me up' routine, I see?"

My heart jumped at the sound of his soft melodic voice. I turned and there he was. God, he was beautiful.

"Yep, works a treat as always. I like to call it the HotRod manoeuvre." I said as casually as I could.

"Lawyer?" André nudged Noel with a crocodile skin boot.

"Family Law"

"Blah."

"Yeah, I know, they leave you with a bit of a bad taste in your mouth, don't they? You?"

"MatchU."

"Still getting bites, huh? I'm surprised the authorities haven't put two and two together yet."

"I have my ways."

"Yes, you certainly do."

There was a pause.

"Hannah, I am sorry," he said softly, hesitantly. "I know what I did to you was wrong."

André carefully stepped around some brain matter to stand closer to me. "I was so desperate for you. I truly am so sorry. I would do anything."

His hand came up to my lips and he gently wiped a smudge of blood from the corner of my mouth. My knees trembled.

I found myself teetering on the edge of that abyss once more. I was trying to find something within me that would deny my want to end the hollowness between fleeting moments of comfort in The Communion with humans like Noel. Still that stubborn something stayed me.

I looked down at Noel and then up at André. I turned and walked as calmly as I could down The Broadwalk green and into the night. I yearned for an end to the feeling of loneliness that echoed down vast empty corridors of black. But it was because of André that the darkness owned me.

I could feel his gaze as a physical touch on my back. I wore it like a warm cloak for a long minute before I felt it taken abruptly off me. I shivered. Something was wrong.

Within a few seconds I was back up the fairway. André was backing up the stairs of the DNA tower, defending himself against three men. He had one hand on a stake protruding from his stomach whilst he kicked at his attackers. I arrived just as the point of his boot connected the chin of one unlucky chap, snapping the attacker's head back and knocking him out instantly to take a tumble to the base of the stairs where he lay atop Noel.

Movement to my left made me turn to see a fourth attacker. He had started up the other staircase of the double-helix spiral, making for the first of a series of viewing platforms that gave access to André's set of stairs from above. I sprinted after him, catching him just as he reached the landing.

I yelled something, I can't remember what. His eyes widened as he turned at my shout. I'll give him credit for how quickly he gathered himself. He moved swiftly toward me while he had the advantage of higher ground and lunged with a stake, a *hawthorn* stake no less. A professional. His reflexes confirmed he was trained for this, a 'sports' hunter more than likely. Religious hunters usually tried to stop me by shaking a crucifix and dousing me in holy water. Regardless, this was real life so there were no showy spinning back-kicks, no lightening speed hand-combinations to impress. I fell back on basics and executed an overhead block at the stake's descent as I stepped onto the platform, moving smoothly past him with his wrist now locked in my grip. I bobbed under his arm, twisted his weapon back in on his body, feeling a minimum of resistance as it pierced skin, muscle and organs, moving up under his rib cage and into his lung. The stench of excrement rose to smother the sharpness of his fear and adrenaline. The hunter, now the hunted, doubled over with a grunt. I brought an elbow down on the back of his neck and snapped his spine.

"Hate to stab, jab and run." I jumped over his gurgling body towards André's stairs.

André was still alive, though his prana seemed weaker. My heart hiccupped. The two other attackers still pressed him. I was no good behind him. I jumped the railing and landed on the ground to the side of the stairs. I could see the first attacker had woken up and was making a groggy escape crawling towards the bush. As my feet clanged on the steps the taller of the last two attackers turned and clambered down to meet me. He had long spider-like legs that cleared three steps at a time. He fumbled with something on a utility belt and flung it towards me. Hard lumps bounced off my head and scattered. That was new, someone trying to beat me to death with a garland of garlic.

His misguided manoeuvre gave me time to lever myself between the railings and kick out and up at his knees. Both made a sickening crack in unison as my feet made contact and carried through. He screamed and toppled forward toward me. I bent low and he fell over me. I pushed up and let him slide down my back and off down the steps. I nodded then turned quickly back towards André.

"Watch out!" he called. I flung myself to the balustrade as the last hunter slid, jerking, past me with a stake skewering the top of his head.

I ran up to André. He was grinning like a devil.

"Are you alright?" I said, sitting on the step below him and tugging at his shirt to inspect the wound.

"Where's the stake?"

André touched the top of his head and indicated the last hunter.

Buttons popped as I ripped his shirt open. His smooth contoured torso exposed a wound that had almost healed. A black ugly scab had formed next to his belly button where a gaping hole should have been.

"Whoa! Can I do that?"

"Yes, my night flower," he said, softening his smile.

"Pah," was all I had to say, but I couldn't help but smile too.

He took my hand from his stomach and moved it to his heart. His body was alabaster; cool, white and smooth. His heart beat a little fast though strong and steady.

"These months without you have been desolate, Hannah. What can I do to make it better between us?" His voice was a whisper.

I stood and pulled him to his feet. We picked our way carefully down the stairs and over bodies. I led him down towards the Women's Memorial Fountain that had the best views of the river and city. There was a full moon rising and the night was singing.

"Well," I said with a smile. "You could start by asking me out on a proper date."

PRIDE AND TENTACLES

D. C. WHITE

"That is not dead which may eternal lie,
across strange aeons, even purple prose may die."
—Necronomicon, Phase One (In Which Doris Gets Her
Oats)

IT is a truth universally acknowledged that a single man in possession of a good fortune, must be in want of a wife."

Yog-Sothoth looked up from the open book. He glanced around the circle. There was silence. The Elder God got the feeling that things were not off to a good start.

"Well?" he asked.

There was a bit more silence.

"Well, what?" Nyarlathotep mumbled from the other side. Of the circle, that is, not from the other side of reality. Technically, being in the common room in sunken R'lyeh, they were already there.

Yog-Sothoth put his book down in his lap and sighed pointedly. He didn't like Nyarlathotep. He never had. He knew very well that the other Elder God didn't like him. Still, Yog-Sothoth was damned if he was going to let Nyarlathotep's petty bickering ruin the first meeting of the Sunken R'lyeh Romance Bookclub.

"Well what does everyone think?"

No one spoke. Yog-Sothoth, eternally optimistic, cast his eyes about the room, finally lighting on Hastur the Unspeakable. He distinctly remembered Hastur being quite agreeable to the idea of the bookclub last week when they were both watching *The Love Boat*. Surely he'd start things off.

"Hastur! Anything to say?"

The Great Old One's head shot up in surprise. His eyes (such as they were, being on the ends of tentacles) looked around the circle nervously. He shook his head.

"Look," pleaded Yog-Sothoth. "This isn't going to work unless we talk about books. This is a book club. The idea is that we all read a book and then we all talk about them. Why don't we go around the circle and each introduce yourselves and your books? I'll go first, okay? How's that? I'll get the ball rolling."

He stood up and held up his book in his right crab claw. As he did so he saw that the book had turned a bit green at the edges. *Bloody ichor gets simply everywhere*, he thought ruefully.

He cleared his throat and beamed around at the rather bored faces around him. "I'm Yog-Sothoth, and I read *Pride and Prejudice*."

He looked to his left in a meaningful fashion. With some trepidation, the heaving mass of pseudopods and what looked like random phlegm next to him spoke.

"Hello," it said in a great blubbery sound that conjured up images of early John Carpenter films. "I'm Shub-niggurath, and I read *Sex And The City*."

Across the circle, someone giggled. Yog-Sothoth couldn't be sure, but he had a feeling that it was Nyarlathotep.

"Good," he told Shub-niggurath, pointedly ignoring the interruption. "Did you enjoy it?"

Inasmuch as it was possible for a large mass of writhing tentacles to appear manly and indifferent, Shub-niggurath managed. "It was okay, I suppose," he said slightingly. "For a girl's book."

Nyarlathotep giggled again.

This time, Yog-Sothoth's patience broke and he whirled around to face the recalcitrant Elder God. "Now look here! The whole point of this was to get us in touch with our feminine sides."

"Oh really?" said Nyarlathotep in an oily tone as he leaned back in his chair. He stroked his van dyke in a pretentious manner. Yog-Sothoth rolled his eyes. Elder Gods couldn't grow beards, so Nyarlathotep had bought one instead. By mail order. He told everyone who would listen that humans thought goatees were evil. Yog-Sothoth had pointed out that what with his face being a shapeless mass of roiling fog, Nyarlathotep didn't really have anywhere to put it, but he had made some snide remark about Yog-Sothoth's knitting and walked off. Ever since, he'd somehow figured out a way of making the beard hover in front of the main bit of fog. Yog-Sotthoth thought the whole endeavour quite ridiculous.

"Our feminine sides?" If Nyarlathotep had eyes they would have narrowed. "You said it was to get us in touch with our human sides, so that we could know more about people before we eat them."

There was a murmur of agreement around the circle. If there were ever a romance book club where the thought of eating people was a hot topic, this was it.

"Well, some females are human as well."

Nyarlathotep became obstinate. "I don't see why we couldn't have read a book that I like."

Yog-Sothoth brought out the big guns. "Because not everyone likes books about hungry caterpillars!"

There were a few muffled gasps from the circle and a clatter as Hastur dropped his Rubik's Cube.

"That's it. I'm leaving." Nyarlathotep stood, his grey, ethereal bulk gleaming even in the ghostly half-light of sunken R'lyeh.

"STOP," boomed a voice, before even Yog-Sothoth could say anything. Both Elder Gods turned to see the dread Cthulhu standing in the doorway.

"Oh, er, your foulness," grovelled Nyarlathotep with the instant obsequiousness he seemed to do so well. "I didn't realise that you were joining us."

"OF COURSE I AM, JUST A BIT LATE, THAT'S ALL. YOU WOULDN'T BELIEVE IT, BUT I GOT HIT BY A SHIP!"

"Goodness," declared Yog-Sothoth. "Whereabouts?"

"THE FOC'SLE."

Everyone winced.

"That's nasty," agreed Yog-Sothoth, looking him over. "But you're walking alright now, I see."

Cthulhu regarded him with a jaundiced eye. "NOT A NAUTICAL BEING ARE YOU, SOTHY?"

"Not really, sir, no. Well, apart from living my entire life under

— 199 —

the ocean, having a face like a giant squid and squirting ink when I get angry."

"CAPITAL. THAT'S A GOOD CHAP." Cthulu turned away to plonk himself down in Yog-Sothoth's chair. "I SAW THE FLYER FOR THIS GROUP IN THE LUNCH ROOM AND THOUGHT I'D JOIN. I LIKE A GOOD BOOK, I DO."

"Oh, er, excellent," said Yog-Sothoth, a little perturbed by the intrusion but quite pleased that the boss was taking an interest, "Well, we were just about to ask Hastur The Unspeakable what he was reading." He got himself another chair and insinuated himself next to Cthulhu.

Hastur opened his mouth, but was cut off.

"HASTUR?" Cthulhu wrinkled his nasal tentacle. "YOU WON'T GET MUCH OUT OF HIM. BEST MOVE ON, OLD BOY."

"Well, next is Azathoth. Azathoth, what are you reading?"

Azathoth stood up, dripping a bit of ectoplasm. "I read *Far From The Madding Crowd* by Thomas Hardy."

"Excellent," beamed Yog-Sothoth. "Did you enjoy it?"

"Not really," Azathoth told the circle.

"What was wrong with it?"

Azathoth looked embarrassed and sat down. "Um, I just didn't care for it, alright?"

Yog-Sothoth sighed. He could guess why. *There's no point in letting this drag on*, he told himself, *let's just get it right out in the open.*

"Was it because it didn't have anyone getting eaten? Was that it?" he asked through gritted fangs, tapping his tentacle on the stone floor.

At least Azathoth had the decency to look embarrassed. "Um... that was major point of contention, to be honest, yes."

"We've talked about this, haven't we? You can't just read books about people getting eaten. You've got to expand your horizons. That's why we're here, to read decent books about love and feelings and things."

"Poof," someone muttered. Again, to Yog-Sothoth's ear it seemed to come from where Nyarlathotep was seated.

"All right Nyarlathotep," Yog-Sothoth declared. "It's your turn. What did you read?"

Nyarlathotep held up his book. "I read *The Time Traveller's*

Wife, and before you ask, it sucked."

Yog-Sothoth was a bit taken aback. "Why?" he asked. "I was rather looking forward to reading that."

Nyarlathotep scowled. "Despite the title, it had bugger-all time travelling in it," he told them. "*And* it wasn't even written by who I thought it was written by."

"Who?"

"Arnold Schwarzennegger. I was really disappointed with that."

Nyarlathotep sat down again. "Your turn," he said, nudging Tsathoggua next to him.

"Um," said Tsathoggua, standing. His bright red shiny carapace gleamed in the half-light. He held a book up with one of his antennae. "I read *Bridget Jones's Diary* and I really liked it."

"Oh, good," beamed Yog-Sothoth. "What was your favourite bit?"

Tsathoggua thought for a moment. "Definitely when Colin Firth and Hugh Grant have the fight in the fountain," he declared.

There was a silence as everyone turned to Yog-Sothoth. "Colin Firth?"

"Yes. He was quite dishy, I thought."

Yog-Sothoth's shoulders slumped. "You just watched the movie, didn't you?"

Tsathoggua was incensed. "I did not!"

"Yes you did," cried Yog-Sothoth. "And what's more, you watched the sequel! You couldn't even manage to watch the actual movie of the book you were supposed to read!"

"Don't yell at me!" Tsathoggua threw his book onto the floor at Yog-Sothoth's feet. "Just because I didn't read your stupid book! I hate reading! I hate literature! I hate the bloody sight of it! Someone should blow books up!"

"NOW WAIT JUST ONE MINUTE!" Cthulhu roared above the conflagration. "I LOVE BOOKS, AND I WON'T HEAR A WORD SAID AGAINST THEM!"

This quietened things down a bit, and both Yog-Sothoth and Tsathoggua sat back down.

"DO YOU WANT TO HEAR WHAT I READ?" Cthulhu asked.

"Yes please," said Yog-Sothoth in a small voice.

"I READ A WONDERFUL BOOK CALLED *VALHALLA RISING*."

Yog-Sothoth felt a sinking feeling in his stomach. He put on a fake smile. "*Valhalla Rising*?" he asked in a hopeful tone. "How interesting. I expect it was straight out of the Norse Sagas? Two young Viking lovers torn apart by the tides of war?"

"NOT QUITE. IT WAS BY CLIVE CUSSLER. ALL ABOUT SUBMARINES. YOU SHOULD READ IT, SOTHY. DO YOU THE WORLD OF GOOD. HERE, YOU CAN BORROW MY COPY IF YOU LIKE."

Cthulhu tossed a rather dog-eared paperback towards the downcast Elder God, then got up and strode towards the door. "RIGHT, WHO'S FOR THE PUB THEN? LAST ONE WITH A BEER IN THEIR TENTACLE IS A ROTTEN EGG!"

ABOUT THE CONTRIBUTORS

After a theatre degree and a stretch of teaching English twelve years ago, ANNETTE BACKSHALL made the natural progression to professional firefighting and has not looked back. She has an equal interest in the arts and science, which explains her love of science fiction. She thanks her ex-English teacher, Mr Doherty, for introducing her to it lending her his Ray Bradbury classics. She has been an active participant with the Katherine Susannah Pritchard SF Writers Group for about four years. Annette is pleased to present her first published short story, "Date with a Vampire".

DAVID BOFINGER is a lapsed physicist who writes a lot and submits too little. Like everyone else in New South Wales he has been sucked into the gaping maw of Sydney, from whose bourne no traveller returns. David took up a job in defence in the hope that beautiful foreign spies wanting his secrets would queue up outside his bedroom door. This hasn't worked and David suspects they instead collect intelligence by reading biographies in anthologies. So, to the sexy spy reading this—yes, of course Shara is modelled on you. Who else could she be?

Swirling mists, dangerous heroes and damsels saving the world— ASTRID COOPER has been writing speculative romance since she could hold a pencil and her own life sometimes reads like a fantasy novel. Her motto of dare to be different (and *Star Trek*) are to blame! She has met Hollywood stars, movie producers, an Apollo astronaut as well as run many fan groups, conventions and published over 150 fanzines. Writing professionally since 1998, her work regularly hits best-selling lists. When not writing and reading, she organises writing workshops and conferences, and makes medieval/fantasy costumes and accessories. Please visit her website: www.astridcooper.com

FELICITY DOWKER is an Aurealis Award finalist and Ditmar and Chronos Award winning author. Felicity's short fiction appears in *Aurealis*, *Andromeda Spaceways Inflight Magazine*, *Midnight Echo*, and many other Australian and international magazines and anthologies. Felicity is a committee member of the Australian Horror Writers Association, a reviewer for the *Specusphere*, and a member of the ASIM Publishing Cooperative. Felicity's chapbook *Phantasy Moste Grotesk* was released in April 2009, and she is currently working on her first novel.

Journalist, novelist, satirist, BRUCE GOLDEN has published more than 80 short stories across seven countries and inside nine anthologies. *Asimov's Science Fiction* described his second novel: "If Mickey Spillane had collaborated with both Frederik Pohl and Philip K. Dick, he might have produced Bruce Golden's *Better Than Chocolate*." His new novel, *Evergreen*, takes readers to alien world full of ancient secrets and a strange intelligence, populated with characters motivated by revenge, redemption, and obsession, on a quest to find the City of God. You can find out more about Bruce and his works on his website: goldentales.tripod.com

LISA HANNETT lives in Adelaide, South Australia—city of churches, bizarre murders, and pie floaters. She has sold over a dozen stories to venues that include *Clarkesworld Magazine*, *Fantasy Magazine*, *Weird Tales*, *ChiZine*, and *Electric Velocipede*. Her story "On the Lot and In the Air" was recommended by *Locus* this year. She is a graduate of the Clarion South Writers Workshop, and hopes to complete her PhD in medieval Icelandic literature before she grows older than her subject matter.

DONNA MAREE HANSON resides in Queanbeyan, NSW, Australia. Her short fiction appears in anthologies: *Machinations*, *Elsewhere* and *Masques* by CSFG Publishing and *Belong* by Ticonderoga Publications and *No One Can Hear You Scream* by Lame Goat Press (forthcoming); and magazines: *Redsine* and *Potato Monkey*. Donna co-edited the CSFG anthologies *Encounters* and edited *The Grinding House* by Kaaron Warren. Under her own imprint, Donna produced *Australian Speculative Fiction—A Genre Overview* and *Johnny Phillips—Werewolf Detective* by Robbie Matthews, which was short listed for best collection in the 2009 Aurealis Awards. Donna usually concentrates her efforts on novel length manuscripts.

Blessed with a lively imagination, SHONA HUSK spent most of her childhood making up stories. As an adult she discovered romance novels and she hasn't looked back. Always fascinated by dark fairy tales and the paranormal, it's not uncommon to get to know spirits, vampires, were-creatures and demigods through her books. In her free time Shona likes to keep fit and get creative in the kitchen. Toblerone brownies, anyone?

Perth-based MARTIN LIVINGS has had over fifty short stories published in a variety of magazines and anthologies. His works have been listed in the Recommended Reading list in *Year's Best Fantasy and Horror*, and had stories in *The Year's Best Australian SF & Fantasy*, Volume Two and the 2006 and 2008 editions of *Australian Dark Fantasy & Horror*. His first novel, *Carnies*, was published by Lothian Books in 2006, and was nominated for the Aurealis and Ditmar awards. www.martinlivings.com

NICOLE R MURPHY has been a primary school teacher, bookstore owner and journalist. She grew up reading Tolkien, Lewis and Le Guin; spent her twenties discovering romance and lives her love of science fiction and fantasy through her involvement with the Conflux science fiction conventions. Her urban fantasy trilogy, The Dream of Asarlai, is being published by HarperVoyager here in Australia with book one, *The Secret Ones*, hitting the shelves in July. She lives with her husband in Queanbeyan, NSW. Visit her website: nicolermurphy.com

Born in a little Welsh mining town, Ian Nichols migrated to Australia when he was three years old. He has spent the better part of the last thirty years studying and teaching at various educational facilities, slaving at a chalkboard and developing an understanding of what teenagers are like off the leash. Currently pursuing a doctorate in Writing, he has also dabbled in amateur and professional theatre, psychiatric nursing, modelling, and all the getting-in-touch jobs. Now, happily retired from educational ruts, he tries to write. So far, there's been a YA fantasy novel, a book of short stories and some short stories in magazines. More will come soon, so be afraid, be very afraid. And he wants a pony.

ANGELA SLATTER writes speculative fiction. Her short stories have appeared in *Dreaming Again*, *Strange Tales* II and III, *2012*, *Lady Churchill's Rosebud Wristlet* and *Shimmer*. Her work has had Honourable Mentions in the *Year's Best Fantasy and Horror* anthologies and has three times been shortlisted for an Aurealis Award. She is a graduate of Tin House 2006 and Clarion South 2009, and she blogs at http://angelaslatter.wordpress.com/. She has two short story collections out in 2010: *Sourdough & Other Stories* (Tartarus Press, UK) and *The Girl with No Hands & Other Tales* (Ticonderoga Publications, Australia).

MATT TIGHE lives in Armidale with his beautiful wife. He has had a dozen stories published, and received a commendation in the AHWA 2009 short story competition for his flash fiction piece "Where Waves Die". About "Growing Silence", Matt says 'There is a brooding old Box tree that sits on the ridge behind my sister's farmhouse. I was standing in the yard looking at it early one evening and everything suddenly went very quiet. It was then that I realised I'd been listening to the rustle of leaves in the wind the whole time, and I hadn't noticed it until it was gone. This story grew from that.'

KYLA WARD is a Sydney-based creative who works in many modes. Her novel *Prismatic* (co-authored as 'Edwina Grey') won an Aurealis Award for Best Horror. Her short fiction has appeared in *Ticonderoga Online, Shadowed Realms, Borderlands, Gothic.net, Aurealis*, and in the Agog! anthologies amongst others. Her work on RPGs including *Buffy the Vampire Slayer* saw her appear as a guest at the inaugural Gencon Australia. Her short film, *Bad Reception*, screened at the 3rd annual Vampire Film Festival and she is a member of the Theatre of Blood repertory company, which has also produced her work. Poetry, feature articles, art; if you can put undead in it, she probably has. To see some very strange things, try www.tabula-rasa.info

D.C. WHITE is a resident of Noarlunga, South Australia. His work has been published in magazines including *The Picture*. He has won several awards for writing in South Australia. As well as horror and comedy, D.C. also writes in the crime and historical genre. This is his first professional anthology publication. He would like to stress to the bookclub to which he belongs that any resemblance to themselves they may find in the following story is purely coincidental...

Acknowledgements

"The Anstruther Woman" copyright © 2010 Nicole R. Murphy

"Fade Away" copyright © 2010 Ian Nichols

"Bread and Circuses" copyright © 2010 Felicity Dowker

"Black Widow" copyright © 2010 Shona Husk

"The February Dragon" copyright © 2010 Angela Slatter and L.L. Hannett

"Growing Silence" copyright © 2010 Matt Tighe

"The Hidden One" copyright © 2010 Astrid Cooper

"A Darker Shade of Pale" copyright © 2010 David Bofinger

"The Valley" copyright © 2010 Martin Livings

"Cursebreaker: the Welsh Widow and the Wandering Wooer" copyright © 2010 Kyla Ward

"Heat" copyright © 2010 Donna Maree Hanson

"Phaedra" copyright © 2010 Bruce Golden

"Date with a Vampire" copyright © 2010 Annette Backshall

"Pride and Tentacles" copyright © 2010 D C White

Thank You

The publisher would sincerely like to thank:

Elizabeth Grzyb, Nicole R. Murphy, Ian Nichols, Felicity Dowker, Shona Husk, Angela Slatter, L.L. Hannett, Matt Tighe, Astrid Cooper, David Bofinger, Martin Livings, Kyla Ward, Donna Maree Hanson, Bruce Golden, Annette Backshall, D.C. White, Terry Dowling, Simon Brown, Jonathan Strahan, Peter McNamara, Ellen Datlow, Grant Stone, Jeremy G. Byrne, Sean Williams, Garth Nix, David Cake, Simon Oxwell, Grant Watson, Sue Manning, Steven Utley, Bill Congreve, Jack Dann, Stephen Dedman, the Mt Lawley Mafia, the Nedlands Yakuza, Shane Jiraiya Cummings, Angela Challis, Kate Williams, Kathryn Linge, Andrew Williams, Al Chan, Alisa Krasnostein, everyone I've missed ...

... and you.